Thanks for
the support

Tales From The Lou

Tales From The Lou

Lea Mishell

Teresa Seals

Myron A. Winston

Mary L. Wilson

Neva Saw it Comin' Copyright © 2010 Lea Mishell
Tattooed Souls Copyright © 2010 Teresa Seals
By Any Means Necessary Copyright © 2010 Myron A. Winston
So St. Louis Copyright © 2010 Mary L. Wilson

Published by Red Bud Ave Publications LLC
P.O. Box 6227, St. Louis, MO 63106

Sale of this book without a front cover may be unauthorized. If this book is without a cover, it may have been reported to the publisher as *unsold or destroyed* and neither author nor the publisher may have received payment for it.

All rights reserved. No part of this book may be reproduced, stored in or introduced into a retrieval system, or transmitted, in any form or by any means electronic, mechanical, photocopying, recording or otherwise, without prior written permission of both the copyright owner and the publisher of this book.

Publisher's Note:

This is a work of fiction. Any reference to historical events, real people, living and dead, or to real locales are intended only to give the fiction a setting in historic reality. Other names, characters, places, business and incidents are either the product of the author's imagination or are used fictitiously, and their resemblance, if any, to real life counterparts is entirely coincidental.

Library of Congress Catalog No.: Pending

ISBN 10: 0-9844397-3-0
ISBN 13: 978-0-9844397-3-7

Cover Design: Sabrina Hypolite

Printed in the United States of America

About Red Bud Ave Publications LLC

Red Bud Ave Publications LLC is more than just a name. This is where Teresa Seals along with her business partner, Aaron Taylor, grew up. When Aaron and Teresa were discussing a name to come up with, they both came to a unanimous decision to call the company *Red Bud Ave*. Their plan is to be the voice, which will speak for all who refuse to have their life choices limited by the environment into which they are born. They are here to promote prosperity.

Red Bud Ave known to many as the "Bud" is located on the north side of St. Louis City. Throughout the years, various individuals have lost their lives and many have served long prison terms behind it. The neighborhood has changed since the two of them have become adults. So in honor of their fallen friends and the new generation the name of their company was established to pay homage to the past and a tribute to the future.

Lea Mishell's Acknowledgments

Above all, I thank **God** for giving me the gift to write for you. Without Him, nothing in my life would be possible.

Teresa Seals, thank you for inviting me to be a part of this project by editing this manuscript as well as contributing my short story. I've been a fan of your work since *Taylor Made* and as much as I looked forward to reading more from you, I never imagined working *with* you! This could be the start of something big for all of us!

To my **family and friends**, thank you for your love, support and understanding when I become engrossed in my writing. You all know this is my passion and I couldn't get this far without you!

Contact info:
Lea Mishell_Author@yahoo.com
http://LeaMishellAuthor.tumblr.com

PeaceLoveHappiness
Lm...

Mary L. Wilson Acknowledgments

This book is dedication and proclamation that my Lord and Savior Jesus Christ is able to do exceedingly and above anything I can think or imagine. Without you I wouldn't be able to display this gift you've anointed me with. Every breath I take and every word I write is confirmation that you've inspire me to do. So Father I say thank you and you are awesome. My life is yours. Continue to use and bless me how see you fit.

My children Anitra, Tony and Maunel the years have passed us by and you all are now young adults. Know that, we wouldn't be where we are today if we had not been through mishaps. Through it all, it made are us strong, we stuck together and we're still here, together. I want nothing but the best for my princess and princes. I love y'all unconditionally.

My sweet grand-boy Jayden, I miss you so much. The time God allowed you in my life was joyous beyond words. I know you're the angel that's looking down on us and smiling. MeMa loves you further than terminology can express.

Mama, Patricia Hatton I'm so glad God has restored our relationship and nothing can damage it ever. Thanks for always being that strong, black, independent woman that showed me how to stand on my own. I so value you and love you for everything that you've done for me.

Russell Lewis, my father, its better never late that never and I'm grateful for what God has blessed us with. We can only get better, Love you old man. My siblings Lamont, Tammie, Jermon, Adrienne, Lil Russell, Shanquita and BJ I love y'all. Shanquita just know that you're not the boss of me. I'm the big sister. My nieces and nephew TeTe love you all. My aunties Jerline and Evelyn thank you for everything. The Lewis family much love.

My best friend Curfrances (Shorty) Wright you know, I valve our friendship and your honesty even more. Thanks for always and when I say always, that's exactly what I mean, for having my back, front and side. You're my straight ride or die bitch for real. A true model of a BEST FRIEND. My God-daughter, JaNise, I'm so proud of you Big Baby.

Family, you all know it's a millions of us, and with that said, I love you all.

To my down chicks Tonya C., Mary Mac, Tiffany R., Monica B., Danielle M., Jeannen M., Kelly R., Pamela M. (OG), Paulette B. (OG), Auntie Squeaky (OG), Theresa M., Denise P. and Lizzett M., y'all gutter baby.

My fellow authors and St. Louis authors, I wish you all nothing but blessing and much success. Teresa Seals you are truly one of my down chicks, my crony and my friend. You have proving your loyalty so many times in the past. You're going to put the Lou on the map. Let no one discourage you and Red Bud Ave Publications is going to expand beyond you and Mr. Taylor's wildest imagination. Teresa you's a go-getter sister and I love your drive. You guys keep up the good work. Jason Poole and K'wan you guys are some cool dudes. Endy, you're my girl without a doubt. Keep grinding hard ma.

Toodie's Hair Salon, Girl y'all gets it in. I love what you and your son are doing for the community. As I said before, and I'll say it again, if you ever need me, I'm just a phone call away. Hey, Kim, Morris and Leo.

The Mckinney's, The Bright's, The McClendon's, The Yates and Johnson's. My hood, my Facebook fam, and anyone else that I failed to mention, thanks for your support.

My readers, without you all there's no Mary L. Wilson and I want to thank you all from the bottom of my hear sweetie.

Haters, HATE ON ME ALL YOU WANT TO BITCHES…..

Teresa Seals Acknowledgments

I have to acknowledge **God** for blessing me with this gift and opening the doors that he has opened for me. I can't continue without acknowledging Aaron Taylor. World he came out the gate getting things cracking. Lea Mishell, Myron A. Winston, and Mary L. Wilson this wouldn't have happened had you guys didn't have that magnificent peace of faith. Therefore, **we** thank you all.

Tiara, Antonio, Trenay, Johnniece, and Jaylon you guys give me the strength and the motivation to have that motto *ain't no sleeping till I'm dead*. April, Ashley, and Aliyah you guys well-being makes me push even harder. Alicia even in this short time you hold a special place in my heart as well.

To my grandmother, parents, friends, family and my extended family I love you all for supporting me in all my endeavors.

Sabrina Hypolite I wish I could dedicate a whole book telling you how much I appreciate you. I thank **God** that you are a part of this team. Robert Ford you gets it in and one day the world will see. To the readers, my FB fam, the book clubs and so on and so forth thanks for supporting.

If you are reading this…THANK YOU, TOO!

Tales From the Lou

Neva Saw It Comin' by Lea Mishell (13)

Tattooed Souls by Teresa Seals (93)

By Any Means Necessary by Myron A. Winston (150)

So St. Louis by Mary L. Wilson (201)

Neva Saw It Comin'

Chapter 1
Raven

"I wish I could find *one* faithful man!" my sister Imani lamented as she sulked in the passenger seat of my 2008 Chevy TrailBlazer. Just moments before, she and I caught her boyfriend Vincent Wheeler at his apartment with another woman between his legs.

"Damn *that*!" I nearly screamed as I started the ignition. "*No* woman should go through this hell! I wish any man that cheats on *me* drops dead in the other woman's pussy!"

I smirked as I saw Vincent's half naked body in my rearview mirror as he shouted Imani's name. Just as Vincent was joined by his female companion, I yelled out the window as I peeled out of the parking lot.

"Watch your back cuz if I *ever* see you around my sister, *I'll fuck you up*!"

"RAVEN!" Imani exclaimed as a bolt of lightning flashed across the sky. Sudden weather changes in St. Louis didn't faze me or my driving skills. Instead, I braced myself for the thunder. Not from the storm but from *Imani*! "How could you *say* such a thing?!?"

"Because this isn't the first time this has happened to *either* one of us not to mention countless others, both male and female. I mean *REALLY*?!? Is it *that* hard to be faithful to *one* person these days?" I inquired as a roll of thunder echoed over us. It was at least a decibel lower than my sister!

"That doesn't mean you should wish harm on someone," Imani stated as she turned on my car stereo. "Remember what goes around…"

"Comes around," I finished, gently swatting Imani's hand as I turned the radio to Foxy 95.5FM to listen to *The Michael Baisden Show*. With a raised eyebrow and instantly piqued interest in what my sister was implying, I asked, "So are you saying that *you* cheated on Vincent?"

"No!" Imani blushed as much as a mocha skinned sista could. "I mean that what you put out comes back to you and because I was faithful in my relationships, *including* with Vincent, the Lord will send me the man that's right for me."

Holding back a giggle at Imani's Pollyanna attitude, I couldn't help saying, "But I thought *Vincent* was your 'man sent from God'. Are you telling me you were *supposed* to be cheated on?"

"Raven, you're twisting my words," Imani huffed.

Seeing that I was upsetting my sister, I dropped the subject and instead focused on the radio show. And wouldn't you know that today's topic was about cheating mates!

I still wish a man would dare to cheat on me and think he'll get away with it!

Lightning flashed simultaneously as thunder rolled overhead. Deftly, I navigated the chaotic St. Louis traffic to guide us safely to my favorite *Steak 'n Shake* location.

"It's my own fault," Imani said quietly, looking out of the passenger side window.

I didn't respond until seconds later when we paused at a red light. "How is it *your* fault, Imani? Did *you* make him put that skank between his legs with her head all buried up in his lap?"

My sister looked at me and rolled her eyes, no doubt at my crass choice of words. "I shouldn't have shown up unannounced."

"Are you fucking kidding me?!?" I shrieked as my anger resurfaced. I nearly peeled out of the intersection the moment the light changed to green.

"Raven! Do you *have* to use profanity?!?" Imani exclaimed in disdain.

"Look, you are only a *few minutes* older than me so quit trying to be Mother!" I snapped back. "And all this hostility you're throwing at me needs to be directed at Vincent's cheatin' ass!"

After a deep breath, Imani apologized. "I know my feelings are misdirected. It's not your fault that Vincent had another woman at his place today. Forgive me?"

Pulling into the *Steak 'n Shake* lot, I accepted my sister's apology. "All I can say is Vincent is damn lucky to have had you because his tires would've been hella flat not to mention he'd have a few busted windows by now if he was *my* man!" I said before humming Jazmine Sullivan's "Bust Your Windows" while pretending to bust the windows on my windshield.

Imani smiled sweetly. "I'll be sure to keep you at the top of my prayer list, Sis."

As we entered the restaurant, you would've thought it was a scene from *Cheers* when the whole bar shouts out "Norm!" except we heard "Raven!" Whenever my office did a lunch run, whoever had the best coupons won and most of those times it was my best friend Monique Clifton with her ever present *Steak 'n Shake* coupons. She and I used the absence from the office not only as an opportunity to get away from our desks but also to get some midday flirting in. Who knew fry cooks could be so damn sexy!

Moments after Imani and I sat ourselves in my favorite booth, our waitress came to take our orders.

"Welcome to *Steak 'n Shake*. I'm Aisha and I'll be your server this afternoon," she said to Imani.

Looking up from her menu, Imani replied, "I need a few minutes but in the meantime, I'll take a cherry Coke, no ice."

"Sure thing," Aisha said before turning to me. "Your usual, Raven?"

"Put my food order in with hers but I'll take my shake now," I smiled. "Thanks Eesh."

"No prob, Ray," she smiled back.

Looking dumbfounded, Imani watched as Aisha walked away. "She didn't even wait for you to tell her what kind of shake you wanted!"

Chuckling, I stated, "Imani, as much as I eat here, I wouldn't be surprised if they started preparing my meal the minute we walked in and had it finished before we sat down in this booth!"

"Oh!" Imani blushed as Aisha returned with our drinks.

"Ready to order?" Aisha smiled attentively at Imani after placing her drink in front of her.

As my sister ordered her lunch, her cell phone rang. Imani sighed in exasperation after looking at the caller ID display.

"Vincent?" I asked without looking up from my banana mocha side by side shake.

"Yes," she replied flatly. Imani's phone chirped to let her know that she had a voicemail message. "I'm not in the mood to deal with him right now. Ray, since my car is going to be in the shop for another week, I'll need you to go back with me to get my things."

"Of course, Sis," I said patting her hand.

We ate our late Sunday afternoon lunch and chatted about work, men and our mom, all in between Vincent's phone calls, voicemails and text messages. Eventually, I reached across the table and turned off Imani's phone.

"Raven, what am I doing wrong?" asked my sister as she pushed away her half empty plate.

"The only thing you're doing wrong is thinking that *you* are doing something wrong!" I replied. "Up to this point, has Vincent done or said anything to make you think he would cheat on you?"

"No," Imani said, frowning as she looked out the window just as the sun's rays broke through the grey clouds above.

"So why would he suddenly do this? Knowing you have access to his apartment and can walk in at any moment, why would Vincent cheat on you at his place?" I asked, against my better judgment, considering that *I* had no idea why Vincent would be so foolish!

"I don't really know why, Ray," Imani said turning her gaze toward me. The pain in her eyes made me want to go back to Vincent's and make him hurt as bad as my sister was feeling right now. I tried to keep the rest of our conversation on lighter fare but Imani's thoughts were clearly elsewhere.

In an effort to change the subject, I inquired about my sister's writing.

"Are you still doing spoken word at *Legacy*?" I asked.

"Not lately," Imani half smiled. "With everything being so crazy at work, it's been hard to settle down long enough to write but I keep my notebook and pen nearby at all times."

"Sounds like me," I said as I reached into my purse for my writing essentials: a pen and a mini-notebook. As I flashed them for Imani, I imitated the credit card commercial. "I never leave home without them!"

It was nice to hear my sister's laugh.

Later that evening as I prepared for bed, I received a text message from an unexpected source.

BSTJ74: *Hey Beautiful. Whatcha doin?*

"What the hell?" I said, looking at the cell phone.

BLACKBIRD: *Nuthin. Goin 2 bed.*

BSTJ74: *Can I be your pillow?*

Sighing in annoyance, I waited a minute before replying as I thought back to the last time I'd seen Brian St. James. While he seemed to be happy with our Booty Call arrangement, I was at a point in my life where I needed more than the occasional touch of a man and instead desired the security of a stable and faithful relationship. Brian didn't act like he wanted a full time girlfriend so we parted ways.

BLACKBIRD: *No time 4 games. U know what I want. U're not ready.*

BSTJ74: *Who says I'm not?*

I couldn't believe I actually got excited from his response!!

BLACKBIRD: *Don't play Brian*

I'd been messing around with Brian for the past couple of years. Since he didn't act like he wanted a serious relationship, he was the ideal Maintenance Man for me while I was in between boyfriends.

Brian was respectful of any situation I was in but no sooner than I'd broken up with my *l'amour du jour*, any time I got that *itch*, Brian was there to scratch it! Eventually, I wanted more than just casual sex and, compared to the ones before him, I knew that Brian was the right man for me. But, being the intelligent sista that I am, I wasn't about to waste my time convincing Brian if *he* wasn't already on the same page!

Been there, done that. Not playing that game anymore just to get hurt again.

BSTJ74: *Raven, I need you*

"You need me?" I said quietly aloud. I got warm shivers from reading those words!!

Could Brian be just as ready as I am to be in a committed relationship?

BSTJ74: *You still there?*

BLACKBIRD: *Yes*

BSTJ74: *Can I come over tonight?*

BLACKBIRD: *2moro's betta*

BSTJ74: *After work?*

BLACKBIRD: *Yes*

BSTJ74: *See you tomorrow Beautiful*

Grinning, I slipped into my queen sized bed with thoughts of a real relationship with Brian.

"I wonder if Brian is as good outside the bedroom as he is in it," I said to myself as I settled into bed, preparing to let the TV lull me to sleep as ideas for our first date popped into my brain.

"He said 'Raven I need you'," I said as I re-read our text conversation. Finally, I had hope for Brian and me.

Shaking my head, making my locs swing back and forth, I came back to reality.

Just because he said he needs you doesn't mean he's not talking about sex. That was Randy's line, too, remember?

Damn! It's a good thing my conscience kicked in! I was liable to do the same thing with Brian that I did with my ex-lover, Randy Boorman.

No more half-assed relationships, Raven. Either you're the only woman or you're nobody's woman!
Smiling to myself, I said, "Amen to that!"

Chapter 2
Raven

Since our entire association was behind closed doors, I debated on how I would explain Brian to anyone. I didn't know exactly where *he* stood so I decided to keep my mouth shut. However, the constant smile on my face hinted at happiness for Raven.

"Looks like someone got a visit from her Maintenance Man this weekend," teased my best-friend-since-high-school, ex-college roommate and co-worker, Monique Clifton as we stood by the printer/copier/fax machine.

"Actually he didn't come over but he did text me last night," I grinned as I picked up my copies.

"OK," Monique looked puzzled. "You're Cheshire cat grinning over text sex?"

"Nah girl!!" I swatted at the back of her head as I walked past her on my way to my desk. "But I don't want to jinx it so just stay tuned."

"Ah'ight," Monique said before I went back to the article I was editing. Curiosity must've taken a nibble because she started again with the questions. "So do I at least get his name?"

"No, Moni," I said sternly as I put the final edits on my article.

"Fine," she said deflated. "Well, I had to put Ted out again."

Rolling my eyes, I asked, "What happened *this* time?"

"He came home late Saturday after visiting his Baby Mama," Monique sighed.

"Which one?" Monique's boyfriend, Ted Downes, was a chronic baby maker. With the way Monique talked about his bedroom skills, I could see why but I'll be damned if I'd let him knock *me* up when he already had two Baby Mamas and four kids with one on the way.

"Nikki," Monique scoffed in reply.

"Is that the one with three of his kids or the pregnant one with the toddler?" I asked suppressing a giggle.

For the life of me, I couldn't understand how women could get caught up with men like Ted. True, these women have a man or at least a piece of one while I sit here single but I'm single because I've chosen to be selective when it comes to who I share my body with. Whether I was in a relationship or not, at no time did I have more than one man at a time. I treated every lover like a potential husband. I wouldn't cheat on my boyfriend so I fa damn sho won't cheat on my husband. I cannot share my body, life and dreams with anyone that isn't on *my* level.

"The pregnant one," Monique said with irritation.

"Maybe he was just checking on her, Moni," I said in Ted's defense and to my surprise. "Nikki was seven months pregnant when you and Ted hooked up and she's due any day now. You may as well get used to him being with her if nothing else to see the baby after it's born."

"He said he was only going for an hour but he was gone half the day!!" Monique frowned.

"Did you two have plans that day?" I asked, playing Devil's Advocate.

"Well, *no* but…"

Sighing, I asked, "Did Ted answer your calls cuz I know you blew up his phone."

"Yeah but…" Monique replied weakly.

"Moni, quit borrowing trouble," I warned. "Maybe Ted was spending time with his son and making sure that the mother of his child was OK. Isn't Nikki the mama that's cool with you?"

"Ray, you don't understand!" Monique declared.

"What's not to understand, Moni?" I asked. "Ted has a bitch of a Baby Mama in LaShaniqua and he wasn't near *her* but you're trippin' off him bein' with Nikki even though he answered *all* of your calls? There's more to this, Moni."

Monique pulled me into her office and closed the door. In a hushed tone, she said, "Ray, I think I'm pregnant."

I looked at Monique like she'd lost her ever lovin' mind!

"Oh girl!" I said as I shook my head.

"And there's a good chance that it's not Ted's. I've been seeing someone new. While Ted was seeing his Baby Mamas, I was getting to know Giovanni," Moni said, hanging her head.

"I guess I don't have to ask how *well* you know this Giovanni since there's a chance you might be pregnant by him!" I replied sarcastically.

"Not to mention that I was planning to break up with Ted anyway because I can't deal with the constant calls from LaShaniqua or her kids with them calling me 'Bitch' and 'That ho' as if that's my given name and Ted's punk ass doesn't say a thing about it!" Monique exclaimed.

"Moni, as your friend, I have to tell you that you are wrong on so many levels with this one," I began. "How many times have I advised our friends not to cheat on their mate? Quit holding on to what you have when it's no longer any good for you. Plus you already have backup so it's not like you'll be alone although *that* isn't a bad thing. Everyone should take a break between relationships, especially ones as toxic and mentally stressing as yours!"

"Ray..." Monique started.

"How can you possibly be mad at Ted *if* he's cheating on you when you've already cheated on him and possibly gotten pregnant by another man?!?" I inquired sternly.

Even with all of Monique's book smarts, sometimes she was clueless when it came to men. A good hit of dick and she become an amnesiac! She *knows* she shouldn't hold on to one man while reaching for another one. Then to get *pregnant*?

Wow.

Monique's eyes filled with tears as my truthful words sunk in. "You're right, Raven. I should've just left Ted but I didn't get serious with Giovanni until a month ago."

"Dayum Moni! You've been creepin' for a month and I'm just *now* hearing about it?!? I thought we was girlz!" I joked, trying to ease the tension. "OK, seriously. Let me ask you this. When you met Giovanni, did you tell him about Ted?"

"Not at first because I didn't want to look like a cheater," Monique said meekly. "But I did tell him eventually."

"Strike one. You started the relationship on a lie," I said shaking my head. "Next question. Did Giovanni know about Ted before or after you two had sex?"

"After," Monique said without looking at me.

"Why didn't you tell him before you had sex?" I felt like a mother scolding her teenage daughter.

"Because he told me his last girlfriend cheated on him and he didn't want to get hurt." At this point, Monique began to cry. "Raven, I really like Gio. And I thought that he could be so much better for me than Ted but I like Ted, too, and I didn't want to hurt him."

"Girl, this shit is worse than a bad soap opera," I laughed. "Your ass is gonna end up on *Maury*. As soon as you say, 'I don't know which one is the father', the audience will laugh your ass off the stage cuz *you're* old enough to know better!!"

"You've always given me honest and straightforward advice, Raven." Monique straightened up and looked directly into my eyes. "And *that* is why you'll be perfect for the position."

Astonished, I said, "What position?"

"The Senior Advice Columnist gig," Monique smiled as she dried her eyes.

"Wh-what?" I said in shock. "That's Geri's spot and she's been here forever and a day!"

"And she's retiring at the end of the quarter which means the spot is up for grabs!" Monique cheered.

"Hold up! How do *you* know all of this?" I asked in surprise.

"I'm not the Senior *Gossip* Columnist for nothing!" she winked.

"So... you're *not* pregnant?" I asked cautiously.

"Girl nah!! You *really* think I would play myself like that? Ted already had enough babies to take care of!" Monique scoffed. "And who's to say that Nikki and LaShaniqua are the *only* Baby Mamas he's got?!"

"What about Giovanni?" I asked, trying to remember all of Monique's details.

"There never was a Giovanni," Monique grinned. "But I *am* leaving Ted. I'm following your advice and my gut especially since Nikki the 'Nice Baby Mama' texted me the messages Ted sent her talkin' 'bout how much he loves her and wants her to take him back. I don't have time for games, his or hers, so I'm out."

That explains why Moni was less than pleasant when she said the name of her "favorite" of Ted's Baby Mamas.

"Glad to hear that you're ready to move on. If Ted wants Nikki, let them self destruct on their own. No sense in you adding fuel to the fire," I advised. "Besides, if they get back together, who's to say he'll be faithful to *her*? Do you really think Ted only has one chick on the side? He probably has backups for his backups! Leave that drama for his Baby Mamas!" As I began to walk out of Monique's office, I had to ask. "I met Nikki but I never met LaShaniqua and with a name like that, I was *sure* she didn't exist!"

Monique walked over to me and patted my back. "Oh trust me, she's real. A real BITCH! *Another* good reason to leave. When I met Ted, he said he had children. I was cool with that. He said he had them by two women. I was hesitant but still wanted to see where things went with Ted. I told him that as long as he didn't bring any drama into *my* life, we were good. In less than two months, he let all hell break loose and I don't like to repeat myself so I'm letting him and *them* go!"

Smiling I hugged my friend, relieved that my girl hadn't completely lost her mind! Before I could verbally respond, Monique's cell phone rang.

"Hello? Oh hi Ted," she said, rolling her eyes. "I'm at work and we'll talk about it later." After closing her flip phone, Monique said with a smile, "He wants to talk this out. Any advice?"

Laughing to myself, I said, "Just be honest and talk to him in a public place. You don't want him in your space in case he decides to flip out and act a damn fool. At least in a public place, security or the police can take him away if he gets out of hand."

"Great advice as always, Ray! Thanks girl!" Monique said before hugging me back.

"Just doin' my job of takin' care of my girl," I said as I opened the office door. Leaning inside the doorway, I added, "One more thing."

"What's that?" Monique said as she walked back to her desk.

"Give yourself some time to get over your relationship with Ted," I suggested. "I know you're looking for Mr. Right but get to know *you* and what you want, need and like before you go looking for someone to fill those empty spaces in your heart and life. Or better yet, talk it over with God and trust that He will send you your man."

Now why did that sound like something Imani would say?

"I'd do as she says."

I turned to my right to see Geri Shannon, our magazine's Senior Columnist, both in age and tenure, standing behind me.

"Raven, I wanted you to know that I will be retiring soon and I suggested your name as my replacement," Geri announced.

I'd always admired Geri's sage advice before I began working for *Another Black Experience Magazine* and felt blessed just to be one of her readers! Once I started working for *ABE*, Geri always made my days fly by with her motherly advice and sista girl attitude. But the thought of her leaving gave me mixed feelings. While I looked forward to the possibility of stepping into her shoes, Geri's spirit would be sorely missed in our office. She only came in once each month to have lunch with her grandson and our Editor-In-Chief, Shelby Roberts, but Geri made it a point to speak to everyone present in the office on the days she'd visit.

"Thank you so much, Geri. I feel honored that you would nominate me," I said sincerely.

"I've been keeping up with your blog and I love the advice you give," Geri commented.

My cheeks felt warm since I wasn't aware that Geri even knew about my side "gig" as an amateur advice columnist. In addition to my paying job as a researcher for *Another Black Experience Magazine*, I also dispensed advice online through my Tumblr blog.

"Didn't know I knew about *Kickin It with Ray Ray*, huh?" Geri smiled warmly.

"Actually, no I didn't, Geri," I replied hesitantly.

"Me either," said Monique with a shocked expression that matched my own as she joined Geri and me in the doorway. "Somehow I don't picture you in front of a computer screen reading blogs."

"My granddaughter told me about it a few months ago, about the time I started thinking about retiring," Geri explained. "Whenever a new question would arise in your blog, I would read your response as well. I must say I am very impressed that a woman your age can have such vast knowledge on so many subjects."

"I visit with my mother and grandmother often and we talk about everything. They've both taught me that one of the best ways to help someone is simply to listen," I smiled as I thought of my elders' advice over the years.

"They are wise women that raised a very thoughtful and intelligent young lady," Geri said. "I feel confident that Shelby will be seeing you soon to make an offer. Hate to cut this visit short but I've got a date with my grandson. I'll see you ladies next month."

"Bye Geri," Monique and I called out in unison.

After Geri's departure, I looked at Monique. "Do you know how great it would be to get that promotion? Not just the title but my own office!"

"Not to mention the raise, the personal assistant and best of all, you'll be two doors down from me!" Monique smiled. "Just like in college. Well, that is until we convinced our roommates to share a room so we could be roommates instead."

"Things are looking up for ya girl, Moni," I grinned. Just then my cell phone rang, emitting my current favorite ringtone, Beyoncé's "Single Ladies". By the time I got to my desk, I'd missed a call from my sister.

"What's up Sis?" I asked when I returned Imani's call.

"I just wanted to know when you can take me to get my things from Vincent's. It's not much but in case he's there, I'll need your support to keep me from doing something I'll regret."

Like take him back...

"This evening works for me," I said, mentally checking my calendar for my availability. "And afterward we can celebrate."

"Sounds fun. What are we celebrating?" Imani asked with interest.

"I'll tell you when I see you," I replied. "I'll swing by right after work, around four."

No sooner than I'd hung up with my sister my cell phone rang again.

"Hello Beautiful," came the seductive baritone on the other end.

My cheeks instantly warmed. "Hi, Brian."

"Are we still on for tonight?" he asked.

I totally forgot!!

"What time were you thinking of coming over?" I asked hoping that I wouldn't have to postpone our date. Then again, I'd waited this long for him to want me, I could wait a little longer to make sure my sister was squared away first.

"I'm on my way to the studio to lay down a couple of tracks but I was hoping I could come over after that," he offered.

"How late are we talking because I don't want to be up too late," I stated in an effort to eliminate setting up a booty call encounter.

"Is eight too late?" Brian asked.

Let's see. Leave work, pick up Imani, get her stuff from Vincent's and have dinner with my sister before dropping her off.

"Nine works better for me."
"Cool. I'll see you tonight, Beautiful."
Once again, my face told the world how happy I was.

Chapter 3
Imani

"Thank you so much for going with me, Ray," I said as I stepped into my sister's TrailBlazer.

"No problem, Sis," she replied as she popped in a CD. Within seconds, we were surrounded by the throbbing bass beat of Family Affair's "You Gon Luv Tha Family". All the way to Vincent's apartment, Raven and I bobbed our heads and followed along with the twin rappers Mr. R.E.P. and QB the Classic of Family Affair, a local St. Louis rap duo.

As Raven pulled up into Vincent's apartment complex's parking lot, Family Affair's single, "Senseless" was just ending.

"Ray, don't you find it odd that we, a pair of twins, are fans of twin rappers?" I giggled more to myself since it seemed that so many things that I thought, did or had mirrored my twin sister in one form or another.

"Not really," she replied nonchalantly. "It's to be expected since we both have such excellent taste."

"Yeah, for everything but men," I bemoaned before exiting the vehicle.

Locking and securing the TrailBlazer, Raven replied, "Unfortunately that's one area we *both* need to work on. But let's get your stuff so we can discuss that over dinner."

Just when we had the last of my things in the living room, I heard a key in the door. Before I could shush her, Raven let out her classic line...

"FUCK!!"

"Baby!" Vincent said upon seeing my face. "I'm so glad you finally came home!" he exclaimed as he walked toward me.

Halting his attempt to hug and kiss me, I put my hand on his broad chest.

Be strong, Imani. Do not think about the pecs under the shirt!

"Vincent, if it's not obvious, I'm leaving you."

"Imani, let me explain..." he started.

"Yeah, Vincent. Explain to my sister why your dick was repeatedly going in and out of that trick's mouth!" Raven blasted.

"Raven," I said calmly. "I'll handle this. Thank you."

"Ah'ight," Raven replied, sitting down in the middle of Vincent's sectional couch. "But let's wrap this up and keep it quiet cuz if need be, I will have our brother Austin here in a matter of seconds." Raven's eyes were locked on Vincent as each word flowed from her lips.

As my sister sat down on the couch, the image I caught of Vincent with his ex-girlfriend, Shawnaé, between his legs came bubbling to the surface.

"You were saying, Vincent?" I urged sweetly. If I wasn't mistaken, I could swear I saw fear in Vincent's eyes! Whether it was because of Raven's fiery temper or my quiet demeanor, I couldn't be sure. While I had his full attention, I debated whether I'd speak my peace. "You know what? Never mind because you're just going to tell me more lies."

"Lies? Imani, when have I *ever* lied to you?" Vincent asked defensively. "Why would I start *now*?"

"Because you know that I am a good woman and I have always given you the benefit of the doubt. I've been with you through good and bad times, layoffs and promotions and *this* is the thanks I get!" I looked at Vincent's pathetic expression. "There's nothing else to say."

Without a word, I picked up my bag and headed for the door. Raven stood up from the couch and held Vincent back as he began to say the most remorseful explanation I'd ever heard. I didn't even bother to stick around to hear anything after he called my name. By the time I reached Raven's truck, she caught up to me.

"You OK, Sis?" Raven asked as she unlocked the doors to the TrailBlazer and took my bag from me to put it on the backseat.

Looking up at the sky, I watched as the dark grey clouds parted to reveal the azure sky above.

"I am *now*." I allowed my body to relax into the passenger seat as Raven navigated through St. Louis' Central West End to head back to the South Side. "I don't know what to do, Ray."

"About..." she asked without taking her eyes off the road.

"About me," I sighed. "I keep making the same mistakes with men and the only common denominator is *me*."

"Mani, it's not all you," Raven began to explain. "True, you are a common factor in each of your relationships but what I believe is happening is that you aren't seeing the common things in the men you date. As discriminating as you are, you don't have many past relationships to compare but if you look back on each one, you will find similarities. Let me ask you this. Did you break up with them or vice versa?"

"I ended it with them," I said after some reflection. "If it wasn't one thing, it was another. One had a drinking problem. Another had a gambling problem. And the one before Vincent was living with the mother of his children yet he swore up and down that they weren't together as a couple, just roommates."

"Men that you can't or shouldn't be with. Sis, this may sound like a dumb question but why did you end the relationships?" Raven asked as she slowed to stop at a red light.

"With the drinker, it started out fine. We met when he helped me with my groceries one day and we started talking and everything seemed great!" I began. "Then as time went on, I noticed he was spending more time at my place and less time going to work yet he always found money to get him a can of beer EVERY day or a bottle of liquor every weekend. One day I asked him if he would mind cutting down on the drinking but he immediately turned violent."

"Did he hurt you?!?" Raven exclaimed as she entered the intersection, narrowly missing a car making a left turn in front of us.

"No! No! I would never let it get to that point especially without you or Austin hearing about it!" I replied as I used my hands to make sure my seatbelt was fastened. Raven's near miss caught me off guard and I wanted to make sure that I stayed safely secured in the SUV in the event of an accident. "When I'd had enough, I packed up his things, put everything outside my door and had my locks changed before I called and told him it was over. At first he denied any wrongdoing but quickly I reminded him that from the jump I didn't like it when people had uncontrollable addictions and if he couldn't control his drinking that we wouldn't last. I guess he didn't believe me. I saw him recently, looking way worse than I'd ever seen him but immediately I prayed that his life was better now that I wasn't in it."

"OK, so what about the gambler?" Raven said as she pulled into the restaurant's valet station.

After a valet driver opened my door, I emerged from the truck, smiling in response to his cordial manner. When I met Raven at the door of the restaurant, I continued.

"Within a couple of weeks of meeting the drinker, my debit card went missing when he did and I found myself calling the bank practically every day about charges that I didn't make. I didn't bother to question him. I just cancelled my debit card and called the police to have him arrested for theft. I mean, our first date was at Harrah's Casino! True, they have a decent buffet and I figured he was being cost conscious but he barely ate and couldn't wait to get to the tables! Almost every time he took me out it was to a casino!"

Raven informed the hostess that there were two in our party. As we sat in the lobby waiting for a table to become available, I filled my sister in on the last wrong man I dated.

"As nice as he was, I just couldn't forgive his lies. And you won't believe how I found out about his situation!"

"She called you," Raven said nonchalantly. "A woman with a cheating man will not hesitate to snoop to find out what he's doing. What gets me is that once they have evidence that their man is no good, not only do they confront the other woman instead of their man but they *stay* with their cheating mate! I seriously don't understand the logic in that! Are we as women so desperate to have a man that we'll keep the worst one for ourselves? I know not all men are bad and there are some women that are just as scandalous but *still*. We *have* to do better! When you know he is not the one for you, let him go!"

"He and I had just come back from dinner and he was still at my place when she called me. She claimed that she wanted to know how well I knew him because she found my number in his phone but didn't recognize the name. The kicker was when she asked me if he told me that he was married to her and that they had two young daughters. He only said he was living with a woman and here is this stay at home mom taking care of *his* babies while he's out cheating on her. I was nice enough about the whole situation considering her man was sitting right next to me as I answered her questions. Needless to say, he and I were done before I handed the phone to him to let him explain himself to his *roommate*. Ray, it's amazing the Lord's timing because that was the night that he and I had decided to finally make love after dating for three months."

"Wow Sis! I never would've assumed any of this went down cuz you never said anything about this!" Raven said. "When did all of this happen?"

"While you were in Texas," I said quietly.

"But Mani, I was only down there for a year!" Raven stated. "How did you have three bad relationships in ONE YEAR?!?"

"Honestly, I was trying to get out there and meet someone, *anyone* so I opened my horizons and tried to date outside my circle," I confessed. "Once I met Vincent, I thought I'd broken the cycle and yet look how *that* turned out!"

"Ladies, your table is ready," our hostess announced pleasantly, temporarily interrupting our conversation.

Politely, we thanked the hostess before following her to our table.

"Mani, just because you've had a bad streak doesn't mean that *all* men are bad," Raven said to assure me.

"I can only pray you are right, Raven," I replied.

I can only pray you're right.

Chapter 4
Raven

Moments after we were seated at our table, Imani headed for the Ladies Room. Once I was sure that my sister was out of earshot, I called Vincent.

"How *stupid* are you? Did you *want* to get caught?" I asked.

"Ray, I tried to explain to Imani but..." Vincent began.

"But my *ass*, Vincent!" I spat. "How in the hell you gon' ask me to help you pick out an engagement ring for my sister one minute, the next minute you got some chick's lips wrapped around your dick?!?" I tried to keep my voice at a restaurant appropriate level but Vincent's transgression had me *heated*!!

"Shawnaé came by out of the blue and I told her *then* that I was going to marry Imani," Vincent explained.

"And?" I asked waiting to see how he talked himself out of this shithole.

"Shawnaé laughed and said that Imani couldn't do to me what *she* could," Vincent added. "The only thing Shawnaé has on Imani is..."

"Giving you a job," I said as I spotted Imani heading back to our table. Knowing my sister, I wouldn't be surprised at how limited her sexual experience was. She refuses to watch porn with me and actually cringes and looks away during sex scenes while we're in a movie theatre!

"Exactly! Shawnaé knows how to give fire head and once she went down there, I tried to stop her just as you and Imani walked in," Vincent finished weakly just as Imani sat down.

Choosing my words carefully in my sister's presence, I asked, "So are you going back to your old job or moving on to the *best* one?"

"Imani's there with you, isn't she?" Vincent asked.

"Yes, sir," I replied while looking over the menu.

"Raven, I *need* Imani. Everything she said is true. Imani *is* a good woman. I love only *Imani!*" Vincent declared. "When do you think I should call her?"

"I don't know but right now I'm out to dinner so I'll get back to you later. Bye," I said before smiling at Imani. "Ready to order?"

"To be honest, I don't have much of an appetite," Imani said, placing her menu in front of her on the table.

"Sis, I know you don't eat when you're stressed or upset but you have to eat," I encouraged.

"Girl, you and I both know I can stand to miss a meal or two," Imani said pinching her sides.

"OK, so we're a little fluffy," I grinned at our word to describe our beautiful yet larger than average bodies. "You know the only men that want bones are dogs."

"And that statement perfectly explains why Vincent did what he did," Imani said coldly.

Why in the hell did I say that?

"I can't *believe* he had that skinny little home wrecker on him like that!" my sister seethed.

"Imani, about Vincent," I began.

"No, Raven. I don't want to talk about Vincent or *any* men for *that* matter," Imani said as she snatched up her menu.

So much for telling her about Brian and me.

Just then our waiter appeared. "Good evening ladies. My name is Antoine and I will be your server tonight. May I start you both with a drink and an appetizer?"

"I'll have a Grey Goose martini," Imani replied to my surprise since the hardest thing she usually drank was a glass of chardonnay.

"And *you*, Miss?" Antoine smiled at me.

"I'll have the same," I replied. After watching Antoine's ass as he scurried away, I had to ask. "A Grey Goose martini? Whatchu know about the Goose?"

"You'd be surprised at what I know," Imani smirked while studying the menu.

"Well, Sis, if you're anything like me, I wouldn't be *that* surprised!" I laughed.

After quiet conversation and a lovely meal of stuffed chicken and linguine followed by tiramisu, Imani and I headed back to her apartment. It was there that my sibling brought up the subject of Vincent.

"I don't know what went wrong, Ray," Imani said as she prepared a cup of chamomile tea. I declined her offer of a cup for fear of being too groggy to talk to Brian later that evening.

"Cheaters don't cheat because of who they are with," I explained. "Cheaters cheat because of something inside of *them*. Even a gorgeous woman like Halle Berry was cheated on so it's not *you*, Imani."

"But what gets me is that I never saw it coming!" Imani looked at me as if I had all the answers. "When he wasn't at work, he was over here or I was over at his place. When would he have *time* to cheat?!?"

"Who's to say that Vincent *was* cheating, Imani?" I inquired.

Ray, even you know how dumb that sounded!

"Did you see Shawnaé in front of him on her knees?!? Did you see him pushing her away?!?" Imani exploded as she slammed her cup of tea onto the mahogany coffee table.

"What I meant was that if Vincent was going to cheat, do you think he would do it in his apartment to which you have a key? How long have you and Vincent been together for you to give up after one mistake?" I asked, praying that I was keeping Vincent *out* of the doghouse. "Imani, the pain is too fresh for you to think about the good in Vincent but be glad it was just a blow job, if *that* even happened. If he'd gone further, you'd be on your way to your doctor for HIV and STD tests!" Feeling a vibration inside my jacket pocket, I retrieved my vibrating cell phone to discover that Brian had sent me a text. "Excuse me, Sis."

"Go ahead and check your messages," Imani said as she cleaned up the tea she spilled before turning on her TV. An episode of "Two and a Half Men" was just starting.

BSTJ74: *I'm about to leave the studio and head to your place*
BLACKBIRD: *I'm at my Sis'. I'll be home shortly*
BSTJ74: *Can't wait to see you, Beautiful!*

Smiling at his response, I looked at Imani. "You gonna be ah'ight or do you need me to stay longer?"

"I'll be just fine, Raven," Imani smiled back. "I've got plenty of work to occupy me so if I don't see you before then, I'll see you at Mother's."

In a flash, I hugged my sister before heading home. A quick hop onto Highway 44 East to I-55 South and I was home within minutes. Just as I turned down my street, I watched as Brian's 5'11" frame emerged from his 2010 Cadillac Escalade which he parked right in front of my duplex apartment building. After I parked behind him, he walked over to my truck and opened my door.

"My, aren't we a gentleman tonight," I smiled as I emerged from my vehicle.

"Always... in the streets," Brian winked. "And you already know how I am in the sheets."

My cheeks grew warm at his comment. As we walked to the door of my second floor apartment, I tried to get a feel for why he *really* wanted to see me. "It's a lil early for a booty call, Brian."

"Just reminding you of one of the perks of having me around more often," Brian said before pulling me to him. When our lips touched, it felt like every nerve in my body was on fire! His kiss was soft and gentle like when he initiates our sexcapades. I had to step back and catch my breath!

"I kept thinking about the last time I saw you and the conversation we had kept playing over and over in my head," Brian began as we walked up the stairs to my apartment. "Raven, I don't expect you to believe me but ever since that night, I've been trying to figure out how to tell you this."

Turning on a lamp in my living room, I looked at Brian. "Just spit it out."

"I know this sounds like it's coming from nowhere but Raven, *I need you*. I want to see where this goes," Brian replied.

Looking into his warm brown eyes, I said, "Just like *that?*"

Brian looked confused. "What do you mean, 'Just like that?'? I'm serious, Raven. I've never wanted anyone as much as I want you!"

Sitting down on my sofa, I looked up at Brain. "Interesting because I figured you only wanted me for sex. In fact, when we first met, you said I was sexy for a big girl as if I wasn't meant to be sexy at my size. Why the sudden interest in monogamy?"

"Raven, I can explain..." he said, joining me on the sofa.

As old hurt feelings came flooding back, I interrupted him. "Brian, if you really wanted and needed me, why haven't we gone out on a date? Why do you only call me late at night? Are you ashamed to be seen with me? Is it because I'm a big black girl and you're a sexy lil white boy?"

"Beautiful, I never said..."

"Why am I good enough *now*, Brian?" I asked. "I'm no lighter in weight or skin tone since the day we met and the only side of me you've seen has been in the bedroom. What's so different *now?*"

Brian took my face in his hands and kissed me. Smiling, he said, "If you'll hush for a second, I can answer your questions."

I sat back and waited for his response.

"I'll admit that when I first met you, your attitude did make me pause on stepping to you. But it wasn't a *bad* attitude. Raven, you have a self-confidence that I have never seen in any woman other than my mother which is something that I love about you. You're the first woman I've been attracted to that I really *wanted* to be in a relationship with," Brian started. "Of all the women I've met, you were the first *real* woman that intrigued me enough to see all that you had to offer. I never saw you as black or thick. I see you as beautiful and ambitious but our first conversation was so sexual and flirty that I thought that *you* only wanted us on the low."

Dumbfounded, I sat in silence.

"As for my calls, I work until late at night and when I emerge from the studio, the first face I want to see is yours," Brian explained. "It's not all *my* fault that we're all over each other the minute I step through your door. And *you* told me why we don't go out but I see you don't remember."

Surprised by what Brian had revealed so far, I was afraid for him to refresh my memory but, as we all know, curiosity killed the cat and Fluffy is standing on the edge of the ledge.

"'The only things open at night are legs and hospitals' is what you told me," Brian reminded me. "If you recall, after you said that, I didn't call you for a while and that was only because by the time I had any free time, it was very late and I didn't want to disturb you."

"Brian..." I said quietly.

"I've always wanted more for us, Raven, but *you* continuously gave me the impression that all you wanted was sex," he finished.

Thinking over the entire relationship, Brian was right. I always talked dirty with and around Brian and we *always* ended up in bed when he'd come over to my place. Not once did I call to see how *his* day went but he never missed a chance to ask me about my day. That is until I blasted him for treating me like a mistress when in reality I gave Brian no reason to expect more than sex from me since Day One!

"Amazing," I replied quietly.

"What's that, Beautiful?" Brian asked, slipping his arm behind my back and tenderly squeezing my waist as I looked up at him.

"My Granny once told me that the way you start is the way you finish," I answered. "I didn't know what she meant until *now*."

"Can you enlighten me because I'm clueless," Brian smiled before softly kissing me on the cheeks, lips and neck.

"We started off flirty and sexual and that's how we always were until I realized my worth and the one guy I wanted didn't feel the same way about me." I looked into Brian's eyes. "Or so I thought."

"Now you know how *I* felt," Brian said softly. "I wanted you so bad that I took whatever you gave me and if the sex wasn't so damn good, I wouldn't have stuck around *this* long!"

Smiling, I said, "My sentiments exactly."

"And as you can see, it's not too late to catch a movie or go to a club. I have the rest of the week off and I need to show off lady tonight," Brian grinned.

"Your *lady?*" I blinked, unsure if I heard him correctly.

"I'm sorry. I didn't ask properly." Brian knelt down on one knee and took my hand in his. "Raven Powers, can I be your man?"

I couldn't help laughing. "Boy, you are so *silly*! Before I say yes, have you told me the truth, the whole truth and nothing but the truth?"

His serious expression put me on guard. "There is *one* other thing. I must warn you about something," he started as he rose from the floor to sit on the sofa.

Oh hell. Here we go.

"Come on Brian. What is it?" I asked anxiously, interrupting his dramatic pause.

"I am going to love you like no other," Brian smiled. "Think you can handle that?"

"Brian!" I laughed with relief. "You made it sound all serious!"

"Loving you *is* serious!" Brian said as he smoothly pulled me to him before kissing me again. "Don't worry. I'll wait while you catch up."

"Are you saying you love me, Brian?" I asked with romantic hope mixed with hesitation.

"Yes, Raven, I love you," Brian replied. "When I'm not with you, I miss you. And when I see you again, my breathing returns to normal because I know the good Lord has let you live one more day."

"OK, don't take this the wrong way but I'm gonna need a drink after that declaration," I admitted as I stood up and stretched.

"No problem. The choice is yours, my lady," Brian said as he rose from the couch before leading me to the front door.

Who would've thought that my Maintenance Man would become my One and Only Man?

Chapter 5
Imani

Over a week passed before Vincent appeared at my door.

"Can I come in?" he asked.

"No," I replied from the safety of my chained door. Not once had I stopped thinking of Vincent and me but thinking of Vincent reminded me of Shawnaé and the visual that refused to delete itself from my memory.

"Imani, we need to talk," Vincent said, trying to touch me through the opening.

"What is there to talk about Vincent?" I asked, pulling my hand out of his reach.

"Baby, I don't want to get into this while I'm standing out here," Vincent stated. "If I can't come in, will you at least come out here? Or answer your phone? Please?"

"Goodbye Vincent," I said firmly before slamming and locking my door. I half expected Vincent to call out to me or at least knock on the door but I heard nothing but the sound of a car driving away. When I looked through the peephole, Vincent was gone.

I hated to admit it but I regretted not hearing Vincent out. Was I being too hard on him? After all, this was his first major error in judgment in the two years we've been dating.

My fingers trembled as I dialed his number.

"First of all, I'm sorry for slamming the door in your face. There was no reason for me to be rude," I began.

After a brief pause, Vincent chuckled. "Apology accepted."

"OK, what did you have to tell me?" I asked trying to sound more in control of my voice than I sounded.

"Can I come back so we can talk?" he asked.

I sighed because I knew I would be stronger with the phone line between us. "You can't say what you have to say on the phone? I'm on my way out the door."

"This will be better in person," Vincent replied. His deep bass voice made everything sound sexy and the more he talked, the more I wanted to give in to his request.

"I'll call you after I get back from dinner. I'm meeting Raven at my mother's in a few minutes."

Why did I tell him that? He's not allowed to know my whereabouts anymore!

"Please tell Mom and Ray that I said hello," Vincent said. "Just call me when you're ready to see me."

"OK. Bye Baby." Before I could recant my statement, Vincent said he loved me and hung up.

Gathering my purse and jacket, I headed out of my apartment to the parking lot. As I approached my 2008 Mitsubishi Eclipse, fresh from its vacation with the dealership's mechanics, I smiled as I thought back to the day that I bought my car. Vincent talked the salesman down to the price that I could afford and even managed to have a few extras thrown in for free. When I realized I was smiling about Vincent, a frown quickly covered my lips.

Shortly after arriving at my mother's, I pulled my Eclipse behind Raven's TrailBlazer. While our mother continued to dress for dinner, I told Raven about my phone call with Vincent.

"Was that a Freudian slip or did you really mean to call him 'Baby'?" she asked as we sat in Mother's kitchen, nibbling on snickerdoodle cookies.

"To be honest, Ray, I don't know," I confessed. "You're right about Vincent. This is the first time in our two years together that he's really made a big mistake. He remembers and celebrates our little anniversaries more than I do. He cooks almost as well as I do. He's the closest to perfect for me that I've ever had, Raven."

"So whatcha gon' do?" my sister asked in one of her comical voices. I had to laugh because she sounded like Goofy and Scooby Doo mixed together.

"I don't know, Ray," I sighed just as our mother emerged from her bedroom. As always, Jamila Powers was a vision of grace and elegance.

"Something tells me we're not going to *Hometown Buffet*," Raven joked.

Our beautiful mother smiled. "No, my Babies, we are certainly not going to any buffet. Are we ready to leave?"

"Yes, Ma'am," we respectfully chimed.

"So how have you two been?" Mother asked once we were on our way to *Antonio's* in her 2010 Mercedes-Benz S400 Hybrid sedan.

"It looks like Geri Shannon is retiring and guess who she wants to replace her," said Raven from the front seat.

"Oh Sweetheart, that's wonderful!" Mother cheered.

"Wow! That's great news, Raven!" I agreed, sincerely happy about my sibling's announcement. "Is that the good news you were going to share with me the other day when…"

"Yeah," said Raven as she turned to glance back at me. "But we were handling other things that day."

I was so thankful that Raven didn't go into details about my situation with Vincent in front of Mother.

"Well, how about *you*, Darling?" Mother asked, turning her attention to me, watching me in her rearview mirror.

"Nothing new on my end, Mother," I replied, praying that Raven wouldn't suddenly decide to rat me out.

"How are you and Vincent doing?" Mother asked, this time with her eyes on the road.

"Vincent is fine, Mother. So am I," I replied, looking out of the window while praying that my mother was done with her interrogation.

To my relief, Mother didn't press the issue further.

Raven's cell phone rang as we pulled up to the valet station at the restaurant. After she gave the caller our location, tentatively, I asked, "Raven, who's coming to dinner?"

My sister laughed at me!

Then Mother let out a small ladylike giggle.

I guess I missed the joke because I didn't see anything funny about my question.

After Mother handed her keys to a valet driver, Raven and I followed her into the restaurant. At the hostess stand, Raven announced that the Powers party had arrived.

Just as the hostess prepared to seat us, a tall attractive young white man approached Raven. Her face lit up when she turned to face him, letting me know *she* knew him.

After the young gentleman kissed her cheek, Raven introduced us. "Brian, this is my mother Jamila Powers and my sister Imani Powers. Mother, Imani, this is my boyfriend, Brian St. James."

Mother, ever elegant and reserved, offered her hand, which Brian promptly kissed. "Nice to meet you, Brian," she said, smiling at his gesture.

"It's my pleasure to meet *you*, Mrs. Powers. Raven speaks so highly of you. I am honored to meet you in person," Brian smiled as he pulled her in for a hug. "Everything Raven told me about you doesn't do you justice."

Mother blushed! Before I could fully appreciate my mother being flustered, Brian turned his attention toward me.

"I've heard so much about you, Imani. I feel like I know you!" the exuberant young man said as he bear hugged me.

"Wish I could say the same about you," I said as Brian set me on the floor. Before I could grill my twin, Raven swiftly took Brian's hand and followed the hostess to our table where an older gentleman was already seated. To my surprise, he rose and walked straight to Mother. After he kissed her softly on her cheek, she introduced him.

"Warren, these are my daughters, Imani and Raven and Raven's boyfriend, Brian. Everyone, this is Warren Greyson."

At least he's not her boyfriend. But then again, would Mother come out and say that in public since this is the first mention of him even being in her life? Of course, not! So who's to say he's anything more than a friend? And why do I suddenly feel like a fifth wheel around these couples? If things weren't so shaky with Vincent and me, I would call and ask him to join us.

"Which side is winning?" Raven asked, gently nudging me.

"Huh?" I said, caught off guard by the interruption of my conversation with myself.

"Looked like you were having an internal discussion," Raven explained. "Don't worry, Sis. I have them all the time. That's how I make decisions. I just hope your conversation wasn't anything that was going to keep you from enjoying tonight."

Before I could respond, I realized the hostess led us to a table set for six.

"Is there a reason why we have an extra chair?" I asked looking from the hostess to Raven to Mother.

"You'll see," Raven replied mysteriously.

Looking to my mother for clarification, she simply smiled at me.

I smell a trap.

I sat across from Raven, leaving the empty chair between Mother and me.

"Did Mother mention Warren to you before tonight?" I whispered to my sister as I laid a linen napkin across my lap.

"Not a word," she whispered back, smiling politely in Mother and Warren's direction.

"Just like the Mystery Man to your left," I pointed out.

"I tried to tell you about Brian the other day but *you* didn't want to talk about *any* men," Raven said before grinning like the Joker.

"Mm hmm," I smiled back.

"Am I late?"

I turned my head to see Vincent standing behind the empty chair!

"No, Vincent. We just arrived," Mother replied. "Please have a seat."

After Mother introduced Vincent to Warren and Brian, he turned his full concentration toward me.

"Why are you *here*, Vincent?" I asked through clenched teeth before he could subdue me with his killer smile.

"I was invited," he answered after brushing my cheek with his lips so lightly I dare *not* confuse it with a kiss.

"By who?" I inquired with curiosity.

"*I* invited him," Mother replied as she leaned around Vincent to look me in the eyes. "Vincent called and asked to speak with you but you hadn't arrived at my house yet so I suggested that he meet us here. I'm sure you don't mind, right, Darling?"

Looking from Mother to Vincent, I remained calm. Leaning over as if to kiss him, I said to Vincent, "This isn't the time or the place."

"OK," he smiled as this time he did kiss my cheek.

Minutes after we ordered our meals, everyone at the table became engaged in multiple conversations. Raven and Brian were talking with Warren and Vincent comparing today's music to what we used to listen to when we were young. Who knew we were old enough to see our music become considered as Old School!

"I'm so happy that Al B. Sure! finally came back to show these youngsters what *real* love makin' music sounds like!" Raven exclaimed.

"Tell me about it," Brian chimed in as he shook his head. "'Boyfriend #2' is *not* a song to inspire someone to be in a loving and faithful relationship. Give me Kevon Edmonds or Brian McKnight any night of the week!"

After I switched seats with Vincent, Mother and I began to discuss soap opera updates which prompted Raven to jump in to remind us yet again why she stopped watching *The Young and the Restless*.

"I left when Shemar did. I followed him to the CW when he did *Birds of Prey* then back to CBS for *Criminal Minds*," Raven commented.

At this point, Brian and Vincent jumped to Raven's topic to discuss the popular CBS crime drama. Since Raven, Mother and I all watch the show together either in person or over the phone, once the guys heard us discussing recent episodes, *Criminal Minds* became the table's main topic of discussion until dinner was served. With all the camaraderie of the evening, not once did I think of the pending discussion I would have with Vincent later that night.

As if he read my thoughts, my boyfriend leaned over, turned my face to him and kissed me.

"I love you, Imani," he said quietly. He looked at me as if the entire world only consisted of him and me. "You said this isn't the time or the place but I have to disagree."

Oh no no no!! Please! No drama! Not here in front of my mother!

Vincent slipped down from his chair onto bended knee.

"Winifred Imani Powers, will you do me the honor of becoming my wife?"

"Oh!" Mother exclaimed as I looked back to see her bringing her hands up to cover her mouth.

I looked over at Raven to see her nodding as if she approved of this. Even Warren and Brian seemed impressed by the gesture.

But Vincent didn't propose to any of them. He was proposing to *me*!

"Vincent... we need to talk," I replied.

Hesitantly, Vincent rose from the floor, took my hand and announced to the table that we would be right back. Leading me toward the entrance of the restaurant, Vincent was mute. Once we were outside, he spoke.

"Tonight's dinner was planned weeks ago. You can check with Raven and your mother. The day you saw me with Shawnaé was the day after Raven and I picked up your engagement ring. I was just getting dressed to go to the gym when she stopped by which is why I didn't have my shirt on. Nothing happened with Shawnaé."

"Why was she between your legs when I walked in?" I asked fighting back tears at the memory of the image.

"Baby, the closest she got to me was when she knelt down in front of me after she pushed me down onto the couch," Vincent explained. "When I told her that my future is with you, she laughed talkin' 'bout how a big girl like you couldn't come close to her skills in the bedroom."

"What?!?" I snapped. "We've done practically everything and I've never heard you complain once!"

"I know, Baby, I know," Vincent said as he pulled me to him. His strong arms felt so good around me. "There's only one thing she's better than you at."

Quickly, I pulled away from Vincent. "Oh, really? And what is *that*?" I asked cringing because I knew I didn't *want* to hear the answer.

"Giving me no reason to ever fight for her," he smiled. "Shawnaé was only with me when I was on top of the world but when I lost my job due to corporate downsizing, she took everything and bounced. When Shawnaé left me, the *last* thing I wanted was to be rejected again so I didn't even pursue a relationship with anyone.

"But when I met you in that coffeehouse, up on stage reciting one of your spoken word pieces, I had to at least get to know you," Vincent continued. "I never dreamed we'd go from friends to lovers so quickly but I thank God that the only available seat that day was at your table and that you were nice enough to let me join you."

"All of that still doesn't explain why Shawnaé was between your legs," I pointed out.

"She must've heard about my promotion at the bank. Now that I'm on my feet again, I guess she figured she could sex her way back into my life," Vincent stated before tilting my head up to kiss me. "I had just finished my shower when she stopped by. I don't know why but I guess she thought her key still worked because I heard her fumbling with the doorknob. Thinking it was you, I opened the door without even checking first or getting fully dressed.

"With me just in a towel, she had easy access but I wasn't havin' that! So I threw on some pants so I could be a bit more decent since Shawnaé said she just wanted to talk. When I came back to the living room, she quickly got to *her* point and went straight for my dick, probably thinking that I would come back to her after a blow job. Sex is her only weapon, Imani," he assured me. "When you walked in, she had just pushed me down onto the couch as she dropped to her knees. My pants were never undone. She never accomplished her mission. Shawnaé is a little girl playing little girl games. Why would I want her when I have a real woman?"

Once Vincent explained everything, most of my doubts and fears dissipated. As I pushed the image of Shawnaé out of my head, I said, "Yes."

Vincent began to smile. "Yes?"

I nodded my head. "Yes, Vincent. I will marry you."

After a few more kisses, Vincent and I headed inside the restaurant. The look on our faces told everyone what my final answer was. When I looked at Raven, she mouthed the words "Are you sure, Sis?"

Squeezing Vincent close, I nodded my head again.

Chapter 6
Raven

"CONGRATULATIONS!!" the entire office applauded and cheered after my boss announced that I had accepted the position as the new Senior Advice Columnist that will become available once Geri Shannon retired.

Shelby and Geri were the first to personally congratulate me.

"You practically do my job better than I do, Ray," said Shelby. "I know you're inexperienced as a full time columnist but from what I've seen, I know I made the right decision."

"Thank you, Shelby," I said as he briskly shook my hand. "I'm nervous but excited about my promotion."

"I know you'll do just fine, Raven," Geri said after hugging me.

"Thanks Geri. Your support means the world to me," I replied. "So what are you and your husband going to do with your new found free time?"

"You're not old enough to know about *that*, Baby," Geri winked before sauntering away, followed by her grandson.

"Oooo Geri!" I laughed just as my shoulder was tapped from behind me.

"Hey Raven."

I turned to look up at our cute and young intern, Frankie. Standing 6'3", he towered a full foot over me. I was so busy getting lost in his dimples that I didn't hear him speaking to me.

"Huh? I mean, you were saying?" I stammered.

"I was saying congratulations on your promotion." When Frankie smiled, his dimples sunk in deeper! Mmm!!

"Oh! Thank you and congrats to you, too, on getting promoted as my assistant! If you need any tips on anything, let me know," I offered. "I'm sure you'll have no problems filling my spot."

Did that sound as dirty as I think it did?

Frankie laughed lightly. "Are we talking business or personal?" he asked with a wink. Damn those dimples!

Before I could respond, Monique entered my line of vision. "Excuse me, Frankie. I need to speak with Ms. Clifton right quick."

Without waiting for Frankie's response, I crossed the room and headed straight for Monique.

"Dirt Alert," I said, evoking our code word for when we needed to discuss personal business... ours and everyone else's.

Immediately, we entered Monique's office. She was barely inside before we started talking.

"Congratu..." she began.

"Later for that!" I said, cutting her off. "I've got a situation!"

"Spill it Sista!" Monique nearly squealed.

"You know I'm dating, Brian, right?" I asked.

"The one I have yet to meet and approve of? The one whose pictures are all over your cube? The one you've gushed about so much that I want to make a clone for myself, sight unseen?" Monique smiled. "Yeah, I remember Brian."

"Well, the thing is that he's already saying the 'L' word but I'm not quite *there* yet," I admitted. "In fact, I'm not even sure if I want to be exclusive with *anyone* right now. All that time I'd thought I'd wanted monogamy and now that I have it, I'm *still* not satisfied!" I finished, shaking my head.

"Are you saying you've cheated on Brian?" Monique asked as she perked up.

"No!" I declared immediately. "But I'm not out of flirt mode yet either. I was just talking to Frankie and..."

"Mm mm MMM!! Now *that's* a tall slice of chocolate cake I wouldn't mind sinking my teeth into!" purred my freshly single friend.

"Moni! Focus!" I giggled. "Like I was saying, I was talking to Frankie and, as you know, he's taking my old job when I take over

Geri's. Well, I told him that he'd have no problem filling my spot, meaning my Research Assistant position, nothing more."

"OK? So?" Monique asked, shrugging her shoulders quickly.

"He asked me if we were talking business or personal and Moni... I was actually tempted to say 'Both'!" I covered my mouth after my admission.

"Wow!" Monique grinned. "A little office romance?"

"Didn't I mention Brian, my boyfriend, all throughout this conversation?" I asked, looking at Monique with wide eyes to show her that I was looking for my answer... NOW!

"Ah yes. The *boyfriend*," Monique replied soberly. "Well, I don't see your problem since you said you don't love Brian and Frankie might just be flirting with you. There's no law against flirting even if you have a boyfriend."

"I know..." I sighed.

"So why are you in Panic Mode?" she inquired, shrugging her shoulders again.

"Because after all this time of hoping, wishing, and praying for a good man, I finally have one," I stated. "And I don't have the best relationship track record..."

If you can call "a guy stopping by for drive by fucking on his way home to his girlfriend" a relationship because that's all I've got to count at this point, give or take a couple of months of monogamy in between flings.

"I just don't want to mess this up," I finished.

"Girl, you know how it is. When you're single, no one's checkin' for ya but the minute you're unavailable, e'rybody wantcha!" Monique laughed. "Maybe I should just say I have a man so they'll be on *me*!"

"You know you need help, right?" I laughed with my friend. "So basically I'm overreacting?"

"Yes, Ray. Enjoy the flirting but let Frankie know that you're off the market or tell Brian that you're not ready to be in a committed relationship with a man yet," Monique suggested.

"You're right, Moni," I smiled.

"No, *you're* right," Monique corrected me. "That was the same advice you gave me when I first started dating Ted and met that one guy while you and I were out clubbin' one night."

"Wow! Really?" I asked in surprise. "It's amazing that sometimes I just need to follow my own advice."

I just hope I find the right words to say to my boyfriend since I really don't want to rehear my advice on what to do when your man leaves you because you don't love him yet.

"Let me ask you this," Monique began, gesturing toward the sofa across from her desk. As we sat down, she asked, "I know you and Brian started out on the low but why haven't I met him yet? Is it cuz he's white?" Monique leaned in, grinning in anticipation for my response.

"He's white?!?" I yelped in fake alarm, clutching my butterfly pendant, gently tugging at the gold small link chain from which my pendant hung. "Girl, nah, *that's* not why! I've dated white boys before."

Releasing the pendant, I had to stop myself in that lie.

"Let me rephrase. I've fucked around with white boys before. I even went to a prom with one. True it wasn't at my school but that was because my cradle robbin' ass was messin' around with high school boys instead of college frat boys. He told me he was 25 but he wasn't even old enough to buy me a drink at the club. I was so infatuated with his green eyes, hard abs and that tight ass that I didn't trip…" I had to catch my breath as I realized my excitement was being shared with my friend. Clearing my throat, I continued. "That I didn't trip off the fact that his boys were taking care of my drinks when we'd all go out!" I finished, laughing at the memory.

"Ray?" Monique asked seriously as she put her hand on mine. "Is Brian that young boy?"

If I didn't know my girl better, I would've thought she was *serious*. Instantly we broke into uproarious laughter interrupted by a knock on the door. As she gained her composure, Monique walked over to see who was at the door.

"Yes, Frankie," Monique said in her professional office voice.

"Excuse me, Ms. Clifton. There's a call on hold for Ray, I mean Ms. Powers," I heard Frankie say through the opening in the door.

"Frankie, take a message please," I called out before Monique had a chance to say something smart.

"I'm sorry Ms. Powers but he's called several times and refuses to leave a message," Frankie said raising his voice. "Sorry for getting loud, Ms. Clifton."

"If anyone calls for Ms. Powers, divert the calls to her voicemail!" Monique said with a smile. Even seeing her cheeks puff up didn't convince me that Frankie would still have a job when I left this room. "Now where were we?" Monique said as she walked back over to the sofa.

"You were asking if Brian was the young boy I freaked with," I laughed. "No, he's not. And I'm not hiding him from anyone. He's met my family, remember?"

"True, but I usually know about your men before your sister does so how did *this* one slip past my radar?" Monique asked quizzically. "I doubt he's unattractive or unemployed because you don't strike me as the shallow type."

"Actually, Moni, I'm pickier than you would think," I smiled. "I've never spent time with anyone that didn't offer some added value to the scenario. Brains go much further with me than brawn but it never hurts to have something nice to look at when there's no physical or verbal contact."

"I feel ya," Monique agreed. "So what is it?"

"To be honest, Moni, it's fear," I confessed.

"What?!? Get the fuck outta here with that, Raven! You're just as fearless as I am and you know *I'll* do anything once!" Monique stated. "Y'all been kickin' it for a minute. What's to be afraid of *now*?"

"That I can truly be monogamous in this relationship," I replied. "Since we officially became a couple, Brian and I have spent more time out than in but I'm not fully embracing the idea of me with him like he sees us. Sometimes I'll see a guy and smile because I don't have to try to seduce him now that I have someone that loves me and wants nothing but the best for me. A man of my own is what I've wanted forever but I've been the side chick for so damn long, I don't know how to be the main and only woman!"

"It starts with self respect," Monique announced. "You once told me that you should love yourself and hold yourself to the standard that you would expect your man to treat you. Then and only then will you have the right type of men coming your way. I've been watching you Ray and you did just that! When you and I go clubbing, most of the guys are on you and all of them were a serious upgrade from the scraps and scrubs that hit *me* up!"

"That's because I finally got fed up with chasing and decided to just focus on me. If I met someone, cool. If I didn't, no big. But throwing myself at every Tom and Harry with a dick wasn't working for me," I admitted sadly. "Brian and I met from me throwing myself at him but there was something different about him. He didn't text me late at night talkin' 'bout he wanted to 'hit that right quick' before going to bed. On a couple of occasions he tried to take me out but I told him I was doing something else," I said as I thought back to *who* I was doing instead of going out with Brian.

Quietly, Monique spoke to me. "Raven, follow your heart. If you love Brian enough to see where this goes, do that. But if you truly don't feel that it's working out, before you hurt him or yourself, let it go."

"My advice to you?" I smiled.

"Yes, ma'am," Monique said as she gently put her arm around me. "And I believe you agree with me on this, right?"

"You're right. Or I'm right. Whichever, I know what I have to do now," I said taking a deep breath.

~♥~

"Dinner was excellent, Brian!" I said after my last bite of grilled Angus burger and homemade steak fries.

"Didn't know ya man could cook, huh?" Brian asked before leaning over and kissing my neck.

Scrunching my head to my shoulder, I said "Ah'ight now. Don't start something you can't finish!"

"Oh ya know I'll *finish*," he winked as he rose to put our plates in the dishwasher. "Did you want any dessert?"

"You made dessert, too?" I asked in disbelief as I rose from the kitchenette table to walk over to the chaise lounge portion of his sofa in the living room.

"Actually, I haven't made it yet." Brian's tone hinted at thoughts most naughty!

Suddenly the image of Frankie's flirty smile came to my mind.

"How about a movie?" I said in an effort to divert my attention as I scanned Brian's DVD rack.

"Pick anything you like," Brian shouted from the kitchen. Plates and silverware clinked as he loaded the dishwasher.

Browsing over Brian's movie collection was no help in keeping thoughts of Frankie at bay.

Unfaithful. Perfect Murder. Jade. The Last Seduction. She's Gotta Have It.

I settled on *Face/Off* which gave me a dose of two of my favorite Hollywood hunks, John Travolta and Nicolas Cage. Brian joined me shortly after the movie began. During the scene where Nicolas Cage had the undercover agent sitting on his lap, Brian turned to me and mimicked Nicolas' character, Castor Troy.

"Peach. I could eat a peach for *hours*."

The intensity in Brian's eyes sparked a fire six inches below my navel!

"Brian..."

"Yes, Beautiful," he said in a low growl as he leaned in to kiss me.

"How serious are you about us?" I asked point blank.

His reaction let me know that I'd caught him off guard as he sat straight up looking directly at me as he responded. "My plan was to take this one day at a time and somewhere down the line I was thinking marriage, maybe a few kids, a nice house. All with you."

"Is that the answer you think I want to hear or is that how you *truly* feel?" I primed myself for the response.

"Where is this coming from, Raven?" Brian asked, reaching for my hands after turning off the television.

I let him hold them while I explained. "Brian, you and I have been sleeping together for so long that I'm struggling to adjust to seeing our relationship outside the bedroom. We still flirt with each other. We still have sex. But there's something missing."

"And what's that?" he smiled while gently tugging me toward him.

Taking a deep breath, I said, "I'm not ready for a commitment."

"Define 'commitment'," Brian asked as he nuzzled on my ear and neck.

"I mean exclusivity. You, me, and no one else," I explained. "I'm not ready to be with just one man."

There! I said it. Brace for impact!

Brian stopped nuzzling. If I wasn't mistaken, I believe he stopped breathing, too!

"Who is he?" Brian asked calmly as he rose from the sofa.

"There isn't anyone else, Brian," I said to assure him.

"There has to be someone else. Why else would you want to leave me?" Brian inquired angrily. "When you were the one that ended things between us, you said you wanted a relationship. I guess I should ask you what your definition of a relationship is?!?"

"Brian, I didn't say I wanted to leave you. I said…"

"I *heard* what you said, Raven!" he roared as he paced in front of me. "Was it something I did? Something I *didn't* do?"

"No, no, no," I sighed, shaking my head. "It's just that…"

Sitting down next to me, Brian quietly asked, "What is it, Beautiful?"

Looking him in his eyes, I said, "I don't want you to waste your time."

"Hold up!" Brian snapped as he once again stood up. "*You* were the one wanting us to be in a real relationship and now you're saying I'm wasting *my* time?!? How am I wasting my time, Raven?"

"You're already saying you love me while I'm still adjusting to us as a couple," I explained. "I don't know if or when I'll be able to say those words and I don't want you sitting around waiting when you can be out there loving someone else."

Silently Brian stood before me. After a moment or two, he sat beside me. "Love is a very strong and serious emotion, Raven. I'm not expecting you to say anything but the truth. If you don't love me *right now*, that's fine. I'm not gonna let you go because of *that*. But if you love someone else, don't let me block *your* happiness."

"Brian! There's no one else!" I exclaimed, surprising myself with my tone.

"Then let's not worry about whether or not you love me yet. Let's just take this one day at a time," Brian suggested. "OK?"

Relieved, I smiled back at my boyfriend. "OK."

Brian gently pulled me up to stand with him. As he held me close, he whispered, "Didn't I say that I would wait while you catch up?"

Tears welled in my eyes. "Yes, you did," I whispered back.

Kissing my forehead, Brian said, "I meant that. Whatever you decide to do, I'll still love you."

I could almost feel my lips prepare to say the words. Instead, I said a silent prayer.

Lord, thank you for bringing Brian into my life. And, please open my heart so that I can find the love to share with him. Amen.

Chapter 7
Imani

RIIIING!! RIIIING!!
"Are you going to answer that?" I asked, getting irritated by the incessant trill of Vincent's house phone.

"It's just Shawnaé," Vincent said as he spooned me closer to his warm naked body. No sooner than the house phone stopped ringing, Vincent's cell phone started up!

"Oh come *on*!" I snapped as I pulled away from Vincent and sat up in the bed. Looking back at my fiancé, I quipped, "Please talk to her. If you don't, *I* will and I cannot be held responsible for what I say to her."

"OK, OK," Vincent smiled as he slowly turned to retrieve his cell phone from the night stand on his side of the bed.

"Hello? ... Shawnaé, lose my number and forget you ever met me. You're disturbing my fiancée and me. ... Yes, she's here and yes, we're getting married. ... She didn't catch anything but a desperate woman chasing a man that don't want shit to do with her! Goodbye Shawnaé!"

After turning off his cell phone, Vincent rose from the bed, crossed the room and proceeded to remove the receiver from the base of his corded phone. "No more interruptions, my love," he said as he returned to bed. "Now where were we?"

Still sitting up, I replied, "I was about to go home."

"Home?" Vincent replied with alarm as he climbed back into the bed. "Why?!? I thought we had the *whole* day together."

"We did until Shawnaé interrupted the mood," I pointed out as I stood up and picked up my clothes from the floor. "Before you know it, she'll be over here knocking on the door."

"True," Vincent sighed. "I should never have dated a woman that lives in my apartment complex. It ain't like she's gonna just up and move away cuz I broke up with her."

Glancing over at Vincent's naked body stretched out on his king sized bed, I was very tempted to stay and play. "Call me when you've settled things with Shawnaé for good."

"So I can't see you until *then*?" Vincent asked with fear in his voice.

"Not saying that at all," I replied as I walked into Vincent's master bathroom. "But I know she can't bug me at *my* place so if you really want to continue our day together, I suggest you come over because that is where I'm going as soon as I get dressed."

Immediately, Vincent leapt from the bed and followed me into the bathroom. As I placed my dirty clothes in his hamper, Vincent turned on the shower. When I looked back at my fiancé, he was leaning in the doorway, naked as a jaybird, grinning from ear to ear.

"What?" I asked with genuine curiosity.

"You just put your clothes in the hamper," Vincent stated.

"I always do that at home," I replied, not feeling his excitement.

"Exactly!" Vincent said as he walked over and hugged me.

Feeling his bare skin against mine just felt so *right*. Like tossing my clothes in the hamper or putting my key in the door.

"I'm comfortable here with you. I almost feel like I'm at home," I said to his mirror reflection.

"And that's great because I wanted to ask you something," Vincent smiled back at me in the mirror. "How do you feel about us moving in together?"

"As long as you're not suggesting we stay *here*," I said as I released myself from Vincent's hold to get into the shower.

"What's wrong with *my* place?" Vincent asked as he joined me under the warm water. "You just said…"

"One word: Shawnaé," I replied as water cascaded over us from head to toe.

Behind me, Vincent groaned as he reached around me to wet his washcloth. "I see your point. But there's another problem."

"And *that* is?" I asked as Vincent soaped up my back.

"My lease isn't up for another six months," Vincent whispered in my ear as if it was a secret.

"Mine is up sooner than that. So what do you suggest?" I inquired with a knowing smile.

"When is your lease up?" Vincent asked, returning to his normal speaking voice.

"The end of next month," I replied as I turned around allowing Vincent access to the front of my body.

"How about this?" Vincent asked as he soaped me from head to toe. "When your lease ends, don't renew it. Move in with me or we can stay at an extended stay hotel and put our stuff in storage. How does that sound?"

"Mmm..." My response was twofold for my fiancé's idea and the fact that at that moment he was soaping my inner thighs. As he rubbed *very* close to a sensitive area, all I could say in return was "Great!"

I looked down to see Vincent looking up at me.

"If you think *that's* great, tell me what you think of *this*," Vincent said seductively.

Immediately, my head snapped back as Vincent buried his face into my Playground. As my fiancé slowly drew circles with his tongue around my clit, I struggled to continue standing!

"B-B-Bay-BABY!!"

"Mm hmm" was Vincent's only response as he continued licking and sucking.

"C-c-can we g-g-go to th-the b-b-bed?" I stuttered.

Again, all he said was "Mm hmm" but instead of letting up, Vincent's *appetite* increased!

"B-B-Baby! I'm s-s-serious!" I laughed, relieved when I convinced Vincent to at least *pause* on his snacking!

"You're all clean now," he smiled as he slowly rose to a standing position.

"I *bet*!" I said in reference to Vincent's distinct attention to detail.

"Shall we move this to the bedroom?" Vincent asked as he kissed my neck.

Before he returned to his downward route, I replied with an emphatic "Yes!"

Without so much as a towel, Vincent hopped out of the shower onto the bathmat, avoiding the cold tile of the bathroom floor, and jumped onto the carpet in the bedroom before sprinting to the bed. Only by the grace of God did Vincent manage to avoid breaking his neck!

Turning off the water, I thought to myself, "Am I really ready for this? Moving in with the man I love?"

Yes, Imani. You are *ready!*

Tentatively, I emerged from the bathroom with a towel covering my wet naked body.

"Drop the towel. Please," Vincent encouraged. "I need to see you. *All* of you."

Smiling, I let the towel slip from my hands onto the floor, which I stepped over before proceeding to walk over to the bed. As Vincent laid spread eagle in the middle of the bed, I gathered my courage as I stopped at the foot of the bed.

You've gone this far. Keep going!!!

Slowly, I crawled onto the bed between Vincent's legs, kissing my way upward.

"Um, Baby, wh-what are you doing?" Vincent asked, sounding surprised.

"Shh..." I said as I continued my journey up to Vincent's thighs to the sound of his deep inhaling and exhaling. Once I'd reached as high as he could take it, again Vincent spoke. Or at least I think he did because I don't recall hearing much after I wrapped my lips around the tip of his penis just seconds before I took in a mouthful.

"Whoa! Yes! Oh Baby don't stop!" Vincent exclaimed to my delight. Considering I didn't have much experience giving oral pleasure to a man, I was pleased to hear Vincent's reaction.

Relying on my conversations with Raven and recalling what I'd seen from flashes of the pornographic DVDs that Vincent watches when he thinks I'm asleep, slowly I bobbed my head up and down until Vincent placed his hands on the back of my head.

"If he puts his hands on your head, that's a good thing," I remembered Raven telling me when I asked her for pointers.

The longer I sucked and the deeper Vincent's penis entered my mouth, the more he moved his hips while moaning deeply.

"Damn Baby! That feels GOOD! Don't stop! Yeah Baby!"

Knowing that I was doing well, I couldn't help smiling. I continued until, just as Raven predicted, Vincent flipped me onto my back to return the favor. Not once have I ever complained about Vincent going down on me and this time was no exception!

Almost every stroke of his tongue sent chills through my entire body. Waves of ecstasy flowed from my pelvis through me up to my arms and down to my legs, out to my fingers and toes. I felt electric ripples of pleasure all over my body!

"Oh Daddy!" I screamed, surprising myself! "Put it in! I want you inside me NOW!!!"

Immediately, Vincent honored my request. As usual, I came upon penetration. With each stroke, I felt my body get weaker yet stronger. Weak with ecstasy and strong with the desire to feel Vincent as deep inside me as he could go!

When I woke up in my fiancé's arms, both of us tangled in the sheets, I looked up at him and smiled.

As Raven once told me, "Never give your man a reason to wander away from home."

"If it means I have to step out of my comfort zone a little to keep things hot between Vincent and me, as long as I still love myself when it's over, so be it!" I thought to myself as I snuggled closer to my fiancé.

Chapter 8
Raven

Standing in my office doorway, I watched my assistant as I gathered my thoughts.

"Frankie, could you come in here, please?"

"No prob, Ray," he smiled before following me into my office. After Frankie closed my door, I began to speak. "I still need those revisions and I have something else for you to look up for me."

"I'll only look if it's under your skirt."

I don't know what caught me off guard more, the seductive tone of his voice or the response itself! Knowing where this could lead and not able to afford the backlash, I chose to nip this office flirting in the bud.

Looking over at my assistant, I said, "Frankie, we need to talk."

Immediately, Frankie proceeded to sit across from me. "Yes, Raven?"

"Frankie, before we stay on the wrong foot, let me set down some ground rules," I began as I slowly paced the floor. "Until I received my promotion, you and I were equals so it was a bit more acceptable for us to flirt with each other but now that I'm your superior, we can't be so openly friendly in the office. Do you understand?"

"Yes, ma'am," Frankie said quietly, slumping in his chair.

"I realize it's a sign of respect but you don't have to say *ma'am* to me," I smiled as I walked back to my desk.

"No, I think it's best that I do, Ms. Powers," Frankie said as he stood up. "Is there anything else?"

"Just the revisions and that other project but let's focus on the revisions first since those need to be turned in before the end of the day," I replied.

"Yes, ma'am," Frankie replied before quietly leaving the room.

Sitting down at my desk, I picked up the receiver, disengaging the speakerphone. "Was I too harsh?"

"Not from what I can tell but he seriously is into you judging by his responses after you told him to cool down the flirting," Monique replied. "I would see how things go for a few days. If the situation worsens, either with the flirting or his work here, I'd let him go."

Tapping my pen on the desk, I said, "That's what I was thinking. Thanks for the second opinion."

"No prob, Chica. We still on for lunch?" Monique asked.

"Actually Brian is taking me out. Rain check?" I replied.

"Sure," said Monique. "Or you could take this opportunity to introduce me to this phantom boyfriend of yours."

"He just met my family, Moni. Let him recover from *that* before *you* interrogate him!" I laughed. "In fact, I'm late. I was supposed to meet him at the restaurant ten minutes ago!"

"OK Girlie. I'll catch you at the staff meeting this afternoon. Enjoy your lunch and tell Brian I look forward to meeting him!" Monique quipped.

"Will do," I smiled before ending the call as I pictured the moment when Monique's eyes took in the image of me with Brian. She has nothing against interracial relationships. Monique is against *relationships*. Period. How she managed to stay with Ted as long as she did is beyond me unless of course she was doin' it like I did with my ex, Randy Boorman.

Randy had a girl he was living with but he'd stop by my place to fuck before going home to fuck her. And no, I didn't think about his girlfriend. According to Randy, she gave him babies but I gave him passion! Besides, as long as I got my fix, I was satisfied.

To Monique, THAT was a relationship.

She's my girl to the end but even *she* admits that she's not the most monogamous woman she knows and she makes no apologies for that. As for me being with one man, Monique will be fine as long as I'm happy.

And the fact that he looks like Robin Thicke's doppelgänger doesn't hurt either!

On my way out of the office, I grabbed my jacket and purse. As I passed Frankie's desk, I informed him that I was going out to lunch and would return as soon as possible.

The restaurant we chose was across the street from my office and yet I was still late! Typical Raven!

When I arrived at the hostess stand, I was greeted by a friendly smile.

"Good afternoon and welcome to *Keetah's*," said the hostess. "Do you have a reservation today?"

"Yes, I do. Powers, party of two," I replied.

"Raven Powers."

I turned around to see where the familiar baritone voice emanated. In the shock of seeing him, I nearly dropped my purse as I steadied my knees.

Randy Boorman.

"It's great to see you," Randy said after kissing me softly on my cheek. "How are you, Raven?"

Sound still hadn't caught up to me leaving me looking like a mute bobblehead doll as I looked at the Devil that I'd just spoken of.

"Did I catch you at a bad time?" Randy asked.

Dammit Raven! Say something!!!

"Um, no! Not at all, Randy! I'm great. Doing well. I'm just on my lunch break," I babbled.

"Picking up something to go or can I invite you to stay and dine with me?" he asked.

Feeling my full body strength and courage return to me, I replied, "Actually I'm meeting my boyfriend for lunch."

"Hey, in that case, take my number and just call me when you get a minute," Randy offered, not giving me the opportunity to politely turn him down as he placed his business card in my hand before kissing me again, this time on the opposite cheek. "It was great running into you. I miss you. Call me!"

Neva Saw It Comin'

Before I could fully register the exchange I'd just had with Randy, Brian walked through the door, just barely running into Randy as he walked out.

"Hello Beautiful. Sorry I'm late. I called your office but your assistant said you'd already left," Brian said before leaning in to kiss me. Unintentionally, I moved my head back as Brian was about to kiss the cheek that Randy had just touched. "Everything OK?"

"Huh? Oh! Yes! Everything is just fine," I said. "My editor said that I can take an extra bit of time for lunch so long as I'm back for the staff meeting at two."

"Ah, the perks of moving up the corporate food chain. Well, that works for me because I have to go to the studio a little early today, like right after our lunch," Brian said as he pulled me in to try to kiss me again. This time I allowed him to finish. "But not a minute before I spend some time with my Beautiful Lady."

As much as I tried, I couldn't shake the image of my ex-lover from my thoughts. It had been so damn long since the last time I saw Randy that I thought for sure that I would never see him again.

I see I was wrong.

During lunch, between texts and calls from the office and Brian prattling on about how well his favorite sports team was doing, I tried to remain focused on the present while fighting memories from the past.

"Raven. Did you hear me?"

I looked up to see Brian and our server staring intently at me. "I'm sorry."

"Did you want any dessert?" Brian asked, looking concerned.

"No, thank you," I declined. "I just need to get back to my office. I'll see you tomorrow, right?"

"Um, I thought we had plans *tonight*," Brian pointed out, sounding confused.

"No," I said, going into Organized Raven mode as I pulled out my BlackBerry. Checking my agenda for the day, I continued. "You're going into the studio early today but you didn't think that you would get out any earlier than usual and tomorrow is your day off so you suggested that we spend the day together then. You wanted to have lunch today because you didn't want to go too long without seeing me."

"Oh! Right," Brian said, deflated. "Well, I hardly had lunch with you *now* so I was hoping we could get together tonight and talk about what's on your mind, if that's OK with you."

Instantly my thoughts returned to Randy.

"Nothing to talk about," I smiled, hoping to convince Brian to halt his questioning.

While Brian informed the waiter that we were ready for our check, I excused myself to go to the bathroom. After checking the stalls to see if there were any extra ears, I called Monique.

"Why me?!?" I lamented, barely giving Monique the chance to announce herself on the other end.

"Why you what?" Monique asked apprehensively.

"Just when I nip the office flirting in the bud, I run into the last man I ever needed to see in my life," I replied.

"The Devil?" said Monique knowing exactly who I was referring to as she was there when I first hooked up with Randy, going through all the ups and downs he and I went through. "Where was he?"

"Here at the restaurant. Just before Brian walked in, Randy kissed me on the cheeks and handed me his business card, talkin' 'bout 'I miss you. Call me'. As if *that* will ever happen!" I could feel my chest tighten at the idea of being in such close proximity to the one man that I thought I'd spend the rest of my life with only to be passed over again and again as he would fall in lust with someone else, all the while keeping me in the background. Just when I finally forgave him because I accepted that a person will only do what you allowed them to do, he returns. What is he up to?!?

"Did you introduce him to Brian?" Monique asked. I could hear the deviousness in her voice. I'm sure she was hoping I'd had a Jerry Springer moment.

"No," I smiled as I busted her bubble. "They passed each other as Brian came in and Randy was leaving."

"Well, now that Randy's back in the picture, whatcha gon' do?"

Monique, forever the Instigator.

"He's not 'back in the picture', Moni," I said just as I heard the bathroom door open. "We'll wrap this up when I get back to the office."

Abruptly, I closed my phone, washed my hands and exited the bathroom. I was greeted by Brian standing in the restaurant's foyer, holding my jacket.

"I'll be over tonight," Brian informed me.

"But you said it would be late," I retorted.

"It's never too late for me to come home to my lady," Brian said before kissing me full on the lips. "Enjoy the rest of your workday. I'll be home tonight."

As we went our separate ways, I couldn't help taking a quick look back at Brian. Before I could stop staring at him, he looked back just after crossing the street. Quickly I blew him a kiss before entering the office building. Just as I reached the elevator, the doors open. No sooner than I'd pushed the button for my floor did I feel the vibration of my cell phone. Looking at the screen, my mouth broke into a grin.

BSTJ74: *I love you, Raven.*

Still smiling, I said to myself, "If you keep this up, I could fall in love with you Mr. St. James."

Chapter 9
Imani

By the end of my workday, it dawned on me that I hadn't received a single call or text from my sister. Any other day I would be fine but for some reason, today I grew concerned.

"If Brian is there, I'm hanging up because I don't want to interrupt them but Raven and I rarely go a day without speaking. I just hope nothing is wrong," I thought as I dialed Raven's home number. Silently I prayed for my sister as the phone rang three times.

"Hello?"

Furrowing my brow, I asked, "Raven, are you crying?"

"Sis, don't start," she said before blowing her nose.

"Raven, you don't cry. Ever. Something is seriously wrong for *you* to cry. Talk to me," I implored.

What Raven revealed to me floored me to the point that when she finished and I opened my eyes, I was on my knees.

"Remember when I went to visit my girl Charlie in San Antonio?" Raven asked.

"I think you spent that Christmas with her the year we graduated from high school. You called to tell us that you changed your mind about going to Saint Louis University because you wanted to stay in Texas, right?" I replied.

"Right but before I went down there I had one last fling with Randy," she confessed.

"That jerk that was chasing after you while he had a girlfriend the entire time?" I asked with ire. "Hold up! Did you just say you had 'one last fling' with him? You mean to tell me you continued to sleep with him while he had a girlfriend?"

"Imani, focus on what I'm about to tell you because that plays into this," Raven said seriously. "While I was in San Antonio, I was so busy partying with Charlie that I didn't notice that I hadn't had my period for the first two months! I took a pregnancy test and it was positive. That same day, I called to tell Randy the news about the baby but he beat me to it when he told me that his girlfriend was pregnant. I told him that I couldn't have his baby and he was fine. Or so I thought.

"After I had the abortion, I came back to St. Louis only to run into Randy. He told me that he was looking forward to the baby that we'd conceived together and that he loved me. Sis, that was the first time he'd ever said it to me! Hell, it was the first time *any* man had said it to me! And as much as I tried to believe him, I couldn't because every time we were together, I was always the mistress. Never the main and only woman! All the while he's telling me he wants me to be his wife, even though he's admitted to proposing to his girlfriend as well. I loved Randy enough to believe every word he told me simply because he said three little words? And today I ran into him and for a brief moment, I forgot the hell I put myself through to be with him. I've spent the rest of the day wracking my brain, Imani! I've got one man telling me he loves me and another that clearly was simply sex yet I'm drawn to him, too. What the hell is wrong with me?"

God, why didn't she come to me when she was going through this?!? She's telling me now so now *is the point to focus on.*

"I just wanted Randy to love me but when I found out I was pregnant at the same time as the chick he was living with, I didn't want to put a child through that. It was bad enough I was barely out of high school myself with no job or skills to support a baby let alone myself," I lamented. "I wouldn't've even thought about the baby until I ran into Randy today! Then I went back over everything else I'd done with and for Randy and it was all a lie that I'd made up to make myself feel better about the lack of self-esteem I had to think that he was ever mine *knowing* that he was fucking me before going home to his family!"

"Is there anything else you need to tell me?" I asked in shock. "Why didn't you keep the baby or put it up for adoption? And please tell me you at least protected yourself when you continued to see Randy."

"It doesn't take much to get pregnant and even less to take care of *that*," I pointed out. "But no, I wasn't using abortions as birth control. I only got pregnant that one time and I've been making my lovers strap up ever since."

I tried to forget she said "lovers" which clearly indicated to me that my sibling may be mistaking sex for love. "Why didn't you call me when you were going through the pregnancy decision? I could've been there for you."

"You probably would've talked me out of the abortion," she stated.

"Raven, you were fresh out of high school. You had scholarships to Saint Louis University and Washington University. You had so much going for you and you made a choice that changed *all* of that," I stated. "I wouldn't dare choose your path. Only God can do that for you. The most I would've done then and now is be there for you to the best of my ability."

"Thanks Sis," Raven replied quietly. "But that was then. What do I do *now*?"

"Have you talked to Brian about Randy or the baby?" I asked.

"Not yet," she sighed. "We just took our relationship public. I don't know how he'll react to hearing that I've already conceived a child with a man that I thought was the love of my life. Kinda hard to live up to that status, ya know? Then, on top of all of this, I'm late again. I can't believe that I've let myself get so off track that I've repeated one of the worst parts of my history. Brian just came back to me. He might not be ready to add a baby to the scenario."

"Ray, a man is ready to have a baby with you *every time* you two have unprotected sex," I pointed out.

"We get caught up in the heat of the moment and I get knocked up?!?" Raven sighed heavily. "It was just the one time, Mani."

"One time is all it takes, Ray," I said, trying not to sound condescending. "Have you taken a test yet? It might be a false alarm. You know stress delays your cycle."

"I was just about to check the stick when you called," said Raven. "Hold on."

As I waited to hear back from my sister, I prayed.

Lord, I love my sister and I know that a baby is a blessing so if that is what You want for her, I only ask that You give me all that I need to help her as much as possible. Amen.

"False alarm!" Raven announced when she returned to the phone, sounding like she was holding the winning Powerball numbers. "You won't be an auntie!"

"Raven, how old are we?" I asked my twin, dismissing her jubilation.

"Huh? Whatchu mean?" Raven asked in return.

"What I mean is that you and I are too damn old to have pregnancy scares," I pointed out. "What's really going on? Is it Randy? Is Brian pressuring you?"

"Brian isn't pressuring me and... and I don't know what to say about Randy," said Raven flatly. "I haven't thought about that man for months and suddenly he's back in the picture just when things are starting to get normal for me?"

"Normal?" I asked. "Ray, I'm getting confused."

Sighing, Raven explained, "You and I are complete opposites, Sis. You are the good girl, I'm the bad ass. You were outside playing with our friends while Mother was either whoopin' me or grounding me. You got all the good grades, I was constantly in detention."

"Quit trying to make yourself look bad, Raven. You went to detention to get caught up on homework before you went to work at the daycare," I smiled. "OK so you didn't get into the National Honor Society like me but I was the academic one. You were the fun one that everyone wanted to hang out with. But you're getting off track. What do you mean by normal?"

"While I was in San Antonio, I got a little wilder than I would around you and Mother and that carried on once I came back," she explained. "You never saw me with anyone because the men I was involved with were either just for sex or they already had situations at home to deal with."

"Like Randy?" I asked.

"Exactly. Just when I thought I finally loved someone and was blessed to have their child, I find out that I'm not the only one about to make him a father. I didn't want my baby competing for his father's love and attention just because his father wasn't with me on a full time basis and I'm not the one to use a baby to trap a man. Yes, I could've put the baby up for adoption but I was only 18. I'd just managed to graduate from high school kid free and there I was about to become a single mother. Teenage pregnancy. Abortion versus adoption. None of that was in my plans, Imani."

"Raven, to be honest, I noticed that you and I were drifting apart during our senior year of high school but I figured you were finding your way. I didn't realize you were getting completely off track," I said as tears formed in my eyes. "You and I used to be so close then suddenly I lost you. Right about the time…"

"… that I hooked up with Randy. I know. I put him before everyone!" I could hear Raven crying on the other line. "I wanted that one man so bad that I did everything I could for him. Whatever he asked for, if I had it to give, I gave it. And if I didn't have it, I did all that I could to get it as long as I kept thinking that I was getting closer to being Randy's only woman. It took me so long to realize that people will do as much to you as you allow them to. I mean the sex was off the chain but at what expense? My self-esteem was already low because I was the largest of all my friends. When I would go out with them, even though I was just as pretty as any of them, the guys would flock to my skinny ass friends instead of me and I couldn't figure out why I wasn't getting any numbers until I became more promiscuous. The more I put out, the more attention I got. True, it wasn't positive attention but it was something when I had *nothing*! The only time I didn't mess around was when I was with Randy which is ironic considering *he* was the one messing around on his girl!

"When I came home from Texas, it was about a month after the procedure. I needed to be near you and Mother but Randy was the main reason why I came back," Raven admitted. "He told me he was looking forward to having a baby with me and that he was falling in love with me. He kept telling me that when the time was right, he was going to leave his girlfriend to be with me."

"Would this be the same girlfriend that was pregnant at the same time as you?" I asked, shaking my head as I waited for the response.

"Yeah," Raven replied. "And like a dumbass, I believed him. Do you know that was over five years ago? And for three of those years, I was there for him when he needed me. Money. A place to stay. Arms to hold him. A pussy to fuck. I gave him everything just for the *hope* of him giving *something* back to me. I feel so stupid for all the times I waited up for him, cooked dinner for him, made sure I was available for him yet he couldn't be bothered to do one simple thing: choose me!"

"Raven, you already have a man that chose you. You waited for him and he came in the form of Brian," I pointed out. "God knew what you needed and He provided it. Just open your eyes and see the blessings you have!" In the background, I could hear someone ringing Raven's doorbell. "You go ahead and get that. It's probably Brian."

"It shouldn't be. He's working late at the studio tonight," Raven replied. I patiently listened as my sister walked downstairs to answer her door. After a brief pause, she whispered into the phone, "It's Randy!"

"Randy?!?" I repeated. "Raven? Raven?!?"

The line went dead.

Chapter 10
Raven

"Randy?" I asked as I looked out of the peephole on my front door.

"Raven, I need to talk to you. Can I come in?" he pleaded. "It's important!"

Why didn't I move out of here when I had the chance? Should've known he'd show up here but TODAY?!?

Opening the door, I asked, "What's so important that you felt that it was suddenly OK to just drop by? I could've been busy with my boyfriend. You shouldn't be here or are you not familiar with the act of being loyal and faithful?"

"Actually, that's what I came to talk to you about," Randy said as he tried to walk into my apartment.

"Uh, excuse you!" I said as I pushed him back out the doorway onto the porch. "You can talk just fine out here," I finished, crossing my arms under my chest as I stood firmly in my doorway.

Taking my hand, Randy led me to the top of the steps and proceeded to sit down. "I remember a day when we sat out here talking."

"Yeah, one of those rare days when you weren't here for a fuck–and–run," I pointed out as I stood off to the side of him. I relaxed a little as the warm late spring breeze blew past my face.

"Raven, can you please come and sit down? I need to discuss something serious," Randy said, twisting around to look up at me.

Huffing, I joined Randy on the step. "First you show up at the restaurant, now my apartment? What's going on, Randy?"

"Don't worry, I'm not stalking you, Ray," he chuckled. "Actually, I'm kind of nervous. It's been a minute since I've seen you. You still look great."

"Happiness does that for a person," I smiled, thinking of Brian.

Glancing at my watch, I urged Randy to get on with whatever he came for. I wasn't expecting my boyfriend to come over anytime soon but I didn't feel comfortable with the idea of an ex being around when my man wasn't there. Not that I have much experience with having a man of my own but putting myself in Brian's shoes, I'd be damned if I would be happy to hear about this!

"It's a bit early in the day for a *visit* so what's up?" I asked coldly.

"Raven, I've known you for a long time. You're not only my lover but you're one of my best friends. I love just chillin' with you and talkin' or watching a ballgame with you. You were even cool when we hung out with my boys. You never nagged me or bothered me. Always kept it sexy and wet for me. You were always there when I needed you even though I rarely returned the favor. Ever since that last night we spent together, I can't get you off my mind and every time I think of you I smile," Randy said with a grin. "I know I wasn't the best boyfriend but…"

"I can't speak for your girlfriends," I interjected. "But as your *ex-lover*, you were at your best in the bedroom and that was fine for us. I wanted more than you could offer and I never pressured you for anything. I simply took whatever you gave me. As much as I thought I was winning your heart, I was losing everything else including my self-respect."

"And our baby," he said softly. "When you told me you were pregnant, I was so excited about being a father to our child. I never wanted you to do that and I wish I could've shown you that I would be there for you both."

"Don't you think you already had enough of that at your place? Or was I supposed to forget that your girlfriend was pregnant at the same time I was?" I asked as I stood up to walk back to my door. "Look, Randy, that's all in the past. As much as I loved you, I couldn't keep that baby knowing that we would only make things worse for you. You seemed to have made things work for your family so leave me out of it. I'm done being your mistress."

"I'm not asking you to be my mistress, Raven." I looked back to see Randy down on one knee. "I'm asking you to marry me."

Laughing, I looked down at my ex. "Not funny, Randy."

Standing, Randy said, "Raven, I'm serious. I'm not happy when I'm not with you. I try to get through my day without thinking about you but I just think more about you. Every morning I pray you'll forgive me and take me back and if you won't do that, I just want you to be happy."

"I *am* happy," I said looking directly into Randy's chocolate brown eyes. "Now if you'll excuse me, I'd like to get back to my happy life."

Randy took my hand in his and slipped a ring on my finger. "Were you *that* unhappy with me? You just said I was great in bed. Let me show you that I'm better than the man you think I am. I've changed. Please forgive my past mistakes. I want to share my life with you. Raven, marry me."

"Am I interrupting something?"

I looked past Randy to see Brian standing behind him.

"Sis?" I said weakly as I tried to focus my eyes. No matter what, whenever I was in trouble, I always looked for Imani to come and save me.

"Right here, Ray," Imani replied softly as she reached for my right hand.

Scanning my surroundings, I was startled.

"How did I get back in my room?" I said as I closed my eyes and tried to block out the throbbing pain in my head. "Oh my God! Brian! Where's... Where's Brian?"

"I'm right here, Beautiful," said Brian as he entered the room with a cool washcloth which he promptly draped across my forehead. Gently, he squeezed my left hand while he sat on the other side of me on the bed.

"The last thing I remember, you walked up just as Randy was proposing to me," I said then I gasped again. "Randy..."

"He's in the living room," said Brian smiling at me. "He and Imani explained everything."

"So you know that..."

"Yes, Raven," Brian replied before kissing me softly on the cheek. "I love you too much to let anyone come between us. He can love you all he wants but as long as you'll have me, I'm yours and I'm not going anywhere."

"Speaking of going somewhere, I need to get going so you two can have some time together," said Imani as she rose from her chair. The wood legs scraped against the floor as she dragged it back to the table on the opposite side of my room.

Any other time, that sound would grate my nerves but today it was a friendly reminder of someone that loves me no matter what.

"Tell Vincent I said hello," I said as Imani headed for the door.

"Will do. Love you, Lil Sis."

Brian spooned with me as my sister departed.

"Baby, I honestly don't remember what happened after you found me with Randy," I said just before he put a finger to my lips.

"Shh, Beautiful. I'll tell you but you need to rest," Brian said as he pulled me closer to him. "You hit your head pretty hard when you passed out."

"I passed out?!?" I exclaimed as I tried to remember what happened.

Randy came over and asked if he could come inside to talk to me. I kept him on the front porch because I figured there's less chance of slipping up outside in public. We started talking. He asked for forgiveness and proposed with ring and bended knee. Brian asked if he was interrupting us. Pitch black.

"Damn!" I exclaimed as I rubbed the lump on the back of my head. "OK well, I may have passed out but how long was I out for Imani to be here and how did I end up in bed with *you?*"

Yeah, that *sounded romantic!*

Chuckling, Brian replied, "I tried to catch you but Randy was closer and I thought he had you until I watched you slip out of his hands. I picked you up and carried you into the apartment. Had to fight ya boy off us. Guess he didn't realize I was your boyfriend and not just a friendly neighbor. As for Imani, she showed up shortly after I brought you inside. She said that you two were on the phone and the last thing you said was that Randy was here then the phone went dead. When you didn't answer her calls after that, she came right over to check on you."

"Brian..."

"Raven, like I said, he can love you. I'm not mad about that. And if you want to be with him, I'm not stopping you. I'm just letting you know that whatever you decide, as long as you're happy and honest with me, I'm happy," Brian said as he looked deep into my eyes.

"OK, so exactly what happened after I blacked out?" I asked, trying not to focus on the throbbing bump.

Tenderly pulling me close to him, Brian began the tale. "As I said, I brought you into the apartment. Randy protested all the way up until Imani showed up to identify me. He followed me to your bedroom asking me 'Nigga, who the fuck is you?' When I said that I was your man, he said 'Nigga, you white!' The whole time I answered his questions, my only thought was you. Once I had you comfortable on your bed, I directed him to the living room to finish the interrogation because I was curious to know who *he* was! Randy explained that he's your ex-boyfriend from high school and that when he ran into you today, he wanted to catch up with you. I guess he thought I was supposed to get pissed since he didn't mention that you told him about me."

I smiled hard when I heard Randy being described as my ex-*boyfriend*. One movie at Union Station to see *New Jack City*, a couple of nights with Chinese take-out and *years* of fucking on the low do not make you my boyfriend and *that* fa damn sho don't give you a solid foundation for marriage! How could I possibly think that what Randy and I had was *love*?!?

I turned to face Brian when he paused. I wasn't going to verbally admit that I'd mentioned Brian to Randy. I just wanted to see his face when he spoke.

"I told him that I'm your *current* boyfriend and that he was welcome to catch up with *us* anytime, if you wanted to," Brian said before softly kissing me on the lips.

Confession time.

"Baby, I've chased Randy for most of my adult life. I'm not saying that Randy is a bad person but he's never treated me with as much love, dignity and respect as you do. Until today, I never knew he wanted to take us beyond the bedroom! I don't want to hurt you by having lingering thoughts of him. I have to have closure with that relationship before I can fully focus on this one. OK?"

Quietly, Brian replied, "Take all the time you need."

"I think it'll be pretty quick," I said as I swung my legs over to the side of the bed, ignoring my spinning head. Gazing back at my boyfriend, I said, "You said Randy was in the living room, right?"

Perking up as he sat up, Brian said, "Yeah."

Taking his hand, I led Brian to the living room where we found Randy looking at my photo album on the coffee table. I smiled to myself as I imagined the look on his face when he saw nothing but pictures of Brian and me.

"Sorry about the intro, man," Randy said as he walked over to Brian to shake his hand. "Ray mentioned that she was seeing someone but I didn't realize you were…"

"Randy!" I nearly fainted again! I wasn't sure where he was going with that comment but it didn't sound like it would be politically correct and I certainly didn't want these two bangin' in my apartment!

"It's cool," Brian said as he walked over to the couch.

"Randy, I need to tell you something," I said as I joined my boyfriend.

"OK," Randy said glancing at Brian.

"He's staying. You're not," I said plainly. "I have no reason to go back to you for anything more than the pain you're sure to cause me. When I was with you, I loved you more than I loved myself which is why I overlooked the fact that you always had a girlfriend while you were sneaking over to see me. I didn't spend holidays with you because you were someone else's man and had to be home with her. I thank you for coming back into my life today because I needed the reminder of why you need to stay away from me. As much as I care for you, I don't love you enough to keep hurting myself." I gazed over at Brian and smiled as I looked back at Randy to continue.

"Randy, you and I have a history and that's fine. I've grown from my time with you. I've become stronger as each day passes but when I think back to the woman I was when I was with you, I didn't like me then. I love me now! I know you love me and want me to be happy so you will understand when I say that not only can I not marry you but I can no longer be friends with you," I finished as I took Randy's ring off my finger to hand it back to him.

Randy and Brian were both speechless.

"Randy?" I asked, hoping that I hadn't shocked him into a heart attack since I didn't know which girlfriend to return him to!

"Yeah... um, I'm just... stunned," he replied.

Quickly, I looked over at Brian who looked like he was suppressing a smile before turning my attention back to Randy.

"I mean, you said you had a man but that never stopped us from getting back together before," Randy explained. "I guess you finally found the happiness I could never give you. And I have to respect that because I love you."

Brian and I rose as Randy prepared to leave. Walking over to Brian, Randy said, "Congratulations. You have a good woman and I wish you both the best."

Kissing me on the cheek, Randy quietly commented, "Really, I'm happy for you Raven. Always."

"Thank you, Randy," I said as he hugged me.

Watching Randy walk out of my door for the last time was one of the best moments of my life. Feeling Brian's arms wrap around my waist topped it instantly.

"I'm so glad I came home early," Brian said as he kissed the top of my head.

"Baby, I love you," I said as I turned around to face my boyfriend.

"Beautiful, I love *you*," he replied before kissing me softly and gently rocking me in his arms.

Chapter 11
Imani

"Vincent! I'm home!" I announced as I entered my apartment. I smiled as I listened to my fiancé singing Usher's "Here I Stand" in the shower. Unfortunately his off key voice traveled all the way through the apartment but it was nice to know he was already at home. After looking through my mail, most of which was Snail Mail Spam, I walked toward the bathroom, humming along as my fiancé continued to sing.

Vincent emerged from the bathroom using a large bath towel to pat his pecs, abs and arms dry, oblivious to the fact that I was standing in the bedroom doorway admiring *him*. No sooner than my grin turned into a cheesy smile, it quickly faded as I looked around the room at the packed boxes! As I fully entered the nearly empty room, startled, I inquired, "Are you moving out?!?"

"Yes, and I'm taking you with me," Vincent grinned as he walked over to me, wrapping the towel around his waist. "Our realtor called just after I finished reading your note saying that you went to see Raven. We got the condo!"

"We got it?!?" I squeaked after the news settled in.

"Yes, we did! The Wheelers are movin' on up!" Vincent exclaimed as he lifted and spun me in a circle. When he placed me back on the floor, I couldn't help taking off his towel.

"I think that kind of news calls for a celebration," I said as I ran my fingers down Vincent's abs to his waistline.

"Ya don't say?" he grinned.

"I *do* say!" I grinned back. "But I have one question. How soon can we move?"

"As soon as we finish celebrating, we'll figure that out," Vincent suggested. "So what happened to Raven?"

"Before I tell you *that*, I need to discuss something," I said sincerely.

"Anything for you," Vincent said as he squeezed me close to his nakedness.

"Recently I found out some things about someone that I love dearly and from hearing what they went through, I don't want to see that happen to us," I began as I sat on the bed. Vincent proceeded to undress me as I continued talking. "I trust that you and Shawnaé are completely done."

"The last time I spoke to her, I told her that my life is with you now and that there won't be any on-the-side liaisons with her or anyone," Vincent said after pulling off my jeans.

"That's good to hear because if you feel the need to be with other women, you and I need to end this because I couldn't be with you knowing that you're sneaking off to see another woman…"

"The only woman I want is you," Vincent said as he pulled me up off the bed and into his arms again. "Shawnaé and I were in lust with each other. Even if she could pull off being a real woman, she's not the one for me. I wish her the best but I have no reason to see her again."

"Did you ever want more for you two?" I asked thinking back to why Raven kept taking Randy back.

"Imani, things were already shaky between Shawnaé and me but when she left at the most crucial point of my life, I knew that I needed more than what I thought I had with her," Vincent said as he held me close. "We both know the Lord moves in mysterious ways and I'm thankful that He's moving things forward in my life with you. You have nothing to worry about from Shawnaé or any other woman. Imani, I am committed to my life with you and no one else. Except maybe a baby or three."

Not needing to hear anymore, I simply prayed.

Father, thank you for watching over Raven and me and for keeping us safe. Please keep people like Randy and Shawnaé out of our lives as we continue on the path You have laid out for us. May the rest of our days be in Your grace. Amen.

Looking up at my fiancé, I knew that my prayer had been answered.

Epilogue

"I'm so glad the weather decided to stay in the 80's this week," Imani commented as she returned to the patio with Vincent and our coffee.

"I know, *right?*" I said as I retrieved Brian's and my coffee cups from my twin and her fiancé. "Writing indoors was working against my creative flow."

"And here I thought I was doing a good job of keeping you occupied until you could play outside," said Brian as he snuggled my ear.

"You did, Baby, but you know writing is my first true love," I smiled before kissing my boyfriend. Turning my attention back to our hosts, I said, "Imani, I love your new condo. You and Vincent found the perfect little nest for you two to begin your lives together."

"Cheers to the happy couple," Brian announced, raising his mug. We all joined in the toast before kissing our respective partners.

"Make that happy *couples*," Imani winked at me. "So how was the cruise? We were thinking of taking one for our honeymoon."

Looking at Brian as he took my hand, I smiled. "It was great! They had so many activities on board and of course we had to try pretty much everything! We almost didn't have time to sleep!"

"But we managed to find our room a *few* times," Brian laughed as I playfully nudged him. "Maybe next time you two will go with us. We could take a nice Caribbean cruise in October for the girls' birthday."

"Sounds like fun," Vincent said before kissing Imani's cheek. "Most of my traveling has been back and forth between here, Kansas City and Chicago. I love living in St. Louis but I can't wait until Imani and I go out of town for some real traveling. I need to see more than the Lou!"

"Raven and I are used to traveling. Mother and Father took us all over the country when we were children," Imani gushed.

As I sat with my sister and our men, my thoughts drifted momentarily to Randy. For as many years as I pursued him and gave him his every wish and desire, I'm blessed to finally come to the realization that he never truly wanted what I wanted for us. Don't get me wrong. I'm thankful for all of the many lessons Randy has taught me. Patience after waiting for years to hear him choose me over every other woman he was with. Cultivating my skills not only in the bedroom but also when entertaining his friends. Granted that was limited in practice but Randy knew he never had to worry about me wildin' out on him while we were out with his boys. Of the few men in my life, Randy was the one that I compared them all to. He wasn't the best gauge but he was the only constant in my life.

Deep down I knew that not only could I offer more to a man than my body but I also deserved more in return than the occasional visit for a quick sex session with someone else's man. Hell, what did I expect when that was all I offered? I mean, really? How would he know if I could cook his favorite meal when all he ate was my pussy? How would he know that I liked to do more traveling than down to his dick? You never know until you ask and that was just something I was afraid to ask. I always believed that if I deviated just *slightly* from my game plan that I would lose any ground that I'd gained with Randy, or any man, for that matter.

As much as I wanted more for myself, I didn't think that I could redirect my life so quickly and, so far, successfully. Then I met Brian. Despite how we began, Brian and I managed to turn our undercover rendezvous into a full time liaison. With everything going so well in my personal and professional life, I couldn't help looking up and smiling, my indication to Imani that I was saying a silent prayer.

First, for years I have an affair with the one man I believed would be the only man I would ever love. He breaks things off with me to work things out with yet another girlfriend that isn't me. I am heartbroken as he has made that decision several times before only for him to return to me with the same empty promises. And every time, I'm there with open arms and legs. Little did he know, to the tune of the Trey Songz hit, that was the LAST time for me. I vowed that day to never to let Randy Boorman help me hurt me again.

Then, through no fault of his own, Brian enters the soap opera that is my life. I was so busy being a freak in the streets *and* in the sheets that I almost lost him! Who knew he was looking for me just as much as I was looking for him?!? I can only thank God that Brian loves me as I am!

Now, we have the ex returning with a marriage proposal coming from left field. At no point did we go past sleeping together so what made him think he could turn this ho into his housewife? Not to mention that I informed him that I already had a man. I guess the years of me saying yes must've warped his brain into thinking that I would jump at a marriage proposal. Especially since it was coming from *him*.

Not.

It goes to show that you never know what plan God has for you. Instead of worrying about what's around the corner, I will thank God for the blessing that is my life. In my wildest dreams, I didn't see Randy proposing to me let alone seeing myself walking away from him or my trifling trampy chick on the side lifestyle to find someone that saw more in me than I ever thought possible. Brian has been such an improvement for my life. Yes, there is more to a relationship than mind blowing sex! And I have no problem letting Brian demonstrate to me just how great our life together will be.

As I turn the page to the next chapter of my life's story, I will move forward with all the lessons I've learned knowing that no matter how I may plan for my future, God has His own plan for me.

Thank you God for giving me the strength and the words to remove Randy from my life.

Stroking my fingers through Brian's freshly cut hair, I instantly thought back to the night we met.

"Beautiful, what are you grinning about?" Brian grinned back at me before giving me a quick peck on the lips.

Giggling, I came clean. "I was thinking of how long your hair was when we met."

His quizzical expression caused me to raise an eyebrow back at him.

"My hair wasn't long," Brian said seriously.

"It was longer than it is now, Baby," I said, smiling as I once again ran my fingers through his ringlets.

"Oh, you just want me to look like that one guy," Brian half-sneered. "So sick of people saying I look like him!"

"Who?" Vincent asked as he practically poured a cup of sugar into his cup of coffee.

"Robin Thicke," Brian and I said in unison.

"You know what? You *do* look like him!" exclaimed Imani. "I guess that's why I thought you looked familiar!"

"Y'all need to quit teasing him," Vincent said in Brian's defense.

Sitting there with my family, I couldn't help expressing my gratitude.

I never thought that after years of living the way I did that I would find a man as wonderful as Brian. Thank you God for bringing Brian to me.

I guess it's like Granny used to say, "Baby, you so busy lookin' the wrong way, ya neva see a good thing comin'!"

Nuzzling in my boyfriend's ear, I thought to myself, "I guess you were right, Granny."

~♥~

Tattooed Souls

Teresa Seals

Chapter 1

"I see you like fucking over folks with yo slick talking ass. You think you can talk mother fuckers up out of their drawers. Snort that shit NOW you lil dope fiend mother fucker. You betta snort it all!" the plump profound player yelled as he enunciated every word with a hardhearted tone.

Looking at the barrel of the loaded pistol, Pete had no choice but to comply. Beleaguered, his eyes *stayed* bloodshot red. Snorting a gram of the purest cocaine hadn't taken total effect to get him to *that* point. It was merely the anger that was overflowing within his soul. This was the fifth time this week that he had been abducted from his spot while out there slinging his poison. His one mistake sent the old player overboard. Pete had rather for him to have buried him alive, instead of humiliating and torturing him.

Pete was trying to let all the up and coming savages around his way know *he* was the man on the North Side. He disparaged everything that came his way. He just happened to get caught belittling the wrong individual. A pure joke came with the ultimate punch line. Killing him was his initial intent for his young worker, Pete. The punishment for this worker, which violated his family, was seeing Pete die slow as he walked the streets as a dope fiend.

Every time Pete raised the glass pipe to his lips or stuck the venom in his vein, he thought about the torture and the humiliation that had pushed him to the point of no return.

##########

Sizzling, crackling, and popping was all that could be heard. Sparks of red, blue, green, orange and silver with the looks of several scrambled rainbows could be seen in the air. The streets overflowed with the sounds of harmonious laughter from the abundant amount of delighted children. They held lit pumps, struck many matches, and flickered large flame lighters as the atmosphere filled with smoke. Every single child that ran around outdoors on this day was sporting new kicks along with their attire on this summer holiday on Saint Louis City's North Side.

"Crow, you betta watch that damn Roman Candle and aim toward the sky!" Skye jumped to the left of Crow as he aimed the Roman Candle at an angle which she felt was way too close to her. She looked down to make sure she didn't scrape her all white leather K-Swiss. These teenagers were enjoying the holiday as well. Any other day you could find Crow jogging around Fairgrounds Park fighting the air as Skye trailed behind on her ten speed bike to show her support. The holiday called for a day off from their workout ritual.

"I *am* aiming toward the Skye!" Crow laughed at his very own sarcastic remark. He always found some amusement as he cracked jokes telling his best friend that the sky is always the limit even though she was so short she was going to have a difficult time reaching it.

The sounds of *Clack! Clack! Clack! Clack!* repeatedly echoed throughout the block. Skye and Crow ducked down beside the car and watched as three men ran out of Skye's home. Skye wasn't even worried about scuffing up her new shoes at this point. Skye's concern was mainly her safety. Even though it was the Fourth of July and the explosion of fireworks were expected to be heard, gunfire had a distinguished sound in their North Side neighborhood. If no one was a victim of circumstance, the reverberation of gunfire was heard like music to most ears on a daily around those parts. It was as if a day didn't go by that shots were not fired followed by someone getting shot up or being taken away in a black body bag.

Although the drug game was very much prevalent, neither of the two primary gangs were organized. Crips claiming one set on one block with the Bloods setting up camp one block over. The peculiar thing to it all was that everyone knew one another from either the grade school or the local recreational activities like little league football. It was either that or being related to one another.

On this particular summer day, the gunfire caught their attention and seemed to be very unusual. The sounds of the barrage of bullets had never escaped from Skye's home. It was known to her that her father owned some fire power but he never had a reason to use it. He let his family know he held on to it for their protection.

Skye looked at Crow with her familiar look of agony. Crow knew that it had to be another problem that had taken place in the Stewart's household. He hated to see Skye wearing that look. It was though he could feel her pain. The problem that took place in Skye's home had to be major because Mr. Stewart was a smooth talker and resorting to violence was the last thing he would do.

Skye was an only child and lived with her mother, father, and her uncle, Pete. With her uncle being a few years older than she was, she grew up like the younger sibling. Everything was split amongst her and her young uncle.

Pete was just seven years older than Skye and twenty-four years younger than his older brother. Skye's grandmother died from complications giving birth to Pete. She had similar complications during the birth of Skye's father and it was advised *then* that she not give birth anymore.

Skye's father raised his younger brother as if he were his very own child. Pete had several problems that drove the Stewart household insane because he enjoyed the street life and getting his nose dirty. Unfortunately, Skye's father always seemed to be the one being preyed upon every time Pete came up short or ventured into something scandalous.

"I wonder who the fuck Pete owe now!" Crow looked at Skye. "Ya know I can kill his ass and yo daddy don't have to keep getting his ass kicked behind him running off with someone's work or their stash. Matter of fact, I'll get Sammy to take care of him. Yo daddy will not have to sweet talk anyone else to save his ass. It wouldn't be much of a problem cause he already dancing with the devil. He might as well join'em!"

Skye smiled at her longtime friend. She admired his sense of protection when it came to her. She wished it could be that simple. With a slight turn of her head, she glanced at Crow. "Then we have to bury my daddy 'cause that dude love his brother mo than he loves me and my mama. Please let's not involve Sammy b.k.a Mr. Ruthless." Skye giggled.

It was a brief moment of silence as they both pictured Sammy thugging. Together, Crow and Skye shared a laugh thinking about how ruthless Sammy could be. Although he was the baby brother, Sammy possessed a big heart that was as cold as steel with the worse venom found within a snake.

Crow started to walk toward Skye's home. "Come on so we can see what's going on." Skye followed behind him. Crow was dedicated to his amateur boxing and his body was fit for it at such a young age. Sanford Louis was his government name and he despised it. He earned the name Crow from his boxing mentor, Chico. His mentor boasted to everyone how successful Crow's boxing career was going to be. Chico was thrilled whenever he heard one of Crow's opponents squeal with a loud sigh whenever he landed his brutal jabs.

Crow's stature was cock diesel and no one in the neighborhood young or old tested him. There were a couple of other boxers from the North Side but Crow's reputation was the loudest. He was allegedly rumored to be the descendant of another well known boxer although it was never proven.

Crow possessed the looks but his brother Sammy had the killer reputation. Crow got mad love from everyone because his hands were known to lay anybody flat on their back in a matter of seconds. Skye followed behind him like a little lost puppy. She admired his demeanor and the way he always seemed to come to her rescue.

Skye's father ran to the door huffing and puffing with his glock .40 in his hand. "If my aim was on point I would've killed every one of their asses! Baby finish packing!" Mr. Stewart yelled back in the house to his wife. "I will be so glad to leave this damn neighborhood. I am sick and tired of these wannabe gangsters coming around here issuing out threats. I'm a kick Pete's ass myself!" Mr. Stewart watched as his daughter and her friend approached him. It was evident where Skye's height came from. Her mother was average sized in height but her father was no taller than Sherman Hemsley. "Skye, you and Crow go see if Pete around there on St. Louis Ave and Sarah!"

Crow slightly turned his head. With the raise of one eyebrow, he chuckled. He and Skye turned around doing what was instructed by Mr. Stewart. "What's *really* going on? Mr. Stewart trying to murk somebody! I knew he had some ruthlessness somewhere in him! I mean damn he trying to get'em by any means necessary!"

When they made it to the corner, it was a ghost town. Wasn't a soul coming or going from the corner that usually had constant traffic the moment the liquor store opened and even long after it closed. Skye looked at Crow and they both knew something was very wrong.

##########

"Crow is hung like a black stallion. I felt like I was undergoing a hysterectomy or something when his cocky ass was up in me! I don't know how long I can keep stringing him along. He took me down through there! I think it's time for me to do what I need to do. He acting like he trying to make me his baby momma!" Skye took a drag off her Newport with her left hand as Chastity squeeze the yellow oblong sponge so the warm water ran down her back. Skye leaned back resting her head on the back of the bathtub. She closed her eyes thinking about how Crow entered her deep dark chocolate petite frame. Chastity kneeled down beside the tub giving Skye her nightly sponge bath just how she liked it. She was waiting on Skye to ask her about her day at the shop, but Skye appeared to have drifted off to Neverland. Chastity removed the cigarette from her hand and tossed it into the toilet. She was so anxious to tell Skye that she could fall back for awhile and let Crow do him. Chastity had a problem with the fact that the only thing that seemed to be popping off with him and Skye was wild sex. She had the feeling that Skye was forgetting what she was actually supposed to be doing. Although she never mentioned it to Skye, Chastity sensed that Skye was enjoying being knocked down by Crow. That was definitely not what was supposed to be taking place.

As Chastity rose from the side of the tub, Skye could feel the movements but didn't want to open her eyes because she didn't want to deter from the sex escapade that was dancing around in her head. Skye could sense the reluctance and figured that Chastity was probably caught up in her feelings. She knew that this sex escapade that was taking place was going to have to come to an end very soon. Crow had put something on her mind and she was not about to let Chastity violate the astonishing feeling she was still having four hours later.

Skye began to feel a moist sultry feeling caressing her right nipple. Chastity knew just how to entice Skye. She enjoyed how wet Skye would become when she caressed all the right spots. Chastity didn't have much territory to conquer because Skye only stood four feet and eleven inches. It was becoming so simple for Chastity to take care of all of Skye's hot spots once she found where they were. She knew what Skye liked and when to just test it out on Skye; it worked every time. Skye opened her eyes trying to figure out how Chastity became undressed so quickly when she was just fully clothed a moment ago.

Skye let out a long hard sigh of satisfaction and Chastity knew that it was okay for her to continue. With a limited amount of space to move Chastity placed her hands around Skye's small waist and pulled her up so that her pearl was directly above her tongue. Skye grabbed Chastity by her bald head.

"Chas, not right now." Skye rubbed her fingers through the small deep curls in Chastity's low cut fade.

"Chas, not right now is all I have been hearing lately. If it ain't nothing to do with cutting your hair we haven't gotten intimate for months. I can count on one hand how many times we have been intimate in the last four years." Chastity was growing jealous of Crow and Skye's relationship. From all the other causalities, Crow was the only one that was taking the longest for Skye to infiltrate.

Chapter 2

"Hey shawty do wop!" All of the barbers spoke in unison as Skye entered Chastity's barbershop. Chastity was the owner of Infinity Styles located in the St. Louis's north county area. She had three barbers that worked for her. Once she opened her shop she didn't have to look far. She persuaded every one of the guys in the neighborhood that was cutting hair in their homes for their friends to come and cut hair in her shop. Derrick, Robert, and Emanuel all grew up with Chastity. Her older brother had the hook up on just about everything so it wasn't hard for them all to acquire their license to work in the shop.

She went after the three people that her brother trusted with his life. They were something like her little crew. Derrick was the quiet chubby one of the crew. Robert was the comedian. He was poised, clean cut, and a habitual chronic consumer. Emanuel was the brains. His demeanor was serene. He was on point at all times. He felt as though he could read people just by observing them. Together the three of them were two steps from being the black *Three Stooges*.

Chastity's demeanor was more masculine than any of the fellas in the shop. No one understood why someone so pretty chose to be a carpet muncher or, as Denzel stated in *Training Day*, the owner of her very own lick-her-license. Even with the deep waves and the low fade, Chastity's beauty was undeniable. Her smooth flawless coffee skin was dominating. Even the small tear drop tattooed under her right eye didn't take away from her beauty. Her curvaceous frame drove the men wild. She couldn't even hide any of those curves with her manly attire. The curves were just as dominating as her hazel eyes. The only thing that Chastity really admired about her body was the fact that she was only a 36A. People couldn't even tell that she even had breasts because they were so petite. She always wore small tight tank tops to press her breasts up against her body concealed under her clothing.

The very first time Skye made contact with Chastity, she thought she was a dude. She couldn't even tell her or her brother apart. It wasn't until Chastity asked if she waiting on a particular barber that Skye realized she was a female. The sound of her voice was agile and alluring.

Skye walked over to Chastity's booth. She stood on her tippy-toes to kiss Chastity on her cheek. Chastity paid her no mind. She already had an attitude with Skye because they hadn't been intimate for a while. She hated that Skye even came in and did that in front of the other barbers. Chastity wasn't ashamed of the fact that she was very much into women, she just didn't want to flaunt it in front of her workers. Chastity was wondering why Skye was even acknowledging her with the kiss. The rules were always to remain that Skye was only her client and it wasn't supposed to be public knowledge that Skye was an alleged lesbian. Chastity was glad that no one was even in the shop to see her bless her with the kiss that instantly made her moist. It would mess up the little charade they had going on. Chastity had cancelled all appointments to go spend some time at her brother's gravesite. Although she was missing money, she was truly happy that no one was there to see Skye land that passionate kiss on her cheek.

"Are we riding with Charles?" Skye asked.

"I am not even sure he's going. In all the four years we have been going, he had not visited Chad yet. The last time he was at the gravesite was Chad's first day there. I think he blames himself for his death." Chastity's facial expression was heartfelt.

"You know you never even told me what happened to your brother." Skye thought about the open tear drop tattooed on Chastity's face and the picture of Chad tattooed on her back on the top portion of her left shoulder. In Skye's world, it wasn't unusual to see tattooed tear drops on someone's face. She had just never seen one on a female. She thought that she had maybe killed someone but Crow let her know that if it's closed that meant that person had a body. The fact that she had an open tear drop merely meant that it represented the loss of someone.

Emanuel sat back looking at the television taking all of the conversation in. Robert was sitting at his booth working his thumbs as he text updated his status on Facebook while Derrick was on the phone setting up a date with one of his many women. They were waiting on Chastity because they never let her go out to the cemetery alone. They would go sit, drink, and reminisce. Emanuel, Robert and Derrick all had matching tattoos on their inner right arm that read: *Chad, we roll to our dying days.*

"I even hate thinking about my brother's death, let alone talking about it." Chastity's eyes began to water. That statement sparked everyone's attention and all of sudden the atmosphere was filled with compunction. Derrick, Robert, and Emanuel had their own regrets about what went down on the day Chad was murdered. It was as though they all looked down at their tattoos and began to reminisce.

The ding of the shop door as it opened sort of broke the monotony. It was though the sound of clippers clipping ceased. It wasn't often that Charles paid Infinity Styles a visit. Everyone was curious to know why the profound player was making this unannounced visit. Skye watched as he wobbled toward her and Chastity. He physically invaded their space as he bent down to kiss Chastity.

"Skye, this is my big brother, Charles. Charles, this is my friend, Skye." Chastity pointed amongst the two of them nonchalantly as her words flowed hastily from her tongue as though she really didn't want to introduce them.

Charles looked Skye up and down. He knew that his sister was into women. He kind of enjoyed it because he didn't have to worry about her fooling around with some bum ass dude in the Lou or some fool bragging about how they were knocking down his little sister. Looking Skye over, he sneered. "You look so familiar to me. Did I ever date your mother or did she used to work for me or something?"

"Work for you?" Skye asked with the swankest attitude. "Only if you go by the name of Bishop because the only work my mother do is for the Lord." The sassiness was very prevalent.

"Yeah I go by Bishop but more like the Bishop Don Juan!" Charles shared a laugh with the other barbers. Charles was a major player in the dope and pimp game. When he started off in the game, things were a bit more organized in St. Louis. Everyone in the game knew their boundaries. Most of the players were chasing the mighty dollar and the only thing that was being claimed was done by the little break dancing crews. Things slowed down for Charles once his younger brother was murdered. He was making his moves to retire because he was tired of the disrespect that was taking place in the city. He was trying to give some guidance to the younger hustlers but his words were falling on deaf ears. The murder of his brother sped up the process. He wanted to start a war but he didn't know who he could trust. The rules had already been violated, but he kept his ear to the street. He was bound to find out who killed his baby brother. In the Lou, the streets were always talking and somebody was always listening. It was bothering him that in four years no one said nothing about what went down. Charles' right hand man, Mike, took over the business. Charles did some investing with his money. Chastity's barbershop was one of his many investments.

Skye wanted to speak on his fatness and see how funny he found that. She chose otherwise because during that entire conversation, Chastity seemed to be elsewhere. She could tell that Chastity was still mourning her brother's death. Since Skye had known her, each anniversary of Chad's death seemed to just become so unbearable for Chastity. Skye didn't understand how someone so scandalous could be so sentimental, but everyone had a weakness. Chastity's family was hers.

"You must be going with me to see Chad. That could be the only reason you have graced me with your presence today." Chastity waited on his response. Emanuel even spun his chair around, looked up and waited to see what Charles was about to say.

"I knew that was where you were on your way to. That's the purpose of my visit. I actually came by to tell you to give that a break. Y'all going there talking to the dirt and crying ain't gonna bring'em back." Charles gave her direct eye contact as he dug the knife in her heart with that statement. "Y'all all around here tatted up with Chad name all over your body. You are not 'pose to mourn this way. Shit, he a lot better off than us!"

"How could you even say that?!? Had it not been for *your* bullshit, Chad would still be here!" Chastity let the tears slowly escape her eyes. She didn't know what happened on that rainy summer night. She felt the need to blame someone and Charles was always the one she gave the case. Even though she was right inside and watched Chad as he walked to answer the door not knowing he wouldn't return, she still gave Charles the case. She had just moved in with Chad and had only been there for a month. She couldn't take any more of her mother nagging about her lifestyle.

Chad and Chastity's place of residence was on Ashland Avenue right across from an elementary school. It was a two family flat that Charles used to house his pharmaceuticals. When the city put out an ordinance on the parameters of drugs near schools and heavy time to go with violating it, Charles decided it was best he changed his location. Chad convinced Charles to let him stay there to entertain his female companions. Although their mother was totally set against it, Charles obliged. After Chad's death, Charles immediately got Chastity out of there putting her up in his condo he had out in the boondocks in a suburban area in north St. Louis County. This was his little hideaway no one knew about it. She had been there for the last four years and wasn't planning on going anywhere else.

Chastity started cleaning up her station, snatching items and throwing them into her black duffle bag. She carried this bag with her needed items instead of opting for a handbag. She signaled Skye with a look on her face to let her know that it was time for them to vacate the barbershop and her brother's presence. Skye had never seen Chastity with this look. All the evil thoughts that Skye held in her heart toward Chastity was put on pause. She was growing with remorse and she returned with the look of "I am here if you need me". Skye continued to observe Chastity's every move. She could tell that Chastity was holding back her tears. She followed Chastity as she walked toward the front of the shop to the exit door. As Chastity grabbed the door knob as she was about to exit, Crow was making his way through the door.

"Hey Chastity! Where are you on your way to?" Crow asked, looking like he just hit the Powerball jackpot.

Chastity twisted her mouth as her upper lip arched high on the right side of her mouth. "Didn't I tell you I wasn't working today?!" Charles had just pissed her off and now the last person on the face of the Earth that she wanted to see was standing before her. The way her words rolled off her tongue, her hate didn't go unnoticed.

"Well little Miss Chastity I forgot." Crow already knew that the animosity amongst them was thick because of his connection to Skye.

"You can come back tomorrow and I will do you up!" Chastity continued to walk out the door. Skye gave Crow a very dry hello and followed Chastity out of the door.

Crow stood in the doorway and watched as Chastity and Skye walked toward the gray Mazda Protégé parked on the opposite side of the street, directly in front of the barbershop. He was trying to figure out why they both were looking so sad.

Charles wobbled toward the door. He placed his hand on Crow's left shoulder. "Dyke One and Dyke Two just need some dick in their life! But anyway, when your next fight? I heard you were on that Corey Spinks and Devon Alexander ticket."

Crow looked at Charles. He was pleased every time someone recognized him. "A date hasn't been set yet. The plan is the Fourth of July, but no one has confirmed it yet."

"Well let me know. I hope I can get the hook up on some seats. I want that front row action." Charles wobbled on out the door.

"I'll do that playa," Crow replied with a Colgate smile.

Crow looked over in Emanuel's direction. "I just need to be lined up."

Robert looked over at Emanuel. "You know how Chas is about fucking with her customers." Emanuel smiled looking like a darker version of Shemar Moore.

Derrick looked at Crow. "Dude, just come back tomorrow. This ain't a good time right now. Chastity is always on edge this time of year. That little lining may just trigger something and push her *over* the edge. We really don't need that right now."

Emanuel wasn't even *thinking* about giving Crow a lining. He was just trying to figure out why every time that Skye came around, Crow always happened to just show up. Emanuel thought about the situation for a minute. He let it go, thinking that Skye had put it on'em so Crow was pussy whipped.

Crow looked around and a sense of uneasiness set in. "I'll just come back tomorrow."

Emanuel took one last glimpse at Crow. "Yeah do that playa. Just come on back tomorrow."

Crow sensed the sarcasm but he knew it was best just to keep it moving.

They watched as Crow exited the shop. Derrick and Robert hopped up not wanting to be left behind and tidied up their booths. Emanuel took his time making sure everything was turned off. He turned off the television, putting the remote up in his station drawer. When he reached the front of the shop, Derrick and Robert were waiting for him. Emanuel closed the blinds, set the alarm, and locked the door behind him.

Chapter 3

"Get it daddy! You like that? Is it good to ya baby?" Skye looked over her shoulder as she threw it back at Crow.

"Yeah daddy bout to bust baby! Uurrgggh!" Crow yelled as his body collapsed on Skye.

"Come on Crow. You already know I have to leave. Chastity is becoming fed up with all this time we are spending together." Skye said as she tried to get Crow up off of her.

"Skye, my mother is starting to complain about keeping Savion all the time. You are going to have to bring all this to an end and come on home. I have had just about all I can take myself." Crow rolled over exposing his nakedness.

"You can take him over to my mother. She loves spending time with him. Baby, you knew that this was going to take some time. We have carefully planned this all the way out and I feel that this is about to come to an end." Skye looked at Crow with discernment. "Just give me a couple of more days. We have made it too far."

"Girl, I am not dropping him off with your mother. She be asking way too many damn questions. The last time I went over there without you, she was wondering was it something going wrong with us." Crow looked Skye directly in her eyes. "Have you went to visit your father lately?" Crow waited on Skye to respond.

"I stopped by my mom's and she said he hanging in there. He just refuses to take his meds." Skye put her head down. She hated that her dad was not able to cope with his younger brother's death.

Mr. Stewart had been diagnosed as a bi-polar depressive and the moment he missed his medication, it took him to the far end. He would become very violent and *anything* triggered his temper. It became unbearable for Skye's mother. When he came down off his trip, Mr. Stewart told his wife to commit him to a mental health facility. It was only for her safety. Ever since that incident on the Fourth of July when those individuals came and violated him as they bombarded their home with hopes of coming out with his wife, things hadn't been the same for the Stewart family.

Crow knew that talking about her dad had become a very touchy subject. He hated sometimes even asking her about going to see him. Crow went every Wednesday and he always took Savion with him. Mr. Stewart seemed to enjoy the hour that they spent with him listening to old street stories on how the Lou once was. Skye's father always ended his stories with, "These tattooed souls begin with love, don't understand loyalty but they somehow find a way to end with betrayal."

"So who is the next vic?" Crow looked over at Skye and waited on her to respond.

"Some dude name Q. She told me about him on our way back from visiting her brother's gravesite." Skye walked over to gather her clothes and put them in the dirty clothes hamper before she walked in the bathroom to take a shower.

"Q? I haven't never heard of him. Where is he from?" Crow grabbed his plaid boxers from the side of the bed and followed Skye into the bathroom.

"He from the CHI or some shit. He knows one of the barbers in the shop."

Skye turned the knobs on the faucet. As she felt the temperature of the water, it was warm enough to get in. She adjusted the shower head and pulled the shower curtain closed.

Crow pushed the shower curtain so he could take a look at Skye and she could see him. "I am the end to this. You need to get this done. One of the barbers know him? Skye that doesn't sit well with me."

"Everything is all good. One of their sisters hooked up with him when they went to the Taste of Chicago last summer sometime. He has been coming down here hooking up with a couple of dudes from out west. Pagedale, or some shit. He 'bout to set him up a lil spot on the south side and call it his second home or some shit. He came to the shop a couple of times. He likes how good Chastity cuts hair."

"Well, he might be a little more of a challenge from all the others. Let me ask around about him. This might not go down as easy as all the others. Most of the time y'all been getting at cats with no heart. This dude might not take that slick shit so easy." Skye could see how concerned Crow was about her safety.

"When is your next fight?" Skye felt the need to change the subject. She was already changing her mind.

"They talking about the Fourth of July. Things just hasn't been finalized." Crow answered with hopes that Skye would consider his feelings this time around and listen to him.

"Well you need to tell your little brother that things are about to go down and I am going to need him on the Fourth of July."

"Didn't I tell you that I wanted to be there?" Crow was not pleased that Skye was trying to leave him out.

"Dude look at here, people don't even know about your grimy ass little brother, Sammy. If things don't go as planned I don't want your name coming up in nothing. All this can jeopardize your boxing career. You need to think about our child. Has Sammy ever let you down? Besides do you know how the turnout to that is gonna be?" Skye waited on Crow to respond.

Crow thought about their child, Savion. He wanted to give him better than what he and Skye grew up with. Sammy had never failed him and came through in the hardest of times and he knew everything would go fine. He just wanted this all to end and it needed to end soon.

Chapter 4

Skye slammed the door as she entered Chastity's condo. Chastity was sitting on the couch Indian style with a white tank top and some red boy shorts watching the Game Show Network. She was playing along with Family Feud as if she was a contestant. Skye walked over and kissed her on her forehead.

"How is your father doing? Is he better than the last time you went to visit him? He must wasn't ready for you to leave." Chastity rolled her eyes assuming and hoping that was where Skye had been that entire time.

"He could be better, but hopefully he will be very soon." Skye retorted.

"Is he in a state facility or is that private?" Chastity was making conversation because she came to a blank as she was trying to call around to find out Skye's whereabouts.

Skye thought to herself, *Why the hell you wanna show some concern about my daddy? You sitting over there grinning, asking questions, and don't even know I am plotting a murder.* Skye replied with, "I don't know of any psychiatric wards that are private. I only know of state facilities. You know something that I don't?"

"What happened to your father anyway? You never quite told me about it." Chastity was trying to call a truce. It was driving her crazy that Skye no longer wanted to be intimate with her. Chastity was trying to figure out why all of a sudden their sex life had recently become absconded. She tried not to pry in the beginning because she could understand somewhat of Skye being so private about her father. Skye had shared a few stories about her father's episodes of going to the deep end. Chastity always thought about the one where he would set a place for Jesus at the dinner table. She didn't like discussing anything about her brother's death with no one. Therefore, she knew exactly how Skye felt about the conversation piece.

"I don't really want to discuss my father." Skye walked over to the refrigerator to find herself something to drink.

"Your plate is in the microwave." Chastity informed Skye.

"Ah yeah. Whatcha cook?" Skye loved the way Chastity got down in the kitchen. She really did her thing when it came to cooking up a home cooked meal. Nothing was ever burnt and happened to be seasoned just right.

"It's nothing special. I just fried some chicken and baked some au gratin potatoes."

"Did you make that special hot sauce for the wings?"

"Just how you like it baby." Chastity smiled to herself. She knew Skye loved the way she made her special hot sauce. The only thing she did to her special sauce was add brown sugar and butter. Chastity would never tell Skye the ingredients though and she never let her see her prepare it.

Skye warmed her food. As the food was warming, she grabbed the ice out of the freezer and placed a few cubes into a large burgundy mug. She cracked opened the one liter of Cherry Coke and poured it in the mug. Skye was watching Chastity to see if she was watching her. She liked the open view from the kitchenette right into the living room. The set up was similar to the apartment she once shared with Crow. The microwave chimed letting Skye know her food was ready. She took her plate out the microwave and grabbed her drink. Skye plopped down on the white leather couch right next to Chastity.

Skye took a bite of the wing and began to lick her fingers. It drove Chastity crazy how Skye always smacked and popped her lips whenever she was eating. Tonight she was going to ignore it the best that she could. She didn't want to upset Skye because she really needed to be held.

"So what's up with, Q?" Skye licked her fingers.

"What you mean what's up?" Chastity didn't even want to discuss the details of the business that they had gotten into. She was regretting that she ever brought Skye into this. Things were going just fine when only she, Derrick, Robert, and Emanuel were involved. Emanuel had convinced her to let Skye in on it. He got a good vibe from her. She appeared to be loyal, witty, and presented a natural look of innocence. Lately, Emanuel began to feel totally different about Skye.

Emanuel figured stuff would go a lot smoother. Chastity felt as though their getting money scheme was going just fine until she hooked Skye up with Crow. Skye hadn't told them the details of his tactics yet. They didn't know what he was moving, if he had a stash spot, or even he had anything worth their time and effort.

"I just want to know when we hooking up. What's all involved? I really don't want things to play out how they did with Ray. I was a tad bit nervous. For a moment I thought Emanuel was going to shoot me. Then Derrick and Robert wasn't pleased with the amount of money they came up on like it was all my fault." Skye was about to complain even more about how that robbery went down, but Chastity cut her off before she went any further.

"Well things are going to be a little different. Y'all gonna hook up like usual. You gone come in the shop as planned and if he says anything about hooking up with you that day we will go from there. I got him coming in next Thursday at two. You know what to do." Chastity grabbed the remote to change the channel. "You need to focus on tying things up with Crow so we can get his ass. That dude got that clean legitimate paper mixed with that dirty money. We probably hit his ass and don't have to do this shit no mo. He got that trap boy money *and* that boxing loot. Plus his lil brother Sammy getting it in, so I know *he* got some stacks on deck!"

Skye almost choked because Chastity was so wrong about Crow. He conversed and associated with cats in the dope game, but his money came from him using his hands in the boxing ring. With the mentioning of Sammy, Skye slightly gagged as though something was pounding up against the top of her throat. She couldn't believe that Chastity knew about Crow's little brother. She was trying to figure out how much she knew about Crow. In one way, it wasn't much because she implied he was in the streets and he wasn't, but Skye wasn't for certain exactly *what* Chastity knew. She knew she shouldn't have pulled that disappearing act and Crow wouldn't have ever wandered into Infinity Styles looking for her. Skye couldn't help to think if Chastity knew she was there plotting her demise.

"Well I will be there at two to meet this Q person." Skye was a little leery now. Chastity didn't give up much information on Q and she threw Sammy's name out there like she knew what Skye was *really* there for.

Skye finished her food and sat looking at the television. That is what Chastity thought she was doing. Skye's thoughts were racing as she was trying to figure out how she was going to find out just how Chastity knew about Sammy.

"Chastity let me pick your brain for a minute." Skye swayed toward the kitchen area to get her attention. She realized she was going to have to give in. She knew Chastity was anticipating sex just from her making the hot sauce. She needed to get her head in the game even though she didn't want to go there anymore with her. She had to step back from all that sexing from Chastity for the simple fact it was times she found herself enjoying it.

"What's bothering you, Skye?"

"How did you get into this lifestyle anyway? I mean you have good clientele coming through the shop so you are not hurting for anything. Charles even looks out for you." Skye waited on Chastity to respond.

"When Chad and I was younger, we used to talk about how we were going to have money just like Charles. Well, Charles wasn't too fond of me getting involved. He didn't want Chad fooling around because he said he wasn't cut out for it. Chad proved himself to Charles so he let him in on some things nothing lucrative. Chad wasn't seeing the paper he wanted to see. Chad acquired a certain taste and the little money that came from him working with Charles wasn't enough for him." Chastity got up from the couch to get herself a drink.

Skye lit her cigarette. She was contemplating her next question. In all the four years they had been around one another, this type of conversation had never taken place. She was not about to let it end. Skye needed more. Just as she was about to speak, Chastity continued.

"Emanuel and Chad met when they were seven. They used to play little league baseball. Although my brother met Emanuel, Derrick, and Robert at the same time, he and Emanuel were closer. Derrick got involved with some other guys and started stealing cars. Robert, he silly as hell, but he ruthless. Dude has had it rough. His parents are not on drugs or anything. It's just a bunch of them. I think his mother got like thirteen kids. Together they all just came up with their own way of getting money." Chastity took a sip of her soda. "Now I don't know how many or who they all robbed from the time they started. But what I do know they was getting dudes that they knew. They were going as far east, west, north and south in St. Louis. Anybody they heard about or knew was getting paper, they were getting at them. How they were doing things got old." Chastity looked over at Skye. She knew she was about to go too far with the conversation but she felt that she needed to come at Skye from another angle. She figured opening up to her would be a good start.

Skye looked over at Chastity. She was thinking about just asking her about Sammy, but Crow was not the topic. It was worrying her to death. She wished she could call Crow and ask him what to do. She decided against it because she didn't even know how she would make the call without Chastity hearing what she had to say.

"Ya know I haven't always been like this." Chastity waited on Skye to respond. Skye was busy in her own thoughts. She was listening but she wasn't really paying her no mind. When Skye didn't respond the way she wanted her to, Chastity didn't know whether or not she should even continue with the conversation.

"I was messing around with Crow's little brother, Sammy." Skye turned to look at Chastity. She knew she had Skye's undivided attention. Chastity thought Skye would be a little disappointed with the fact she was involved with a male once before. That was *far* from what Skye was thinking. She was so relieved that she didn't have to come up with a way to find out what Chastity knew about Crow.

"So you been knew Crow?" Skye needed to know if she knew anything about her or Savion.

"No. I didn't know him. I just knew of him. Sammy and I was at the movies one day. I can't recall what we went to see, but that ain't important anyway. It was the day after Crow had won his match against some Puerto Rican dude. An older fella by the name of Pete congratulated him and told him to let his big brother know he was proud of him. Sammy was this private type of guy. He didn't mention a family and we had been kicking it for about eight months. I can remember that day like it was yesterday. He smiled at the fella letting him know that he would pass that message along. All of a sudden his mood changed and he told me he needed to drop me off. That was the last time I had heard from him. Every time I have heard that Crow was fighting, I have had intentions to go to his fights but I never have. Ever since the day Crow walked into the shop and the boys acknowledged that he was the boxer Savion Jamison, I have been anticipating the day to see Sammy. He broke my heart and I vowed that I would never let another man get close to me ever again."

Skye was glad to hear that she had never been to any of Crow's fights because she would have seen her there. Being ditched making Chastity give up the sexual healing from a man had Skye thinking about the pleasure *she* received. It wasn't that serious for her. She sat there wondering how Chastity remembered the name of the man that had spoken to Sammy.

"How long ago was that? You are really good with names. How did you even remember that name?" Skye was curious.

"Well before he dropped me off and got his attitude, Sammy was speaking of how Pete was from his neighborhood. Pete had a scholarship and all kind of scouts were trying to get at him, but he threw it all away chasing that high." Chastity shook her head. "The same thing that happened to Chad. It's just that my brother had given up on baseball long before he started getting his noise dirty."

Chapter 5

"Skye, you really need to let Chastity know you are not up for this one. I asked around about this dude, Q. Now his paper is right, but that dude ain't like those other cats y'all have been setting up. This may not turn out good at all. You need to think about Savion on this one. You got into this shit to get close to Chastity." Crow walked over to grab Skye's hand.

Skye looked over at Crow. She knew that he had to be worried. She wanted to tell him that there was no need to worry. She wasn't going through with it anyway. Q was not letting her see how he conducted business and he didn't floss his paper. As far as Skye knew, he wasn't doing anything illegal, but that was only to the naked eye. He didn't have a mediocre budget, but the simple fact that he wasn't punching a clock meant a little something.

Each time when she had a job to do, Crow gave his approval and let her know it was all good to go through with it. He wanted things to come to an end and fast. He tried to be ruthless but his heart wasn't there and his mentor Chico let him know that he could have a better life if he remained focused on boxing. Before the money came pouring in, he would assist his brother in his life of crime. Crow was used to his baby brother doing scandalous stuff but he was growing tired of Skye even being involved. He hated the fact that some days she would go as if she didn't have a care in the world. Skye could pretty much hold her own but he always felt the need to protect her.

This time, he was totally set against the task she was presented. She wanted to tell him that he could rest because she already knew that Q was of a different caliber. Of all the guys she had set up, he was the first that didn't floss his dough. She had made up in her mind from their first encounter that he wasn't any ordinary lame. She knew the Lou bred the same caliber and *those* she stayed away from. She totally preyed on the weak.

"Skye, you had one intention when you met Chastity. Now when you first approached me with this whole thing I wasn't sure, but I know how you felt about the entire ordeal. All the conditions that came with this I was fine in the beginning even knowing the risk, but this dude Q is a force to be reckoned with." Crow moved closer to Skye as she leaned up against the kitchen counter. "I heard this dude is affiliated with the Disciples and he is a part of some organized crime. That's why he came to the Lou. He trying to lay low. If word get back to his peeps that some bogus shit went down things can take a turn for the worse. Chastity and her get along gang need to think this one through. I want you to know that I am totally against this one. Then you never know y'all both can be plotting a murder!"

Skye walked out the door. Crow's words were dancing around in her thoughts. She thought about the day that she walked in the barbershop and saw Q sitting in Chastity's chair. The small incision on his right cheek made his smooth caramel skin look rough and rugged. When Chastity was putting the final touches on his low cut bald fade and he arose from his seat, Skye walked over as if she was next, so she could get a closer look.

Q walked past Skye looking down on her. "Girl, I'll give yo lil ass a *nice* lil workout. I can carry yo ass all over my spot and tear it up at the same time." Q gave Robert some dap as everyone chuckled. Q admired the sight the first time he saw Skye.

That's exactly what he had been doing for the past four months: tearing it up. She pressed the buzzer.

"Hold on a second, Sweetie." Q shot back through the intercom.

Seconds later, Skye heard the click to let her know that he had buzzed her in. She entered the apartment building, walking up to the second floor. The door was slightly ajar.

"Hey Quincy!" Skye looked around the empty apartment. He had been there four months and the only thing he had bought was a 19-inch television, a DVD player, a box spring and mattress set on the floor; and a card table with four folding chairs.

He had just got out the shower. Apparently, when she buzzed him, he hopped out the shower to answer. He came back to the bedroom and stood in front of Skye and dropped his towel. Skye looked up at him and smiled at his physique.

"You know you need to get that all out of my face." Skye snaked her eyes trying to act as though the view was not admiring.

"Girl, you know you love this. Just wait till it grows. He little right now, but you know when big dog gets big..."

Skye gave him a slight push as he stopped talking in the middle of his statement.

"Skye, don't make me get ugly." Q giggled.

"Now that wouldn't be hard to do!" Skye laughed at her sly remark. Q wasn't fine as Jamie Foxx but he wasn't bad looking by far.

"What's on the agenda for the day lil lady?" Q asked.

"Quincy, I really think we need to talk." Skye was letting Crow's words run rapid through her mind. It was as though he was sitting on her shoulder telling her to just walk away.

"What's on your mind?" Q sat down beside her. He admired her innocence and confidence. He found pleasure in countless women, but none was like Skye. She didn't ask a bunch of questions, was able to hold a decent conversation, and she went right along with the flow of things. She showed no fear and he loved how bold she was exploring every nook and cranny of his body.

"Now you promise to let me say what I am going to say and it's going to stay between us?" Skye looked up at Q with her sad puppy dog eyes.

"Girl, what you gotta say? Gone say it. I am not the one for games." Q was curious to find out what she had to say.

"I am here to set you up. I'm supposed to find out the inner workings of your business and once I have all the details they are going to come in…"

Skye was not allowed to finish. Q put his index finger over her mouth. He wouldn't have taken this lightly had he not growing feelings for Skye. He felt some sort of connection and for her to tell him what was supposed to take place actually meant something to him. He appreciated her gratitude. His family back home would have felt he had gone soft for letting her slide on that.

"Who supposed to have the guts or the balls to walk up in my spot and take my shit?" Q asked with the least bit of aggression.

"Robert, Emanuel, and Derrick." Skye held her head down.

"Who idea was this in the first place? You know what I don't even want to know the details. This is what I want you to do."

Chapter 6

The other day I had Obama on my t-shirt
Looked down thought about the situation
...Cuz we are here now...

The speakers were blaring the sounds of Murphy Lee from Nelly and the St. Lunatics. Robert pranced around jerking his body to the beat as he was sweeping the hair into one large pile in the middle of the floor. Derrick, Emanuel, and Chastity were all putting the finishing touches on each of their customers.

All of sudden Robert spun around with broom in hand, bending over dipping the broom as if it were a human. Everyone looked around as if he were crazy. Being amused by his foolishness, everyone shared a laugh at his expense. Chastity was finished first so she sat down to watch Derrick and Emanuel as they finished up. One by one, each of their last customers began to leave the shop.

The door clanged as the local salesman came into the shop tugging three black duffle bags. One was full of socks ranging from colorful women's socks to all white men's socks. His next bag was full of deodorants, soaps, toothpaste and anything else to help with personal hygiene. His last bag was full of the latest bootleg movies and CD's. Everyone checked out the items and made their purchases. He usually stopped by earlier but he was behind from trying to hit up all the beauty and barbershops in the city.

"Emanuel, go ahead and close those blinds and lock that door before some fool walk up in here. I am done for the day and I don't have any more money for anybody that wants to come in here selling shit." Chastity sat down in her chair and grabbed the remote.

"I was looking for me a booster today. I need me some new gear. Anybody heard from Shauna?" Derrick asked.

Emanuel looked over at Derrick. "I heard her boosting ass got caught up in Mississippi. From what I hear, they knocked down three malls and got over fifteen thousand dollars in merchandise. They ditched mall security and was headed to the highway. The driver dumb ass had to stop for gas and the police flagged him for improper plates as he pulled off the lot. He ran everybody's name and Shauna was the only one with a warrant."

Chastity shook her head. "Damn people taking boosting that damn serious."

Derrick chuckled. "Shit, *she* do! She be paying mother fuckers five hundred dollars to take her out of town. Shit I done got paid a couple of thousand fooling with her. She called me talkin' 'bout 'Take to me to Arkansas,' and I was like 'What time?' She hooked a nigga up with some fresh gear and kicked me down five crisp hundred dollar bills!"

Chastity looked over at Derrick. "You mean to tell me this bitch hit the highways to steal? It ain't even that *serious*! What, she doesn't know how to drive or something?"

Emanuel fixed his eyes on Chastity's direction. "Girl, everybody in the Lou got some type of hustle and they gone get that paper by any means necessary!"

Derrick was frowning from the aroma that was filling the air. He stood to his feet and with a frown on his face he yelled, "Robert, we smell yo funky ass all the way out here. You could have spared us and saved that until you got home."

Emanuel laughed as he reached for the lock on the door. As he was about to turn the knob, he saw the doorknob turn. "Dude we closed for the day!"

Chastity spun around in her chair. Before she could speak to vouch for Emanuel that the shop was closed, she was looking at four individuals dressed in jeans and white tees pointing their artillery in her direction. Chastity knew this day would eventually come, but she felt she would be better prepared. Looking at the clip of the M16, she couldn't believe she was in this situation. Not once had she considered the fact that she would eventually face her final hour. As the individuals stood before her, the thoughts of her and Chad playing in her mother's front yard consumed her. She smiled when she saw Chad's bubbly smile as he jumped from behind the big oak tree. When the individuals walked past her, hearing a familiar voice made her snap out of her vision. Chastity observed as two of the unmasked men walked toward the back of the shop. It was apparent that they were looking for the fourth barber that was supposed to be there.

Robert emerged from the restroom looking down as he fixed his clothing. "Fuck all of y'all. I feel about ten pounds lighter!" He raised his hands to point to his friends. "I'll give it thirty-five to forty-five minutes before you step up in that joint."

"Punk ass nicca shut the fuck up and everybody get face down on the floor! Nobody moves, nobody gets hurt!"

Robert looked around and did as instructed. The next individual walked over to each of them taking their earnings out of their pockets.

"Look through those stations! They may have some loot in'em!" The individual yelled from the back of the shop as he aimed his weapon. Although the individual that was giving all the instructions looked unfamiliar, Chastity recognized the voice. It was the same voice she heard on that rainy day when Chad was murdered.

Skye was enjoying the summer night. It was out of the ordinary for a summer night in St. Louis not to be muggy or sticky. She had made up in her mind that she was going to visit her father. In three days it will be the Fourth of July and it will be the anniversary of the disappearance of her uncle Pete. Her father wrote him off as dead, but her gut feeling was telling her different. She looked down at her G-Shock watch and noticed the shop was closed. She was going to take her chances and stop by the shop to get trimmed up. Chastity didn't have any of her working material at home. All of her hair stuff stayed at the shop and Skye knew that Chastity didn't like bringing her work home.

Skye walked in the door of Infinity Styles. She locked eyes with the individual that was instructing his crew. She was shocked to see him. He didn't have that dope fiend look he had the last time she saw him. It was more like a killer with a vengeance.

"Bitch get the fuck down on the floor! Why didn't yo dumb ass lock the door?" He looked at the other individual that was with him that held the Mossberg pump. He waved his M16 in the air from left to right. "Hurry up so we can get the fuck out of here!" The four of the individuals exited out of the door of the shop.

Everyone stood to their feet as the last individual exited out of the door.

"Motherfucka! They got my rent and bill money!" Robert yelled. It was evident that he was pissed. He walked over and kicked his station. Everything on the left side of the shop trembled from the kick.

Skye didn't know what to say. It had been four years since she had seen her uncle. He was looking pretty good. For a moment she almost smiled showing how proud she was with the way he looked. She knew Emanuel was watching her with his peculiar look he had been giving her lately.

Skye made herself a mental note that she was going to see her father. She really needed to go talk to her father to let him know that Pete was doing just fine and he could stop thinking someone did something to him and left him for dead. He had worried himself insane trying to figure out what happened to Pete. He thought he had been abducted and killed. Skye couldn't wait to tell Crow. Crow kept his ear to the streets. She was taken for surprise when she saw Pete but she could believe that Crow didn't know anything about Pete still breathing.

Derrick looked at Robert. "Dude that hurts like hell. I was scared as a motherfucker. I thought they were going to murk us all. Especially walking up in this joint without their faces being covered with those mothafuckin' assault rifles."

Robert replied, "Man I know. They was holding some heat. They wasn't on no stagecoach type of shit, coming through the door with pistols. How you think I felt coming up out the shitter seeing that going down? I am pissed I didn't have my burner on me! I would have blasted every one of those fools!"

Emanuel was focused on the look that was exchanged between the individual and Skye when she walked through the door. Chastity was sitting there going through her mental catalogue trying to figure out if that face was familiar. Then it came to her. That was the dude she saw when she was with Sammy. He didn't have that brute hard up look he had back then. She wasn't tripping off that fact. They were robbed! She figured it was karma. She shook it off thanking God she was still alive but the thought of what goes around comes around overwhelmed her thoughts. Emanuel wasn't letting that go that easy.

Emanuel gave Skye a subtle glare. "Skye, what is up with Q? You been getting at dude for about four months now. We can get at Crow later, but we need to get at Q ASAP! Ya dig?"

Chastity stood up to let Skye sit down. Skye wanted to give Emanuel the business because she was noticing how he kept glancing at her. She could sense the tension in his voice as he spoke. She knew it had to be a problem because majority of the time when you catch someone looking at you they turn their head. Emanuel wanted her to know that he was looking at her.

Emanuel watched Skye as she took her seat. "So what's up Skye? Whatcha got for us?"

"E, hold your fucking horses. Let her get herself together. Dude she just walked in on a measly ass robbery. She probably shook up." Derrick spoke up.

Skye looked around. "What y'all need to be doing is calling the police!"

"Girl we a bunch of stick up kids! We hold court in the streets! Them niggas walked up in here unmasked. They won't be too hard to find. News travels fast. Charles will know who hit us up before the sun goes down." Emanuel was trying to hit a couple of Skye's nerves, but it wasn't working.

Skye felt it was time to give up a little information. "Well y'all know that liquor store on Page and Sarah that sits directly across from that car wash?"

"Yeah, I know what you talking about." Robert chimed in. He began to explain the whereabouts of the liquor store to the rest of them to make sure everyone was on the same part of town.

Emanuel looked at Skye. "Yeah, what about it?"

"Well guess who the owner is?" Skye smiled.

"Let me guess." Robert declared, "Mr. Quincy?"

"Robert come on down! You are the next contestant to let's get that nigga!" Skye shrieked as she shared a laugh with Chastity.

"This the killa right here." Skye had everyone's attention. "That's how he washes his money. Every Wednesday he makes his purchases for the store. Then on Thursday he gets all the monies together and one of the workers waits on a red Cavalier with a female driver. Once she comes, they give her the money then she meets somebody on Grand and Page at the Ebony Motel." She told the story just how Q told her to tell it.

Emanuel looked at her with a confused look. "That shit don't even make no sense. That's the wackiest shit I ever heard. What the fuck she doing taking money to a motel?"

Skye looked at Emanuel with a very reserved but intent look. Taking a breather, she spoke. "I know it don't make sense. Q don't know why she does it either. He followed her a couple of times once someone told him she was the one making the stop."

Robert looked at Skye. "Who is the bitch?"

"Somebody that works for him. She makes the stop there before she leaves to hit the highway to see one of her tenders. She's married to some old man that's cool with Q and the old bastard refuses to take the blue pill." Skye was dreading another question.

Emanuel wasn't liking the answers she was giving. He felt the story was bogus. He had to ask one more question. "What the fuck is in this red Cavalier?"

"Money!" Skye wanted to cuss him out but she kept her composure.

Chapter 7

Skye had to call Crow immediately after seeing on the nightly news that some men had been gunned down on the city's North Side. They were only able to release the name of Samuel Louis, the only one of the three men whose family had been able to be located and contacted.

Skye sat next to Chastity trying to hold her composure. It was hard. It wasn't any way that she was going to be able to go sleep not knowing how Crow was holding up.

Chastity shook her head. The news coverage only brought back bad memories. She couldn't help to think about how her very own brother was murdered and thrown into the garbage like yesterday's trash. She got up to get herself something to drink. She wanted to be remorseful but that feeling of what goes around comes around emerged.

The abrupt knock on the door took them both from their thoughts. Skye couldn't believe Crow had showed up there. Chastity looked over at Skye wondering who that had to be as she made her way to the door.

"Who is it?" Chastity wasted no time. She didn't even want to look through the peephole. This could be only one of two people, her mother or brother. That was not likely because they both always called before they came.

Skye awaited the response. When the individual responded, she couldn't make out what they were saying because it was short and quick. Chastity snatched opened the door without a thought of considering her well-being.

Q strolled through the door as if he were invited. Skye was trying to figure out how in the world he knew where she could be found. Chastity was about to be pissed but from the bewildered look on Skye's face she sensed that this visit was uncertain and unexpected.

Q took a seat on the couch and kicked his feet up on the table. "I heard you bitches like bumping pussies so I came to see if y'all were down for a *ménage à trois*. So what's up?"

Skye looked him over. Her thoughts were racing. She didn't know her fate or what Q was about to say or do. She was wondering how did he find her and what was he actually there for.

"Skye, you get up on outta here. I don't want you to get all jealous while I am knocking down your little girlfriend." Q looked at Skye raising his shirt exposing his weapon. "Move bitch! Get the fuck outta here!" He stood up and walked over to Chastity who was still trying to make sense of the situation. Q grabbed Chastity by her waist and snatched her toward him. He looked directly in her eyes as he said, "You bout to try dick again!"

Skye didn't know whether this was a game or a set up. She was outraged but she didn't know how to display it. She was trying to figure out what else was going to go wrong. First it was the robbery at the shop now the bold home invasion. Now when they talked previously and he told her what to say about the inner workings of his business, he failed to mention he was going to make a surprise visit. She slid into her black Nike flip-flops and headed for the door.

"Ah, Skye," Q called out. "My mans is sitting in the car. If anyone comes or the police is called, your little girlfriend will be looking at the roof of a church! So my advice to you is to find you something to do for about two or three hours."

Chastity gave Skye a slight nod to let her know to go ahead and leave. Skye was hesitant until she told her go ahead and don't call anyone. Chastity didn't know how this was going to end, but if she came out alive, Q was going to hate that he even knew where she stayed.

Skye was being tormented with the thought of Q telling Chastity about what she said, but she had to find out how Crow was doing. She hopped in Chastity's Protégé and headed toward the apartment she once shared with Crow.

As soon as she entered the apartment, she could sense that it was empty. She could tell that he left in a hurry because Savion's toys were on the floor and Crow was adamant on putting things back. That's when she saw the note on the dining room table.

Skye swiftly made her way through the halls of St. Louis University Hospital. When she reached the room, she was glad to hear laughter over the rapidly beeping monitors.

When she entered the room, Sammy was in the hospital bed with a bandaged head, wearing a smile. "Bustas shot me twelve times. They didn't know real niggas don't die!"

Skye looked over at Crow as he shook his head. She walked over to kiss Sammy on his forehead.

"Boy what happened to you?" Skye asked.

"Girl, I been shot!" Sammy laughed.

"Nigga, she can see that," Crow gasped.

"I was down on the North Side hollering at my boy, Q." Sammy closed his eyes and moved his head from right to left.

Skye looked over at Crow. She wanted to know if Crow had known the entire time that Sammy knew Q.

Sammy continued. "Matter of fact, Pete hooked me up with him. He was from here but he moved to Chicago. His mother's boyfriend was beating her ass and he killed him. Dude family was trying to get at'em so his mother sent him to live with one of her sisters. He was letting me know that he was grimy, getting at all niggas and taking that cake. He and Pete used to work for that nigga Charles back in the day. When he found out Pete was out here tripping he took him back to the CHI wit'em and got'em all cleaned up. You should see your uncle. He don't even look the same."

Skye looked at Sammy. "Nigga, fuck all that! Plus, that stroll back down memory lane! What happened to you? Do you know we got three days to get this shit crackin'?"

"Me and two of my cats from off the Dub were standing on the corner shooting the shit with Pete and Q. Q was telling him about you and that whole ordeal. Then Derrick and Robert hopped out nowhere on us talking about my dudes and Pete robbed them the other day. I was like nigga y'all out here in these streets playing detective, but Q knew Robert so things was going smoothly. It was like Robert pushed Q out the way and Derrick pulled out his burner and popped our asses!"

"The news said three men or some shit." Skye looked at Crow.

"Girl they be having that shit all wrong. I was the only one that got popped! I told your uncle the little plan you had. Pete told me to tell you to lay on back. He is going to handle the rest."

Sammy's speech was becoming slurred. The pain medicine was taking effect.

"Q over at Chastity's spot right now and I think he blowing her back out." Skye looked at Crow with a devilish smirk.

"Straight?" Crow was baffled.

"Yeah Pete was telling him where Charles' honeycomb hideout was. He thought niggas didn't know. I gotta give to him though. His ass is hard to find. Don't a nigga out here know where he lays his head at now. He should know betta than err nigga out here mugs don't miss shit out here in the Lou. You put that ear to the streets and all the right and wrong shit could be heard." Sammy slurred his words as he was barely able to keep his eyes open.

"Skye, we need to talk." Crow sat down in the chair beside Sammy's hospital bed.

Skye looked at Crow. "Dude you ain't gotta say shit. The night of your fight it goes down. Charles is going to feel like my daddy feels. This will be a Fourth of July we all remember! I just got to figure out now how the hell I am going to pull this off with this nicca laying up here in this hospital bed all shot up and shit!"

Crow knew it wasn't no changing her mind. He knew he shouldn't have even listened to the crazy plan of hers when she first brought it up. Now he was trying to figure out how he was going to win his match and talk her out of hers. He had to work fast because he only had three days left.

Chapter 8

Chastity sat on the couch wearing an oversized thick white t-shirt and a smile. The violating feeling she had at first wasn't even an afterthought. She was glad that he made that visit. She hadn't had the real thing in so long she totally forgot the feeling. She was contemplating on making him a regular hook up. Ever since the robbery occurred, she was thinking of changing things in her life. She felt that God spared her for a reason. Becoming another statistic, adding or being added to the murder rate in St. Louis, was something she didn't want.

Skye eased the door open. She wanted to catch Chastity in the compromising position that she hadn't had since way back when to see if she was enjoying it. She quietly opened the door. She didn't know whether she was going to find Chastity knocked off or being knocked off.

Skye noticed her in the usual position on the couch watching television. She called out her name. Chastity turned around with a sense of satisfaction on her smiley face.

Skye paused as she thought for a second. She didn't know exactly what she was walking into. She instantly remembered not even observing the parking lot. She was so anxious in seeing some action she forgot about checking out her surroundings.

Chastity stood up. "Skye, the fight is in three days. I want to hit the mall up and get me an outfit. I wanna go to the fight. I know Sammy is going to be there."

Skye was so confused. Why all of a sudden she wanted to see Sammy? It appeared to Skye that she was flaunting the name Sammy as if she knew more than what she was putting on. Did Chastity know that her brother Charles was the reason behind Pete becoming strung out on drugs? Did she know that Charles was also involved with her dad being in that state facility?

Right then and there, Skye contemplated on completing the task she was there for in the first place. She didn't know what all popped off between the two of them. Skye didn't give Q any information about her connection to Chastity. She didn't know whether or not she had walked into a room that was fulfilled with her destiny. The streets of St. Louis had become so wicked. Even the most loyal cats were getting weak. Honor amongst thieves was becoming a thing of the past and lost souls were finding it their duty to endure treachery amongst their closest acquaintances. Had Chastity figured her out?

Chastity looked over at Skye as she was trying to figure out why Skye was looking as though she had seen a ghost.

She placed herself in close vicinity of Skye. "Girl, that dude took me down through thurr! Ya, hear me?"

Those words were music to her ears. She went from looking lost to content. She was speechless. She didn't have a comeback line at all.

Although, Skye was still a bit nervous about Chastity's intentions of wanting to attend the fight, she suddenly tried to alleviate her look of discernment.

Chastity continued, "You think you can convince Crow to get us some seats. I bet he will have us sitting right next to Sammy."

Skye was reluctant to answer. She pulled her cell phone out. She knew she had to call just in case Chastity started making the connections. She wondered if she knew Pete was her uncle and that was he that led Chad out the house that rainy day. He lost his life protecting his brother, Charles. Chad didn't want to tell where Charles could be found. Pete was making sure no one was going out to hunt for him once they found out he was on the prowl to seek some revenge.

"Hey Crow, what's up wit it?" Skye waited on him to respond.

"Is everything okay?" his concern was felt through the phone.

"You got a brother? Well let me say this, Chastity wants tickets to the fight. She wants to see this brother of yours." Skye looked over at Chastity. Skye had read many a face and the face that she was reading was clueless to her plotting. "Hold on, Crow. I am going to let you talk to Chas." Skye handed her phone to Chastity.

Chastity blushed. "Hey, Crow."

Chapter 9

The traffic was thick. Everybody that was somebody was on their way downtown to the Edward Jones Dome. Throughout the city, smoke filled the air. Crackling, sizzling, and popping were the few sounds that could be heard over the booming systems as the cars cruised by.

Crow was up first. Once the announcer announced him and the crowd cheered he made his way into the boxing ring. He pranced around as his opponent's name, Juan Julio, was called. He looked over to the empty seats that he reserved just for Skye and Chastity. He instantly became concerned when he saw Sammy sitting with a few of their childhood friends.

Crow instantly lost focus as he thought that Chastity had figured the whole ordeal out. He tried to get himself together. He repeated over and over to himself, "Dude, get your head in this ring!"

Juan Julio felt the repercussion of Crow's wrath. Every jab landed. Throughout the first three rounds, Crow continued to glance at the empty seats. Something triggered his thoughts and Mr. Julio felt a blow that didn't allow him to get back up. The ref counted down and the next thing that was heard was, "The winner by knockout!"

Chastity looked over at her gas hand. "We better get some gas. You know this traffic is going to be thick." Chastity pulled onto the lot. She pumped her gas as Skye sat in the car touching up her makeup.

Chastity hopped back in the car. "I hope Sammy is going to be happy to see me."

Skye looked at her and smiled. "He will!"

Chastity pulled to the edge of the parking lot. Right as she was about to enter the intersection a loud noise was all that she remembered.

Crow was calling Skye's cell phone. He was growing with rage because she wasn't answering. He knew that he shouldn't make the next call but he needed to know what was going on. He became furious when Chastity's phone went straight to voicemail. He wanted to watch Devon do his thing but he needed to find Skye. Crow thought about going to get Sammy to let him know that something wasn't right with Skye, but the crowd deterred him.

Once outside, he determined his best way to go. The traffic was still piling into the Edward Jones Dome parking facilities. When he heard the sounds of sirens coming toward his direction, he figured they would be a great help. He jumped right behind the ambulance.

Crow followed the ambulance until the coast was clear. Then the ambulance came to an abrupt halt. Crow couldn't see a thing but a crowd of people and several police cruisers.

Crow picked up the St. Louis Post. He kept reading the headlines over and over again.

Two Killed in Car Crash Near Downtown

Two people were killed the night of the Fourth of July. Witnesses say approximately three cars were traveling at a high rate of speed. It is believed that a drag race was taking place when one of the drivers lost control of their car causing it to hit a gray Mazda Protégé as it pulled off the lot of the Mobil near Delmar and North Jefferson causing the car to rollover several times.

    Crow placed his hand on the tattoo he had gotten of Savion and Skye near his heart right after Savion was born. He couldn't hold back his pain. The abundant amount of tears didn't conceal his grief.

Tattooed Souls

By Any Means Necessary

Chapter 1

"Ay, playa! Tell me who got that good!" Sean asked the slim individual who stood on the corner of Wells and Clara posted up like a security guard.

"Who wanna know?" the so-called security guard asked.

"A buyer, ole clown ass nigga!" Sean snarled.

The individual looked him up and down. He pointed to the door of the house he was standing a few feet from. "Nigga go ahead and knock on that door right there."

Sean laughed as he walked up on the porch. He didn't knock like he was instructed. He opened the door and walked on in. He laughed to himself at what he was witnessing. Rochelle was on her knees sucking the life out the cat he came to see. Rochelle was the good girl that got turned out trying to mess with dudes out of her league. The typical gold digger who, unfortunately, had dug too far. Rochelle was at the point of no return. She began to get her noise dirty so she was doing whatever it took to get her some heroin. Sucking niggas unconscious was the first on her agenda. She was blowing dudes' minds. Several cats wanted to wife her on her head game alone.

"Nigga I literally caught you wit yo pants down," Sean giggled. "You know what I am here to do. So gone give it up!" Sean grabbed the black Spalding duffle bag and headed out the back door with ease.

Dub looked down at his cell phone. He looked at the number, trying to recognize the unidentified caller before pressing the key to answer. It could be anybody because the people he knew used nothing but burner cell phones. Nobody he knew was committed or locked into a contract. He finally decided to answer. "Hello." He awaited a response.

"What up Dub, this Sean. Man I need to holler at you, it's important." From the silence, Sean thought Dub had hung up. "Hello?"

"I'm listenin'." Dub said with a slight attitude. He and Sean hadn't talked for a brief minute. He felt Sean was moving way too fast in the streets. Dub was more conservative and how dudes were snitching, everybody needed to be cautious about the way they moved. Sean was way too relaxed and it bothered him.

"It's important man." Sean pleaded.

"Aight." Dub ended the call after agreeing to meet up with Sean. Dub was irritated by Sean's call, but not knowing if he was in some sort of trouble or not led Dub to agree. After all Sean was his brother from another mother. No matter how sloppy Sean got, Dub could come through for him. He just had to play hardball.

At the age of twenty, Dub was what most call an intellectual gangster. His sloppiness earlier on in life had taught him to be poised and cautious. He was going to Ranken Technical College by day, fathering a daughter by noon, and lurking the streets by night. He felt he had a good front game. He kept a delicate balance of criminal activity and civilized citizen activity. Going back and forth to jail since he was fourteen taught him to be a real covert crook. Dub was on parole for three attempted murders from when he was sixteen. Being five foot seven baring a chocolate complexion, he had a cocky complex that often led to him being on the defensive side. However, for twenty he was well before his time.

Sean stood six feet tall with no facial hair. His brown skin was as smooth as satin. His coal black hair was neatly plaited. Sean was three years older than Dub, but he was the little brother of the two. Sean was one of those happy treacherous gangsters. He was always joking and laughing. Most people thought because he was so silly that he was harmless. They couldn't be more wrong. Just when you played him like a silly fool, he would knock fire out of a nigga! Unlike Dub who had a baby momma and a kid, Sean had nothing but women problems. He liked gangster bitches. The type of chick who would help him fight in the streets then turns around and whoops *his* ass. Even though Sean was skinny, he was swell with his hands. The chick he was currently involved with was keeping him on his toes.

Sean and Dub grew up together on the west side of St. Louis. The west side was a high crime area. A dope infested gangland that made the evening news every night of the week for one reason or another. Sean and Dub would always see the neighborhood dope men in Cortez Nikes, Dickies, and Starter jackets. They wanted to be just like those Jheri curl Cortez Nike wearing thugs.

Sean never had much of a family so Dub's family was his family. As kids, they would skip boxing practice to go smoke joints with the rest of the neighborhood rugrats. Their childhood history is what kept their bond strong.

Dub left his house in north St. Louis County headed toward the south side of the Lou where Sean stayed with his lil chick, Ricki. Checking to see if it were all right for him to proceed toward the oncoming traffic, he turned his '87 Chevy onto Highway 70 heading east to the I-55 south/I-44 west split. The long stretch of the road gave Dub enough time to evaluate as he accelerated the gas pedal.

The nature of the phone call from Sean was weighing him down. It's not strange for the St. Louis streets to turn friends into foes and he prayed that neither one of them would face a tragic situation. He heard many stories of cats being betrayed by their best homies. One could never be too cautious. He couldn't keep letting his negative thoughts consume him because he was feeling the need to turn and go back home.

Dub popped his Scarface joint into the CD player. Right as he got the vibe, his exit appeared. He jumped off the Gravois exit then made a quick right down a winding street that led to Sean and Ricki's crib. Ricki was that latest gangsta chick he was involved with. She was holding him down. She was even working with him. They had simply become a modern day Bonnie and Clyde.

Dub wheeled the Chevy into a parking space right in front of their apartment door. He looked around checking for the unexpected. After five minutes of contemplating his next move, Dub placed the car in park and made his exit.

The moon hid behind the slow moving clouds that were causing shadows every three seconds, making the evening feel very eerie. Dub was slightly nervous and at the same time, conscious of what he had in his pocket. After a few clicks, the door opened, and much to Dub's relief, it was Tez.

Tez was a hustler from the same block as Sean and Dub. Over time, he had proven he was a trustworthy and loyal cat. Tez's hustle was mostly selling weed and pills. He wasn't exactly what those in the hood called "Stomp Down." He was just an average mug. He stayed on the grind for his. He wasn't about to rob anyone. He respected everyone's hustle. Tez wasn't soft by any means though.

He opened the door for Dub and shot up the steps. All Dub could see was the back of a Green Bay jersey as he followed Tez up the steps. Sean was in the living room when they reached the top. Sean was standing there with a big Dr. Seuss grin. Dub was getting mad. With his hand still in his jacket pocket, Dub shouted out, "Man I'm finna bounce!"

Dub was thinking it was some ole family reunion, I miss you type of trip. Nevertheless, as Dub was turning to leave, Sean threw a black Spalding gym bag at Dub's feet. "You always gotta be so fucking serious!"

Dub looked at Sean as if to say, "Don't throw anything at me." He reached down to pick up the bag when that all too familiar aroma arose from the bag. "Yep, chronic!" he thought to himself. Dub couldn't see nothing but green in several zip-lock bags. It was several pounds of weed.

"Still mad at me?" Sean asked with his eyebrows raised, smiling as though he was awaiting a Nobel Peace Prize or worse... a hug. All Dub could do was laugh at Sean's silly ass. Tez looked from left to right. He was trying to get a feel for Dub and Sean. When he noticed both of them looking like they were holding back their smiles, he laughed.

Sean had just robbed one of the major hustlers in St. Louis. It was easier than he thought. He took every bit of thirty pounds of weed from dude. Although he brought his strap with him, he didn't even have to pull it out. He laughed about how things just went down. He thought maybe the next time he saw Rochelle he would thank her for making his task so easy. He was prepared for the retaliation because whatever was going to happen behind the robbery came with the territory.

Chapter 2

In the early June morning sunshine, Dub sat looking through the local newspaper. His reading was interrupted when the phone rang.

"Yo," said Dub, his usual response when he answered the phone.

"It's poppin' man. When you comin' down on the set?"

Dub immediately recognized the voice. It was Beanz, Dub's big homie. Beanz was considered scandalous because he robbed, sold dope and did whatever a street nigga could do to get money. Beanz was one of Dub's favorite people because they both lived by the any means necessary motto. Normally Dub would come whenever he called but he was in the bed with his baby momma, Tangie. She hated when Dub left the house and she expressed her displeasure with eye rolling and neck snapping.

"Man am I gonna have to get this money by myself or what?"

"Hold on," Dub said looking down at Tangie to see if she was listening. As usual, she was ear hustling and eye balling him. She blurted out, "Baby why can't you stay at home sometimes?"

Dub looked at Tangie, biting his lips and told Beanz, "Man look, I'm gone chill wit Tan and the baby. I'll slide through when it gets dark."

Disgusted, Beanz said, "Whateva dawg." Then the phone went dead. Dub looked down at Tangie as she rested her head back on his hairless chest.

Dub couldn't resist his very own personal chocolate Hershey. They were together so much they began to resemble one another. People often thought they were siblings.

Tangie was from North County where the girls were mostly square and preferred bad boys. She and Dub had a nice little home stashed away in the county. A quiet suburban are on the outskirts of St. Louis City. She was very much aware of Dub's lifestyle even though she didn't agree with it. Being as cautious as he was, he kept her well protected. He sheltered her from the details of his day-to-day hustle. Tangie was twenty as well and very much wrapped up in Dub's world. He was her ambition.

Tangie was seventeen when they first met and had never been tampered with. Spending four years on Normandy's High School cheerleading team kept her body tight. Being a bit of homebody, she didn't call for much maintenance. Having short thick luxurious black curly hair kept the hairdresser bill at a minimum. Her self-cut tapered style accentuated her chocolate skin. It wasn't that money was a problem; she didn't mind staying in the house playing wifey.

Later that night, Dub put on his usual: Jordans, jeans, wife beater and white tee. He grabbed the baby, spun her around in the air and kissed her repeatedly.

"Say 'Da Da'. Say 'Da Da,' boo." Dub continued kissing his daughter's chubby cheeks while she squirmed and giggled in his arms.

Tangie was used to the signal. Playing with the baby before he left had become the routine right before he walked out the door. It was if he was saying his final goodbye. Tangie snaked her neck and placed her hands on her hips. "Un mmm, where you going?"

"Baby you know I gotta get this bread," Dub stated. Dub put the baby down and headed toward the door. Tangie followed right behind him. She caught up with him, turned him around, stuck her hand up his shirt, and tongued him long and hard.

Dub released himself from her embrace. "Damn! I almost forgot the Roscoe!" He left her standing at the door to go get his .357. When he made it back to the door, he tried to ignore Tangie standing in his way with her arms folded.

"Do you gotta take that?" she hissed pointing at the dingy chrome .357 revolver in his hand.

"You want me to come back, don't you?" Dub looked at Tan with an "I don't wanna hear that shit" type of look. He kissed her on the forehead and made his exit.

Headed eastbound on Highway 70, Dub was bobbing his head and singing, "I keep my mind on my money, money on mind, finger on the trigger nigga hand on my nine." He was vibing to 2Pac and MC Breed as he gripped the steering wheel with both hands.

Dub never drove drunk but you couldn't tell from the way he swerved in and out of the lanes.

When he finally reached the set, he saw Beanz leaning against Sean's burgundy Thunderbird with a can of Budweiser beer in his hand. Dub parked and got out. The set was popping just like Beanz had said. Sean and Tez were running back and forth out of the alley. The little up and coming gangsters were in the alley with their arsenal and the crackheads were doing their normal wheelin' and dealin'.

In St. Louis, the nights were alive. It was like Mardi Gras seven days a week, 365 days a year. If the block wasn't jumpin', everybody went to the riverfront which was its own little Miami Beach, the muddy Mississippi sparkling as it quietly floated by the Gateway Arch. Folks from north, south, east and west of the Lou congregated for smoking and drinking. The main attraction was the car strip where all the honeys rode past and acted uninterested in the ballers leaning in their car window talking a million dollars worth of shit while their gold teeth were shining.

The blocks were all together different. The hood was like an African safari. When the sun went down, the wolves came out. If you were feeble or similar to a weak deer, it was best you stayed inside. In the hood, everybody knew everybody. The alleys acted as bushes where the lions and hyenas hid waiting on their prey, an unsuspecting mark that was out of bounds. Dub was the lion and Beanz was the hyena.

Beanz was up to his norm trying to run everything and pulling that rusty ass .45 out every time he saw a car. Beanz's demeanor scared most cats. He was darker and huskier than Sean was. Sean was vicious, but Beanz had a bigger bite. He was capable of turning an average trip to the store into a homicide or a robbery. However, for some reason, it didn't bother Dub. He felt as though there was some loyalty amongst thieves.

Most dudes in St. Louis had the attitude of "by any means necessary" or "an eye for our entire head" concept. Sometime other major cities had influence on the culture of most mugs. Los Angeles had a major influence. You see similar dress codes like Dickies, Chuck Taylors and so forth. The only difference was the dialect. Nonetheless, St. Louis had its own breed. Like Beanz, he was a typical St. Louis nigga. He loved drama and storytelling and saying "Ya know what I'm saying" every three seconds.

"What's crackin' cuzz?" Dub said as he greeted Beanz with a neighborhood handshake that people swore was some sort of secret religious code.

"Shit, just lettin' these fools rack up befoe I Debo this alley. Ya know what I'm saying?" Beanz looked Dub over. "So Tangie finally let you out, huh?"

"You know betta than that!" Dub responded.

"So what's good? I heard you made a killin' last week. Sean says you ready to comp again, boy. Plus, I holla'd at Grip and he say he'll plug mugs for the low-low." Beanz took a sip of his beer and continued, "I met this lil broad at the gas station the other night. She says her baby daddy got all work. She pissed cuz the nigga likes to step out on her ass. I can't wait to get at'em! Ya know what I'm saying? Then we can take over the west and knock Grip off too. Ya know what I'm saying?"

Dub just listened as he looked around watching everything. Beanz always had some elaborate scheme and somehow Dub always threw in a smarter strategy. Before anybody noticed, they would vanish into the night. Dub wasn't up for it this night; Dub wanted to make a few grand and get back home to Tangie. That kiss had put something on his mind.

"Hold up fam. Who is that?" Beanz spotted a car with four heads in it. In the Lou, you never know if it was people coming from church or some dudes from another hood ready to shoot up the block to make mugs look at the roof of the church. Luckily, it was the girl Beanz met at the gas station. Beanz put the rusty pistol back in his waistband and went into full Mack mode when they pulled up.

He leaned into the car window. "Damn baby! You missed Daddy huh?"

Sean, Tez and every other desperate fool out there ran up to the car. Dub snuck down the alley and spent his time filling his pockets. Even out there hustling, he had Tangie and his daughter on his mind. He was thinking about what he was going to buy them.

When Dub came out of the alley, everybody was gone. He figured they probably tailed those females to some motel. Dub just jumped in his car and peeled off.

Chapter 3

When Dub arrived at home, he sat in the car in front of the house. He turned off the car and counted his earnings for the night. He never let Tangie know exactly how much he had. Dub split his stacks into two piles and put them in separate pockets. He hastily made his way out of his vehicle with his keys ready to open the front door.

As he opened the door, all he heard was Tangie's favorite CD playing. Tangie was somewhere in the house crying about how weak she gets in her knees.

Thinking she was alone, she sang the words to the song as if she created it or was a losing contestant for American Idol. He observed as she stood washing the dishes in her t-shirt and panties. Dub crept up behind her and kissed her on the back of her neck.

Despite the fact that she instantly became moist from the kiss, Tangie dropped the dishes into the sink, yelping, "Ooh! Boy you scared me!" and tapped her lover on his arm. Tangie's heart was beating rapidly and wetness flowed from her insides. After a few seconds, she calmed down and turned to finish washing the dishes. Dub kissed her neck again. He continued to kiss her neck gently.

He gripped her hips and whispered, "I missed you Tan!"

Dub loved Tangie deeply and he aimed to please her, always making sure she was satisfied completely. She was his only bliss in the cruel world he secluded himself from. When Tangie tried to turn around to face him, he forced her back to face the sink . Both facing forward, he slid his hand around to caress her vagina. Tangie's knees began to buckle as she moaned and purred like a kitten from his tender touch. Dub could feel the wetness through her panties.

She pressed her frame back against Dub. His soldier was at full attention. Removing their clothes in sync with one another, Tangie stood on her tippy toes with an arched back as she leaned over in the sink immediately throwing it back as soon as Dub entered her. Feeling her moist cavity on his hard penis made Dub close his eyes. He penetrated deeper and deeper into Tangie. She loved how aggressive he was. Bumpin' and grindin,' she could feel herself about to climax. She yelled, "Whose is it nigga? Tell momma whose it is!"

With slow deep and long breaths Dub stuttered, "I-I-I-I-t-t-t-s yourzzzz bayyyybbeee!"

Pumping faster, they were almost there but just as Tangie was about to cum, Dub slid his soaking wet soldier out and turned her around. Using both hands, he placed her on the countertop and began licking her gently. Tangie was going wild as his moist tongue flicked her clitoris. With her legs spread-eagle she palmed his head slurring slowly, "Yes, baby, yes!"

Dub gave her clitoris a few more swirls with his tongue; she quivered while releasing her creamy fluid into his mouth. While Tangie continued to shake in his hands, Dub pulled her down to the floor, put her on her back and slid his penis back in. Lying on the white marble kitchen floor, he pumped long and hard as he threw his head back.

"That's it baby! Cum baby! Go ahead and bust baby!" Tangie met his rhythm as he continued to penetrate her cavity. She continued to encourage him to bust.

Dub gave a hard thrust that seemed to move the earth as he shouted and grunted, "AWWW, TAN!!"

She could feel the warmth of his juices inside her. They both lay flat on the floor breathless. Tangie rolled over to embrace Dub. She grabbed his limp solider and slowly stroked it. Even soft, his penis was thick and long. Looking into his eyes, Tangie asked, "You missed momma huh?"

"Momma really do need to finish those dishes!" Dub joked. She playfully slapped him on his chest and he stood before making his way toward the bathroom to wash Tangie's wetness off.

Chapter 4

BAM! BAM! BAM! was the sound that awakened Dub the following morning. The sound was frightening. He immediately hopped up like a firefighter going to save a life from a blazing fire. He ran to the door in his boxers. Still half-asleep, he looked out the peephole and saw Sean's loud and obnoxious gangster girlfriend, Ricki. Her attitude was as thick as her body. She wasn't the average ordinary around the way girl, but she was definitely a ghetto superstar. At thirty, she was very silly and immature. The majority of Sean's friends thought she was too old for him. She maintained her youth. She didn't look a day over nineteen. Pulling her sandy brown hair up in a ponytail, letting the nappy ends stick out, often kept individuals speculating about her age. She was the hardest broad he had ever met.

Dub cracked the door. This was the very reason he didn't want Tangie conversing with Ricki. She had no reason knowing where he laid his head. Rubbing the eye boogers from his lids, he spat, "Damn! What's up?"

Ricki pushed him right out of her way and barged into the living room of his home. She didn't go far because she knew that Dub was not going to stand for too much more. She was looking around the room with hopes of finding who she was in search of when she began to speak very loudly. "I ain't seen Sean all night! I know you know where the fuck he is! Where is he, Dub? He bet not be with no…"

"Girl shut yo loud ass up while my gal and my daughter in there sleep!" Dub was furious. Ricki knew he could get real crazy, real quick. She had Dub a tad bit shook, but he wasn't about to show it.

She stood there with her hands on her hips and her lips poked out as if to say, "I'll be quiet for a minute, but I ain't going anywhere until you tell me where the fuck he is."

It was 7:36 a.m. From his living room window, a wide ray of sunlight floated in and seemed to be filled with dust. Dub figured this would be his easy way out and didn't have to go through the usual routine with Tangie. He went to the bathroom, collected himself, and freshened up.

Dub followed Ricki to the west side to look for Sean. Once they made it down on the set, he took the lead with Ricki trailing behind him. They bent a few corners to no avail. Instantly Dub knew where Sean might have been. He knew that if he called Sean he would answer, but he was not going to make that phone call while Ricki was anywhere around. Dub saw a couple of the youngsters out on the block. He flagged one of them down. He looked in his rearview and, just as he figured, Ricki was tuned in. He didn't ask the young cat anything about Sean. He was just seeing if anything popping. He wanted to appear just as it did; that apparently Sean was not going to be found by either one of them. Dub rolled down his window to wave Ricki to come up to him. She pulled alongside the driver side and rolled down her window.

Dub looked at Ricki as if he was struggling with the hardest arithmetic problem known to man. "Ain't nobody seen his ass, but if I hear anything I will definitely give you a call."

Ricki had a gut feeling that Dub was full of it. She sped off leaving tire marks as she yelled at Dub, "Yeah right! You lying mutha fucka!"

"Silly bitch!" Dub yelled as though she could he hear him. Shaking his head, he took a long gasp of breath and let out a loud chuckle.

What Dub didn't know was the event that took place last night on the set when Beanz and Sean made it back on the block. As soon as they pulled up and got out the car, they were stopped in their tracks as the sounds of an automatic weapon began.

Bullets riddled Sean's car from across the open lot that faced the set. During the hail of bullets, Beanz upped his colt and returned three bangs from behind the car. That didn't stop a thing. More shots came in their direction. Whoever was after them was only sending a message or either needed some target practice. When the gunfire stopped, Sean and Beanz were spread flat on the concrete behind the car breathing very heavily. Each one noticed that the other one was alive. They jumped up and dusted themselves off. From that very hour, they spent the evening night unleashing hell and damnation on everything within a one-mile radius. Sean's last heist was about to have him in his final resting place.

Chapter 5

Dub made sure that Ricki didn't duck around any corners and was laying in the cut, waiting for him to make a move. He bent a couple of more corners to make sure he wasn't being tailed. Once he saw the coast was clear, he pulled up in an alley off of Kingshighway and Page to park. Before he made his exit from his Chevy, he secured his .357.

Dub knocked on the back door to Playa's house. Playa was Sean's cousin. Not really a street nigga, Playa was an all day dope dealer. He broke the most important rule in the dope game. He kept it and sold it where he laid his head. He kept a lot of bread to attest it too. Playa had one of those houses that mugz packed up in and did whatever. Sort of like punk ass Chauncey's crib in *Menace II Society* and the activities were similar to Sugar Ray's in *Harlem Nights*.

BOOM! BOOM! BOOM! Dub stood at the door with his hood nigga knock.

"Who dat?" Playa hollered over the old tune of Ghetto Boys' "Mr. Scarface". After looking through the peephole, making sure it wasn't the police, Playa unlatched the locks.

Dub made his way through the door. "It's me fool! What's crackin' cuzz? Where is Sean's fool ass at?"

"Him and Beanz in the living room going at it on that Madden!" Playa closed and secured the door behind Dub.

Playa earned his name in middle school. He always thought he had more game than Slick Rick the Ruler and Goldie put together. Playa was what the hood called a skinny pimp. He juggled a cell phone, a Playboy magazine, and a crack jar. His business came to him so he could usually be found in the house walking around in a white wife-beater all day long.

Dub walked through the kitchen. He turned his nose up at the unpleasant aroma of cocaine being turned into crack. Playa went back to the stove to work on his whip game as if he had a gourmet meal in the works. When Dub walked into the living room, he saw Sean and Beanz playing the Xbox. They were tuned in like two zombies. Dub plopped down on the couch and began to play with his phone. Beanz and Sean kept right on playing the game as if they never saw him enter the room.

Dub stood up and yanked the plug from the wall socket. Beanz jumped up out of his seat and fixed his eyes on Dub. Through gritted teeth, he spoke. "You lost yo mind, dawg?"

"Sit yo' tough ass down nigga and where the fuck y'all been all night? Dis nigga right here," he pointed in Sean's direction sounding like Katt Williams, "Gal came banging on my mu-fuckin door and shit!"

They both knew Dub had a problem with unexpected guests. Sean looked with a gaze. He wasn't surprised about anything Ricki had done or might do. He knew when he didn't make it home she would come looking for him.

Sean sat back down. "Man, plug the game back up!"

"That's half the problem now. All these ole entertainment systems. It's real out here. While the body count is stacking up and the system is extorting us like cattle, you silly mu-fuckaz is playing Madden!" Dub was starting in on his sermon about the strategy to stay focus. Today they were not about to listen. Beanz rushed Dub growling like an angry linebacker. Upon impact, they both fell on a plastic covered couch with Dub on the bottom. As soon as Beanz raised his hand to punch Dub, he slid from underneath him, reversing the position. Beanz was now on the bottom and still growling. He was jerking his entire body so that Dub couldn't get a firm grip on him. Sean was standing in the corner taking it all in and laughing hysterically. His laugh was brought to an abrupt halt. During the scuffle, Dub's .357 Magnum flopped out and released a loud bang. The bullet exited the chamber, ricocheted the wall and went right into the TV set. Sean was still laughing his head off when Playa rushed his way into the living room.

Playa's skinny ass ran up in the living room like a raging bull. "Man, what the fuck y'all doing? My son in the other mu-fuckin' room sleep! What the fuck y'all in here trippin' off of?" Dub was still on top of Beanz. Beanz was holding Dub's wrists in the air and looking him square in his eyes. Dub snatched his wrists from Beanz's grasp and stood up.

"Who gone pay for this shit?" Playa asked in a very high pitched and passive voice.

Dub didn't take his eyes off Beanz as he reached in his pocket and threw a fifty-dollar bill at Playa.

"Man you have to come betta than that. Fifty snaps?!?" Playa had a look of disgust.

"Dude shut up." Dub had to tell him he already knew that everything in his house he got for the low-low. "Nigga that bunk ass floor model TV prolly cost you twenty dollars from a fuckin' base head." Dub walked back through the kitchen and out the back door to cool off. His body temperature was up. While sitting on the back porch, he collected his thoughts.

It was a warm St. Louis morning with the sun half shining and squirrels running in and out of the dumpsters. Playa's backyard was a simple square with a carport facing the back of the house. In the distance, Dub could hear the 95 Kingshighway Bi-State bus making its rounds. He had to cool down. He wasn't furious with Beanz and there were no hard feelings. The little squabble was nothing out of the norm. Squabbling with your brothers was part of life in the hood.

Just as Dub was about to get up and leave, the back door crept open, and Sean along with Beanz walked out. Together, they grabbed a seat on the steps. With Dub sitting on the middle step, there was nothing but silence among them. The flow of the traffic was the theme music to their thoughts.

Sean broke the silence by saying, "Look we all been making a lil bread lately and I know y'all kinda pissed right now, but listen. I think we got enough money between us to make something happen. I know some people in Countryside who can…"

Beanz had to get in on the dialogue. "If you knew some fools in Countryside then tell me why the fuck we ain't robbed 'em yet?"

It was as though the light bulb popped up over Dub's head. "This is what we need to jump off. We gone put our ends together and comp from Grip. Then we can get at them niggas in Countryside and distribute the work to every mug on the west side." Dub looked at his watch and continued. "We going hard in the paint or we ain't going at all." Dub stood up to leave. "I gotta go take this final." He placed his pointer finger toward Sean. "You need to go find Ricki's crazy ass. You need to either shake her or keep her tied up on something. And tell her to stay the fuck away from my house." He couldn't leave without giving Beanz something to do. Beanz was ordered to get the artillery and they were to meet back at Playa's at 7:30 sharp. Dub walked to his Chevy and all he could think of was him and his boys getting it in that night.

Chapter 6

The whole time Dub was in class focusing on the inner workings of an air conditioner, he was forming a blueprint for this west side take over. Dub had an uncanny ability to multi-task mentally. That was one reason he was enrolled in an accelerated program at Ranken Tech.

Dub was distracted from his thought process as his instructor began to speak with his high impact of country accented broken English.

"Now tamarra' be pa'pared to do shop round six-sa-clock."

Dub shot out the class. He was moving so fast he almost dropped his book bag. Catching it by the strap, he continued to walk as if it were one motion. He made it to his Chevy. With his usual NASCAR driving method, he smashed through the campus parking lot. When he made it home, Tangie was on the couch laying with the baby.

"Hi Boo!" she said without taking her eyes off the television.

"What's up Baby?" Dub said as he hurried to walk over and kiss her and his little sunshine. He thought to himself how he would just die if something happened to them.

Taking her eyes off the television, she noticed that Dub's strides became extremely fast. "Why are you in such a hurry?" Tangie questioned.

"I'm finna go handle something. If anybody calls, tell'em I am over at mom's house fixin' her lock." Dub rushed into the bedroom. Making his way over to the closet, he began to thumb through his clothing options with speed. With what he had planned, he knew exactly what his wardrobe should require: black Dickies, black t-shirt, black hoodie and a black skullcap to match his black Hi-Tech boots.

Dub went to a secret compartment in the closet under the khaki colored rug. While the compartment remained opened, he pulled out three rubber band stacks, a small silver flashlight, and a box of latex gloves. He looked at his watch. It was 7:12 p.m. He put the end of the flashlight in his mouth and closed the lid on the compartment in the floor. Making sure the items were secure, he stood up. He turned and was taken by surprise. Tangie stood firmly with a look of disgust on her face.

Holding her robe with her lips turned up and eyes narrowed tight, she spoke. "So you finna change a lock huh?"

"Baby listen..." Dub tried turn on his normal script but Tangie was not in the mood.

"So what you lyin' to me now nigga! You gonna just try to play me like I didn't just see what you were doing?'

"No baby, listen! I am coming right back," Dub pleaded.

"And you gonna *keep* lyin'?!? Wit yo wanna be slick ass! You really must think I'm stupid huh?" Tangie's voice escalated with each syllable. "While you think you being slick, I know mo' than ya think! I don't wanna see ya locked up or let my baby lose her daddy to the streets! I am begging you not to leave this house! Dub I am serious!" Tangie's volume was way past ten.

Tangie felt that her demands would be heard and understood. Dub hated to see her so upset, but the streets were waiting. What she said was not being ignored, but there was no time for him to even consider entertaining it. With the flashlight still in his mouth, Dub gathered together a pair of baseball gloves to go with the latex gloves and money as he proceeded to make his departure. He pocketed the money before he put both pairs of gloves and the flashlight in the front pockets of his black hoodie.

Being ignored had Tangie ready to explode. "Don't ignore me, Dub! You got all this black shit on and I am 'pose to think you going to change locks! If you leave, don't come back ole lying ass nigga!" She was moving her hands as if she was the conductor of an orchestra and rolling her neck like most women do when they are pissed.

Dub pushed past her, almost knocking her onto the bed. An emotional wreck, she closed her eyes and unloaded a fury of slaps to Dub's back. Feeling the pops, Dub turned and quickly grabbed Tangie up by the shoulders. The fast clench made her close her eyes immediately. Her small frame seemed like a midget in his grasp. Her arms were straight at her side and her robe was opened, exposing her apple shaped breasts. When she opened her eyes, it appeared as though floodgates had been broken. The tears poured out unstoppably. All she could see was a deranged Dub with gritted teeth and tight jaws. He began to shake her back and forth as though she were a rag doll. He had never put a hand on her before so she didn't know *what* to expect!

He bellowed with gritted teeth. "Don't make me fuck you up girl! Calm yo ass the fuck down! Don't ever put yo hands on me! Do you know what I do to a nigga for that?" With a hard thrust, he threw her on the bed. The way she floated, she almost appeared lifeless. When Tangie hit the bed, she just balled up in a knot and continued crying. Dub took one last glance at Tangie as he made his exit.

Tangie noticed that he returned to his task. She didn't care to close her robe as she stormed behind him. She figured her nakedness would sequester his attention. Not wanting to get too close, she pleaded from afar. "Baby I am so sorry! Please, pleaaassse don't leave tonight! Pleassssse! Dub I had a dream this... this morning!" She was sobbing so hard she could hardly talk without her voice cracking.

Dub was hurt, but with money on his mind, he just continued to walk toward the front door. When he entered the living room, he noticed his daughter sitting on the floor. She was oblivious to what had just gone on with her parents. She was in the middle of the floor nibbling on the remote control. Tempest looked at her daddy smiling with clear drool on her chin. He walked toward her and picked her up.

"You know yo daddy don't cha, huh? Who's daddy's baby?"

Tempest suddenly frowned looking at Dub as though she had sensed him upsetting her mother. It was as though it was a vibe of merciless energy hovering over them both. Tempest grabbed both of his cheeks with her tiny brown hands. She smirked with a sigh saying, "Da... Da."

Dub's lips quivered as his eyes began to water. For a split second, he had forgotten about the spat that had just taken place with him and Tangie. He wanted to run and tell her what the baby had just said. Trying to be strong, he wiped the tears that had just fell upon his face. He kissed Tempest on the forehead and placed her back on the floor. He grabbed the remote and placed it back in her little hands. He had vanished by the time she went back to nibbling the remote.

Chapter 7

In the city of St. Louis, just about every street had an alley or two connected to it. On some sides of town, there's an alley every half block, similar to a complicated piping system that wound its way through neighborhoods as it interconnected with street after street. On the west side, every block had an alley behind it. Just as you could travel ten blocks by street, you could also travel ten blocks by way of the alley. These infamous alleys were a criminal underworld. Even the bad ass kids would cut the bottom out of a milk crate and hang it up on a lamppost to shoot ball. The gangsters could also be found conducting their business. The alleys in the Lou have a life of its own.

7:32 p.m.

Dub could feel the loose gravel of the alley floor crackling and crunching as he drove down the alley's path of Kingshighway. Creeping at a low speed, he could see two figures directly in his headlights. He could tell it was Sean and Beanz. They were standing there with their arms folded and legs spread apart looking like two desperados in the old west. Dub pulled smack dab up on them and they didn't budge. He laughed inside his car at his homies. They knew how to make a scene memorable. Still laughing, he hit the lights and hopped out the vehicle. The alley was dark and the temperature was a bit chilly. Most of the alley's lights on the lampposts had been shot out. It would take the city quite some time to replenish them. Dub dusted off his pants as if he had spilled something as he walked over to Sean and Beanz.

"Is my dudes ready or what?" Dub said as he gave each of them some dap.

"What's the deal Dub?" Sean inquired.

"I figure to establish some order, you must create chaos first." Dub replied.

"What nigga?" Sean didn't understand. He was one of those people you always had to break things down for.

"To establish some order, you must create chaos," Dub repeated himself. "Tonight, we unleash a plague of drama and create chaos in Countryside. It's only so we can establish order on the west side. Me and Beanz finna jump this chaos off." Dub reached into the pocket of his hoodie and gave Sean the stacks of money. Giving Beanz direct eye contact, he continued. "And you take that to Grip so we can establish order." Dub smiled a silly "ain't I so smart" smile.

Sean started laughing and said, "Cuzz I'm feelin' dat!" Sean was so excited.

When Dub heard a dog barking in the distance, that's when he focused on Beanz. He was more quiet than usual. He looked at his big homie and asked, "Wat up? You ready? Cause if you scared go to church!"

Beanz looked Dub up and down as if he wanted to get something off his chest. "Nigga, if I am scared, ain't no such thing in that Man upstairs, boy!"

"Then if no gangsta objects," Dub looked at the both of them and whirled his finger in the air. "Mount Up!"

Sean jumped the concrete part of the carport and dashed through Playa's backyard to go holla at Grip. Dub and Beanz hopped into the Chevy and mashed out toward Countryside Apartments. Each red light, Dub placed a latex glove then a black baseball glove on both hands.

The darkness of the night and the glow of the moon made the streets appear shiny. Light shined occasionally through the car as the moon played hide and seek with the buildings as they passed by. All that could be heard was the constant sound of the car moving.

"You cool cuz?" Dub looked over at Beanz and then back at the road. Beanz had a particular look, but he went into a whole other being when he was getting down and dirty.

"I'm straight. I'm just waiting to see this takeover manifest in the flesh. What do you think about Playa?" Beanz kept his eyes on the road as if he were the driver.

"Shit! I mean he good. I don't agree with him having his son living with him in a dope house. He does all that shit where he lays his head and dat ain't cool. And um he ain't nobody I could play the street with, but he good. Why? What's up?" Dub took a look at Beanz and then went around a slow moving car. Out of everybody in the hood, Beanz felt a connection with Dub. He never envied Dub's leadership skills.

Beanz spoke almost at a whisper, "Naw. I was just thinking."

"You need to be thinking bout how many mu fuckaz might be in this apartment." Dub saw the Goodfellow Avenue exit, which would lead him to his destination. He hit his blinker and slid up the ramp with ease. Bringing his vehicle to a slow stop as he looked to his left, then toward the right and proceeded with caution.

7:56 p.m.

When the two reached the complex, Dub let the impeding traffic pass and pulled up to the gate which was being guarded. The security guard was a middle-aged black woman. He noticed that she wasn't wearing a wedding ring. He eased his way out the car and stood at the booth blocking the guard's view of Beanz.

"Excuse me Miss. May I have your name?"

"May I ask just what are you going to do with it once I give it to you?" the guard said with a hint of an attitude. Her caramel skin glistened as her front gold tooth on the right side gleamed.

"Well I know anybody working this booth has to be a woman of courage and I couldn't help but to get a closer look at this superwoman that I've never seen before...."

"Yeah, yeah... Now where are you going in the complex?" she was curious but flattered.

Dub dropped his head as if he were ashamed, and then looked up directly in her eyes, "I recently lost my wife to another man. I mean... I tried to be the man she wanted, but my honesty and compassion lost to a man with money, muscles, and pretty brown eyes." Dub looked like he was going to cry. "And I'm trying to visit a friend so we can drink some wine and start the healing process. Have you been hurt Miss Superwoman?"

She wasn't quite familiar with many men who expressed their emotions. She instantly became sympathetic. She gave Dub direct eye contact. She could see the sincerity in his eyes. She put her lips tightly together with a twist and out came a slight pop as she began to speak. "Awww.... I am so sorry about your grief and what you are going through. You know me and my friend...."

Dub cut her short and told Beanz, "Go on through nephew. She understands." He quickly turned back to the guard. "I am sorry baby, go ahead." He was about to look down at his watch but he knew that wouldn't be a good move. He pretended to listen attentively for the next few minutes. Then he thanked her for her sensitive advice. She allowed Dub to slide between the gates into the complex. Dub ran up to the car laughing and Beanz looked at him sharing the laugh. He hopped back into the parked car.

"Okay, listen. You see that red building right there?" He pointed to the building directly ahead as Beanz nodded. Looking straight ahead, he never took his eyes off the door he was headed for. "Now the third door is the one."

He reached under the seat and handed Beanz a badge and a black cap that read A.T.F. "Some homies in the hood lifted the items from a parked car. Here put this on. We bout to bust up in there like the cops! Yo name is Malone and mine is Riggins."

Dub liked the names, but Beanz was thinking to himself, *"I ain't bout to say nothing but 'Gimme the loot'!"*

"So we splittin' this shit 50/50 right?" Beanz looked at Dub as if he would agree.

Dub blew him off. Beanz always had issue while the crime was in the beginning process. Dub was thinking about the statement wondering if he was implying that they cut Sean out or what!

Nonetheless, they headed toward the third door with caps on and badges ready. Dub had taped the small flashlight on the bottom of his 40 caliber to make it real cop-like. Once at the door, they looked each other in the eyes with their pistols drawn and Beanz counted on his fingers raising them one at a time. It was routine and Dub already knew when his third finger popped up it was time to get it started.

8:12 p.m.

BAM! The door cracked and flew off the hinges. Beanz and Dub forced entry as Dub yelled, "Everybody freeze! A.T.F. got damn it! Nobody moves and nobody gets hurt! Malone, secure the perimeter!" Dub yelled waving his piece in the air.

There were only four people in the entire apartment. Three guys and a girl. Dub stood inches from the door with his eyes going back and forth pointing his piece at the three dudes as they lay down on the floor.

Beanz headed down a short hallway, which lead to a kitchen where a young blonde white girl was trying to throw all the crack down the disposal in the sink. He looked at her as if to say, "Why are you doing that stupid shit?" Beanz cocked the lever back and said, "Imma need you to stop doing that." She was hesitant but she obliged when Beanz yanked her hair up in his balled fist. Before she knew it, she was being drug down the hall. Beanz tossed her to the floor with the rest of the occupants.

"I hate you fuckin' pigs!" the girl yelled as she joined the others on the floor.

Beanz was going through his mental catalogue to remember what Dub wanted to be called. "Riggins, check the house!"

Dub hurried to check the house. This was a lot easier than he thought. The disguise had the dudes shook. Dub walked in the only bedroom in the apartment. Picking the only closet door, he found two duffle bags, which contained cash in one and a ton of dope in the other. He shot back in the living room with the bags on his shoulders. Dub came to a dead stop when he saw Beanz with his gun to the back of one of the dudes head whispering to him. Dub wanted to know what the topic of discussion was.

"Malone, round these suspects up and let's call it a night." Dub didn't know how to digest what he was observing.

"Ten-foe Riggins." Beanz bagged off giving Dub a nod to signal him it was time to make their exit. The two had been in enough raids to know the drill. They ran to the car and smashed out. As they made their way to the security gate, Dub blew the guard a kiss. She waved as she pushed the button to open the gate.

8:27 p.m.

Beanz was driving now. They both laughed and slapped each other's arms like two girls in a schoolyard fight. Heading down Goodfellow Avenue with the rewards of deception, Dub and Beanz rode at a moderate speed. Dub happily turned the radio up and dipped his head up and down. He noticed that Beanz was again quiet and staring at the road as if he was thinking. Beanz still had his pistol in one hand across his lap and gripping the steering wheel with the other hand.

"What's up homie? Put that banger away in case we get flagged." Dub insisted then turned to suck in a deep breath of smoggy St. Louis air from the open window. When he turned back around, Beanz still had the revolver in his lap.

"So… Ugh, we goin' down the middle or what? I mean Sean ain't put no work in tonight." Beanz looked at Dub awaiting his approval.

"Is you serious nigga? We break bread across the board man! Sean ain't gotta put no work in; he doin' his part. You on some other shit, Bruh! We don't pose to move like that! And second of all nigga…" Just as Dub was about to finish his sentence, he saw the white of Beanz's eyes and in one motion watched Beanz point the pistol. All he heard was *BANG!*

Delirious and half-aware Dub felt his entire body burning and then the pressure of something hard. Beanz fired two shots into Dub before pushing Dub out of the car, partially wiping the window off and leaving his homie for dead. As Beanz skidded toward the highway, Dub laid flat on the side of Goodfellow Avenue.

In and out of consciousness, he could see midnight blue skies and the temperature seemed to be dropping fast. With a hole in his chest and one in his shoulder, every breath began to get shorter and shorter. Somehow, he saw visions of Tangie and Tempest. He tried desperately to reach his hand out as if to touch them as his eyes began to become watery. Then with one hard breath, he went cold. Dub laid on the concrete in his all black, motionless. What took a lifetime to gain took only an hour to lose.

Chapter 8

Beanz made his exit off Kingshighway and pulled up to the alley behind Playa's house. He took a minute to clean up the car from the blood stains. Putting the bags in the trunk for security, he changed shirts, and was proud to be in his Beast mode. Sometimes the St. Louis streets had the ability to create monsters from men. Greed can be the anti-Christ masquerading as loyalty. When a street nigga confuses the lines between want and need, not a soul is safe. This is definitely not the city of brotherly love.

When Beanz knocked on the back door, Playa opened it so fast Beanz almost fell through before he could finish his knock.

"Hurry up and come in!" Playa nervously said as he peeked out the door looking from left to right.

"Calm down nigga! What you so noid about?" Beanz was curious now. Beanz stepped in and Playa threw a Penthouse magazine down on the kitchen table and turned off the stove.

"Follow me," Playa instructed.

They walked in Playa's bedroom and the Channel Five News was on. Playa turned it up.

Breaking news flashed across the screen and the reporter was giving the rundown on how two officers on the city's Westside were shot in an attempt to stop a drug transaction near Page Blvd. and Union Blvd.

"The details are sketchy, but we have live footage as one of the suspects has fled in a burgundy Thunderbird. Dan, can we see the sky cam?" The newswoman said as she was holding her earpiece.

The sky cam showed Sean's Thunderbird speeding down the highway with an entire precinct in pursuit.

"Damn Playa! I hope that ain't my dude. You ain't seen Grip?"

Playa turned to answer him when he noticed blood on Beanz.

"Where that blood come from? Where Dub at?" Curiosity grew in Playa's eyes.

Beanz punched him in the mouth. He didn't even see it coming. Playa stumbled and grabbed his mouth. The TV was still following the story. Beanz upped his revolver and lowered his eyes.

"Dub is in the matrix nigga. Now if you wanna keep yo hat, you betta dig in yo stash and break yo' self nigga." Beanz spoke in a low but stern tone.

Playa hesitated from the shock. He didn't know how to respond. Beanz slapped him with the gun.

"Damn it I said now! Move it nigga!" Beanz pointed his banger.

Shaken and afraid like the mark he was, Playa tore the cover off his vent and gave Beanz everything. Beanz took all his shit and grabbed Playa by the back of his tank top.

"Thanks pussy. Now lock yo self in the bathroom bitch ass nigga." Beanz slapped Playa on his ass as if he were a good sport. Playa did as he was told. Happy to be alive, Playa just listened through the bathroom door making sure Beanz had left the house.

Chapter 9

beep... beep... beep...

"Ahhh. GRRR!" was all Dub could say with his dry and hoarse throat. He felt pain throughout his entire body. All he heard were the beeps from the heart monitor. His attempt to get up was of no use. Dub's slightest movement woke Tangie up immediately. She looked at him. Genuinely he recognized her but her normally pretty face was puffy and damp. She had been crying and praying all night.

"Baby, *relax*. I love you so much." Tangie gasped. Her throat was just as dry as Dub's.

"What happened? Where is Tempest? I... I... need to..." Dub was losing his breath. His chest was padded and his arm was in a sling. The hospital room was cold and small with one window overlooking Kingshighway. The TV in the corner was showing an episode of As the World Turns.

"Don't move baby. Relax! The baby is at yo' momma's house. Who shot you Dub? I'm sorry." Tangie shook her head. She didn't care because he survived and he was in her presence. She was mourning but it was only from an injury that he would soon be part of the past. "It don't matter. I just want you home."

Dub immediately recalled what happened. Tears began to develop in his eyes. Worst than his wounds, the betrayal was hurting even more. He thought to himself, "Beanz, how could you?" Tangie reached over to dry his eyes. He smacked her hands away and lay there hurting physically and emotionally. When he lifted his head up, he saw Ricki in the corner chair sleep with a hospital blanket over her. What was Ricki doing there? Dub didn't even care for her. It instantly made him wonder where Sean was.

"Where is Sean? If Beanz... I'm gone ka... ka... *kill him*!" Dub was heavily sedated and very drowsy, so he couldn't speak clearly. He was fearing the worst.

"What do Beanz have to do with anything baby?" Tangie didn't understand.

Just as Tangie grabbed Dub's hand to comfort him, two uniformed cops entered the room. The officers resembled Sean Penn and Robert Duvall when they were in the movie Colors trying to stop gang violence. One had a classic clean cut appearance. The other was more relaxed like he'd seen it all a million times. They approached Dub's bedside.

"Get the fuck out of here! Don't walk in here while he's at his worst! You mutha fuckaz is heartless!" Tangie snapped and she was on the verge of getting real grimy. She thought they were there to harass and degrade him in some sort of way.

Dub's speech was slurred. "Calm down baby. Let these men do they job."

"Excuse us ma'am. David Douglas, do you know who shot you or why? The stolen car report indicates..."

"Wait. Stolen car?" Dub was clueless as he struggled to speak.

"Yes, stolen car. It was the call we responded to. Your animated girlfriend here reported your car stolen around 8:15 p.m. last night," said the Robert Duvall impersonator.

"She did what?" Dub was pissed. He thought about being on his mission then being stopped randomly for a stolen car with his ratchet on him. His drowsiness fogged up his thoughts.

"Baby I didn't know where you were and I had a bad feeling." Tangie pleaded with her eyes, but Dub was furious. "Plus I had a dream similar to this situation. If you were paying attention when you left the house I was trying to tell you about my dream."

"Actually, you need to be thanking her. If it were not for her, we wouldn't have found you. Now can you tell us who shot you and why?"

"I don't know officer. Maybe the carjacker." Dub was now conveniently getting tired again.

The clean cut officer cut in. "Well we found your car parked on Enright Avenue. The suspect was approaching and when our officers confronted him, he fled the scene. Your girlfriend came and picked up the car after we called her." He paused. "We will be monitoring this case closely, Mr. Douglas. If you are involved, we will arrest you." He looked at Tangie and nodded. "Ma'am, have a nice day."

Chapter 10

It was almost noon on July 15th. Dub, Tangie and Tempest were rushing to get ready for his graduation. Dub was feeling like this day would never come. Being shot by Beanz had really put a lot on his mind. It wasn't nothing unexpected because Beanz was that type of dude. Dub just felt that it would never happen between the two of them. Looking at the hood from the rearview mirror was almost the most obvious. Then the thoughts of revenge were prevalent. Thoughts of Beanz coming to finish the job were daily troubles that danced around like sugarplums as though it were the *Night Before Christmas*.

"Baby, hurry up! Shit!" Dub was getting irate. He was ready and anxious to leave. He was suddenly becoming frustrated with his thoughts. He didn't want to be late for a day he long awaited. He checked himself out in his pinstriped Perry Ellis suit. The smell of Hugo Boss filled the air.

"I'm coming! Don't rush me dude!" Tangie yelled from the bathroom. It was not very often that she got out the house so when she *did* leave, she had to make sure she was on point.

"Me and Tempest finna go to the car. Hurry up lil girl!" Dub and Tempest went outside and listened to the radio. He was leaned over the front seat singing and looking at his baby. He sat her down in the back of the car in order to get the car seat out of the trunk of the car. Tempest was bobbing her head as if she understood the lyrics he sang to her.

Tangie ran out and Dub was so impressed. She was looking so fire to him in her black clingy spaghetti strapped dress. The black high heels that showed off her pretty French-tip manicured toes made the attire even sexier. He was ready to go back in to calm his third leg down.

Dub got out the car and said, "Damn baby!" He couldn't find the right words to let her know that she was looking good as that thang.

"You like?" Tan asked with opened arms. She already knew the answer from the look in his eyes. She smiled because she accomplished what she set out to do. Tangie tiptoed to the car as if her feet were hurting. She grabbed the car door. "Stop lusting Boo. Pick ya mouth up and let's go."

Dub was still looking. He couldn't move. It had been a long time since he had seen her look so pretty. It was as if she had recently had a Hollywood makeover. Dub had almost forgotten that he was initially getting the car seat out of the trunk. As Tangie was getting in the vehicle, he was walking toward the back of the car not taking his eyes off of his girl. He opened the trunk and Tangie was no longer in his view as he felt around to grab the car seat. When he finally looked down, he noticed two sets of bag handles sticking up.

"What the..." He could say no more. Dub was in shock. He pulled the bags to the surface. It was the money and the dope from the lick that he and Beanz did. He looked left and then he looked right. He grabbed the bag and carefully ran them in the house. Once inside he laughed. The laughter became loud as he let out a loud sigh of relief. At that very moment, he felt like the universe had dealt him some justice. Dub secured the bags in the attic and ran back outside. He didn't realize he was still wearing a big kool-aid smile. Tangie noticed it. The smile was different from the look he had just given her.

"Why are you so happy all of sudden? You have went from I am sick of waiting on you to I can do it to ya right now and now the look is like I think we won the lottery!"

"Ahhh..." was the only thing he could get out. He was thinking even though he got shot up, he still came out on top. He looked over at Tangie. "Sometimes even when you lose you win anyway." He cranked the engine and headed toward his destination. Tangie looked at him as confusion riddled her soul. She was trying to make sense of what he said along with his sudden happiness.

Nevertheless, the graduation was beautiful. Tangie cried tears of joy. The instructor along with Dub's mother cheered him on as he walked across the stage, brushing the imaginary dirt off his shoulders when his name was called to get his certificate.

Sean was still going through his trial, but Dub gotten him the best lawyer that street money could buy. They talked on a regular. He finally told Sean that Beanz was the trigger man. Sean let him know that that was what he was hearing because the streets had been talking. He just couldn't bring himself to ask Dub about it. It was far out of character that Dub had not opted to retaliate and Beanz hadn't tried to finish the job which was the reason that delayed him from asking.

In the bright sunlight of a perfect July morning, Dub and Tangie sat side by side in two white plastic lawn chairs in the front yard. Tangie was wearing a pink two-piece bathing suit that fit her frame nicely. Dub was in a white wife-beater, khaki Dickie shorts, and a straw hat leaned down over his face hiding his eyes. Dub had convinced Tangie that they should take a vacation so this was their imaginary getaway. Dub was sipping on his tea with a little umbrella, twiddling his toes.

"Baby who is that?" Tangie asked lifting her pink sunglasses that matched her bathing suit.

"That ain't anybody but Tez." Dub leaned back and resumed his relaxed position.

"Now how did he ever find us? I didn't think we would be able to be located on this secluded island." Tangie said in a high-class articulate type of tone. They both shared a laugh.

Tez entered the yard looking at them like they both had just flown over the cuckoo's nest. He chuckled to himself as he began to speak. "Where the hell y'all think y'all at? Oh, let me guess. Is this the Florida Keys?" and he laughed some more.

Dub didn't move from under the hat. He didn't even give Tez any eye contact as he spoke. "Dude you mean to tell me you came all this way and didn't know you were coming to Hawaii?"

Tez held his laughter in. He reached toward his back pocket and handed Dub what he only wanted him to see. "Well since you are on vacation in Ha-Y-E, you have time to read what's going on in your neck of the woods."

Dub grabbed the newspaper and Tez looked at Tangie. "Tan and Dub... Aloha!" Tez exited the yard and was gone just as fast as he appeared.

Dub sat for a few more minutes enjoying the sun. He tilted his hat up and unfolded the newspaper. On the front page, the headline immediately caught his attention: **Barry Walton Found Slain in Westside Dumpster.**

He had to read that headline about twenty times before he opened the newspaper up some more to read the story that followed the headline. At the bottom of the newspaper was a very familiar face. It was the same picture used five years ago when Beanz was wanted for questioning for a robbery he and Beanz committed some time ago. Dub just sighed as he looked at the old picture of Beanz. He didn't even want to read the story because it pretty much lacked all the facts.

"What's with the paper that it was so important that he had to bring it all the way on our vacation?" Tangie saw the headline from her seat. She just felt the need to ask a question, but she already knew it was going to go unanswered.

"Ah nothing. Just another careless St. Louis cat falling victim to the city streets."

The streets of the Show-Me-State are notorious for bringing the worst out of people just like any other city plagued with individuals hungry for the green substance that contains pictures of old white men. In some cases, if he's lucky, a man can navigate his way back to normal life. The streets have a way of sucking your soul dry. But if you're smart, you may be able leave out with what little soul you have left. The Westside takeover was defeated by greed and disloyalty as most schemes are. As for now, the St. Louis streets are undefeated and yet to be taken over. Maybe one day men will give up or continue to have failed attempts. Either way, there's only one way out.

By Any Means Necessary

So St. Louis

Chapter 1

YOUNG POOCHIE & PASO

"*POW! POW! POW! BANG! BANG! BANG!*" was the sound of some major gunplay across the street.

"Get the hell down Paso!" Poochie yelled at her son hoping that the flying bullets wouldn't harm him. "Boy, if I told you once, I've told you a thousand damn times, that bullet don't have eyes nor names. How many times do I have to tell you that?" she shrieked pulling him down with her.

"Ma, that's Fatman'em." Young Paso replied with excitement in his tone.

"I don't give a damn!" She paused only to start again. "And stop focusing so much on this street life. This is not how you want to live. It's better than this, my baby." She continued to chastise Paso with her arms wrapped tightly around him, securing him only how a mother could. She waited for the shooting to subside before she allowed her son to move. This was something that she was used to. "Now go in the basement and read a book. Do something constructive and exclude the video game, knucklehead." She smacked him softly on the behind.

Poochie loved Paso with every ounce of breath in her body. She didn't want anything to happen to him. She was doing everything within her power to get them away from the north side of St. Louis. She had seen *enough* guys lose their lives on Red Bud Ave. She only lived there until she could afford her own spot. If she had a choice, she would have raised her son away from the city life, above all the naughty North Side.

Poochie had big plans for herself just as most young girls did. After graduating high school, she went to Meramac Community College at night. That wasn't her first choice of colleges but that's how things panned out due to an unexpected pregnancy. She had always done well in school and was liked by many. She didn't want to disappoint her family, most of all, her grandparents whom she loved greatly.

The Patricks had lived on Red Bud for fifty years. All three of their children were born and raised in that house as well as Poochie who became pregnant with Paso in her junior year of high school. She contemplated having an abortion but she knew that her heart wouldn't allow her to lie to her grandparents. She knew that she couldn't lie to Lizzie Patrick. You see, back in the day, the old folks knew what was going on in their children's lives. The kids in today's society have too much freedom. For instance, and I'm sure you can relate:

1. You couldn't have privacy in your mama's house. You had to leave your door to your bedroom open at all times.
2. You definitely and absolutely could not have company in your bedroom.
3. If your mother said something you didn't like, she dared you to mouth off at her. Your entire mouth would be bleeding

from that backhand smack she'd delivered. Lastly but not least...

4. Wherever you acted up, you got your ass beat on site. No ifs ands or buts about it. It went down and you were dared to call Family Services.

Lizzie raised her grandchild as she did her children. She knew when Lois became pregnant with Poochie that Poochie would be her and Leo's responsibility. Poochie's mother Lois liked to run the streets and they didn't like the company she kept. Just as she refused to let Poochie go to daycare the same thing applied to Paso. Lizzie kept him until he could talk. That way he could tell if someone was hurting him in anyway. The same cycle was repeating itself.

Lizzie and Leo had raised three children: Lois, Lynn and Lester. After graduating high school, both Lynn and Lester moved out. Shortly after that, Lois moved out and Poochie remained with her grandparents. Poochie wanted to get away from there and build a better life for her and Paso. She could taste the freedom of new beginnings on the tip of her tongue. After high school, Poochie went full time and worked 40 plus hours as a bank teller. She didn't have to pay any bills and most girls would have loved that. Now don't get it twisted. Poochie enjoyed having money to do what she wanted to do, but she wanted a better environment for her kid. Banking a huge amount of her paycheck helped build a nice account. Her granny wanted to make sure that she always had enough money to provide for Paso. Paso was the best dressed kid on the block as well as school. He was fresh to death everyday. Even though Poochie received child support from Paso's father, her grandparents contributed to his large number of the Air Jordan's. There wasn't anything he or Poochie couldn't get from them. Saying that they were spoiled was an understatement. The other grandchildren felt Poochie and Paso were always favored more and they were correct.

Chapter 2

GET IN WHERE YOU FIT IN!

"Hi, welcome to First Community Credit Union, how may I help you?" Poochie asked with a pleasant smile on her face but not really feeling her job today. The man that stood in front of her was stunning. His well-developed physique was captivating and followed by a perfect smile. He gave Poochie a deposit slip with fine penmanship. "How's it going Mahoganee?" he asked, reading her name tag.

"I'm good, Mr. Love," she stuttered, astounded viewing the large number on the withdrawal slip as well as his name.

"How do you want your money back?"

"It doesn't matter. It all spends the same way," he responded arrogantly.

"Sure, would you excuse me a second?" Poochie retorted leaving her station to get approval from her supervisor. He enjoyed watching her from the back and Poochie knew it. She gave him a little show, strutting as if she were on a runway. She immediately returned with his cash.

"Why did you go in the back?" He looked at her with discernment.

"Anything over six grand has to be approved. It's protocol, rules, something we all have to follow one time or another." Poochie proceeded to count ten thousand dollars in large bills back to him.

"Yeah, some of us. I refused to work for the white man anymore." He looked at Poochie with a serious face.

"Well some of us have to do what's needed to survive in this cruel world." She gave him much attitude, continuously counting his cash not missing a beat. "Nine hundred ninety nine and ten grand. Have a good day Mr. Love."

Tyron Love was caught off guard by her last statement. He made eye contact before he uttered another word. "You do the same, Ms. Lady." He replied gathering his money, neatly placing it in a big yellow envelope, housing it in a small black Marc Jacob's briefcase. He turned to leave and Poochie couldn't resist the stimulating smell of his Usher's VIP cologne. She also checked his fresh gear and he was on point. His Brotha' Brotha' Original outfit was fly. The green sleeveless vest with the IZOD design adorned the black button down underneath. The black signature *BBO* loafers put that extra swag in his gear. As he neared the exit, he took one quick look back at Poochie then secured his eyes from the sun light with his Cartier shades. Everything about this ninja was inviting and Poochie accepted his request. Poochie knew what that quick look meant: get in where you fit in.

Chapter 3

WE GOTTA STOP MEETING LIKE THIS!

Poochie waited on quitting time to come but it was moving in slow motion. After counting all of the currency and doing the paperwork for the day, it was time for her to make her exit. Walking to the parking lot, Poochie was displeased with her red 1999 Pontiac Grand AM. She wanted a new car but didn't want the car payment. While riding home, she adjusted her radio to Hot 104.1 FM. Staci Static was jamming "I Am", a track from Mary J. Blige's new CD "Stronger With Each Tear".

Ain't nobody gonna treat you better
Ain't nobody gonna touch you better
Ain't nobody gonna love you better boy than I am

Mary's voice echoed through the speakers. Poochie sang right along with the song, stuck in the five o'clock traffic on Highway 70. Just as she was about to exit on Union Blvd., she saw a familiar face in a tricked out white 2009 Dodge Magnum. She could hear Trey Songz playing in the backdrop.

"Is this ninja following me?" she thought, entering the parking lot of the liquor store where she stopped most days to get Paso a Hostess Ding Dong cake after work. She exited the car and walked across the street to Micheaux's to get her some buffalo fish and Paso some cheese fries. The line was extra long due to it being a

Friday evening and this was the spot for whatever you wanted to eat. Byron had the huge grills going in the front and the pots boiling in the back.

Poochie placed her order before going outside and calling to see what her son was doing while she waited on her food. After she hung up the phone, a recognizable face was near. "Is your lil man cool?" Tyron asked licking his lips.

"He's good, thanks," she replied caught off guard. "Mr. Love, right?" she asked as if she couldn't remember.

"Correct," he responded. "What such a pretty young lady as you doing in a rough neighborhood?"

"Getting my son and me something to eat," she threw back at him sarcastically. "I also live over this way."

"Can you cook?" he boldly asked.

"What's it to you if I can or not?" Poochie displayed excessive attitude.

"No need for the attitude babe. It was just a lil jokie joke, that's all," he told her.

Tyron's cell phone rang to the sounds of Birdman's "Money To Blow".

"Excuse me," he told her, walking toward the corner. Poochie looked at him and admired his appearance from head to toe. He was swagged out in a pair of dark Polo jeans with a dark blue Polo shirt and plaid Polo shoes with the huge Polo logo on the side.

"Damn he's sexy," she thought to herself. Her thoughts were interrupted by the sounds Melanie Fiona's "It Kills Me". She knew it was her cousin/best friend Ceria.

"Hey cuz, what's good?"

"Bitch where you at?" Ceria yelled through the phone.

"Getting Paso and me something to eat, why?" She frowned into the phone wondering why Ceria was yelling like she'd lost her everlasting mind. She continued, "Ceria calm it down, dang. You're about to bust my eardrums with all that damn screaming."

"My bad cuz. You know how I get when I'm excited," Ceria said, smacking her lips. "Bitch," she paused momentarily. "Guess who's coming to Karma Night Club?" Karma was one of St. Louis' newest hot spots. Her voice went up an octave. Poochie didn't say anything. She'd already heard before Ceria could ask who. "Pooch Hall from 'The Game'. You know Derwin Davis, Rookie, Ding Dong with the girlfriend, Girl Melanie." Ceria informed her taking a deep breath after finishing her sentence.

Poochie knew all too well who Ceria was talking about. That was one of her favorite sitcoms. "And," she continued with her sista girl neck rolling. "We in the V.I.P. baby"

"What did you do to make that happen?" she started laughing knowing that Ceria was going to curse her out.

"Bitch what you mean, what I do? Are you going or what 'cause you know I can always find a replacement!"

"Girl, you wish but anyways, when is he coming?" she asked getting just as excited as her cousin.

"Tomorrow night and you better be ready."

"Okay I will. Let me call you when I get home and get situated," Poochie told Ceria, looking in Tyron's direction. He was approaching her quickly.

Poochie adjusted her huge tan Coach bag and began to enter Micheaux's. "Hey Ms. Lady," Tyron called out to Poochie. She turned around unfazed by his statement and looked him in the eye.

"What's good, Boo?" She licked her lips, thinking to herself, "This ninja is fine as hell!"

"I was wondering if I could take you out this weekend. Being that you work at a bank, I know you're off."

"What gives you that idea? I do work on Saturdays," she stated with that matter of fact type of attitude.

"Well I know you're off on Sundays. I would love for you to hang out with me on Saturday night."

"Why don't we exchange numbers and I'll let you know when I'm free." She had her cell phone in her hand ready to retrieve his number as he did the same.

"I hope we can hang out tomorrow and also I will pay for your babysitter. I really want to take you out." He shook his head up and down approvingly.

"I'm sure that can be arranged and I'll be in touch. Oh and another thing, I hope you're not one of those guys that waits on the female to call you first. That's so immature but do know this. I'm a grown woman, it's only one man I play with and he's my son," she told him hardheartedly.

"I got you babe, no games. That's not what I'm about and if you go out with me, you'll see. Hope to hear from you soon," he told her, holding the door for her to enter back into Micheaux's.

"Oh, you will, sooner than later. We gotta stop meeting like this." She walked in front of him going to get her food.

Chapter 4

A Mother's Love!!

Poochie woke up at 7:00am the following morning, as if she was going to work. She likes to get her day popping early. She started her day by making breakfast for the family. The menu consisted of eggs, grits, rice, waffles, sausage and fried potatoes with cheese. If she didn't know how to do anything else she was a skilled cook. Her granny taught her that.

"Paso what do you want to drink?" she asked situating his plate in front of him. "We have orange and apple juice or milk."

"I'll take some milk. It does your body good," he said making a muscle.

"Boy you silly," she said as she began to fix her grandparents' plates.

"Ma, can we go to the mall today? I saw those new Polo boots and I want them, please," he begged.

"I don't have a problem with that but I need to see your progress report." She stopped what she was doing and walked over to Paso. "Look at me," she told him in a motherly tone. "I want you to always know that education is the solution. I want you to excel above the sky. There's no limit to what you can do." She lifted his chin gently to face her.

"Ma I know. I've heard this speech since I can remember," he said, cutting her off. "I understand, I promise that I do." He smiled at her.

"Now let me see your progress report." She stuck her hand out standing back on her legs. Paso removed himself from the table and obliged his mother's request. He wasn't worried about anything. He knew what he had to do to get what he wanted from his mom.

Poochie went back to fixing her grandparents' plates. As she wrapped the last one, shots rang out. Before she could do or say anything, bullets flew through the kitchen window. She moved her head just in time but Paso wasn't that swift. Poochie heard a loud noise and saw her baby boy stretched out on the floor with blood leaking from his little body. Poochie went into a raging fit. "Paassoo!" Her voice screamed waking her grandparents. "Baby, get up!" Tears flooded her face.

"Oh my God!" Mrs. Patrick yelled. "Leo call the ambulance and the police! These sons of bitches done shot my grandboy!" she shouted crying bending down to join Poochie.

"Don't touch him, wait on the paramedics!" Mr. Patrick hollered doing as he was instructed.

Poochie rode in the back of the ambulance with Paso while her grandparents rode right behind them. Poochie always prayed and thanked God for her blessings but today she prayed that God heard them all. Just in case He didn't, she was going to speak with Him right then. "Lord, please protect my baby. The devil is trying to take him away." The tears soaked her pretty face. "Lord I pay my tithes at church, I give to the homeless and I volunteer to feed them once a month. I give back to my community and my heart is good. I respect your word and I try to be the best person I know how to be. Please don't take my baby away from me. If there is anything you want me to do, Lord please send confirmation and I'll obey your word." She finished her prayer and turned to the tech in charge.

"Is my baby going to make it?" Worry consumed her.

"We're doing everything in our power," he responded as he continued setting up the IV. "Ms. Patrick calm down. We need to keep your child calm and in order to do that, I need you to stay calm. He's still conscious of everything of going on around him. Do this for him. I know it's hard." He composed himself reassuringly but on the inside he knew that this six year old kid would not make it.

Poochie rubbed Paso's hand. Just the comfort of his mother eased his small mind. "Ma I'm not gonna make it." Paso told his mom just above a whisper.

"Don't say that baby. I told you, you can do anything you want. We're almost at the hospital. The doctors and nurses will take care of you." She held his hand tighter with tears drowning her face. "You're going to be fine baby."

"Ma its hurts so bad. I don't know how much more I can take. It's even starting to burn." Paso's speech was slow, low and fading.

"Baby, just hold on and be strong. Mama's going to be here. I will not leave your side." Poochie's tears seemed as if they were the size of a golf ball. She listened as the tech call the hospital and informed them of Paso's wounds and condition.

Poochie and her grandparents waited as the doctors operated on Paso. Lois also made it to the hospital accompanied by her siblings, Lynn and Lester. Ceria came as soon as she'd heard as well as LaTona, Lester's daughter. Ceria sat with Poochie with her arms wrapped around her tightly, both with flowing tears. "He gon' make it cuz." Ceria tried to comfort Poochie.

"I hope so. He's all I got," she replied and bawled her eyes out again. Lois walked over to Poochie and grabbed her hand to take a walk with her. Once they were away from the others, Lois hugged Poochie extra tight and they rocked from side to side. Poochie hadn't felt her mother's touch in ages. She almost forgot how it felt but thanks to Mrs. Patrick for keeping the love alive.

"My grandboy is gonna be fine. Watch what I tell you." Lois had huge tears in her eyes. "God is not gonna take your baby away from you. He knows how much you love that little boy." Lois pulled Poochie away from her and looked her in the eyes. "You are such a wonderful parent. You run circles around my parenting skills. I know I have never told you this but you are doing an awesome job with Paso. Yes he's spoiled rotten and makes me want to whip his tail sometimes but I wouldn't trade him or you for that matter, for anything in this world. If I never been here for you, I am today and every day after. I ask for your forgiveness, for not being the parent I could have been. I know the streets seem more important to me than you but they weren't. I was just young and dumb but I'm better now. You can depend on me for whatever. You're my child, not my parents', and I have been jealous of y'all relationship ever since you were born. I'm willing to take a stand and play my position if only you give me a chance." Lois continued to stare in Poochie's eyes.

Poochie said nothing but shook her head in agreement. She had been waiting to hear those words ever since she could remember.

"Thanks Lois," Poochie expressed referring to her by her first name, hugging her mother strongly. "I've been waiting to hear those words for so long." Poochie broke back down crying. That's when Mrs. Patrick came out to see what was going on.

"Everything is fine out here mama," Lois told her mother as she walked up on them. Mrs. Patrick would kick ass about Poochie and Paso.

"Alright, I'm just checking. I heard my baby crying and I wanted to make sure you were not upsetting her more than she already is." She stretched her arms out to Poochie and she fell into them without a second thought. "I love you baby and Paso is gonna be fine." She tried to reassure her, not really convinced herself.

"I love you too, grandma," said Poochie as the ladies walked back into the waiting room.

Chapter 5

Is This Life!!!

Poochie was getting extremely edgy waiting on the doctors to inform her of her son's condition. Lizzie and Leo needed to go home to take their medications but they wanted to know Paso's status. Lizzie had been to the nurse's station several times but each time she was told the doctors will be out to inform them shortly. Paso had been in surgery for over three hours now and they heard nothing. "Papa, take grandma on home and I'll keep y'all updated."

"I think that's a good idea," Ceria suggested.

"Mama, you and dad need to take y'all medication. Go ahead. There's nothing we can do right now. Ceria will stay with Poochie and we're not taking no for an answer," Lois reasoned as well as her siblings. So everybody decided to leave but Poochie and Ceria.

After everyone left, Poochie explained to Ceria what happened to her son. No matter how many times she tried to refrain from crying, the tears escaped her eyes. "Ceria, I'm going to find that punk ass nigga who shot my baby and deaden the shit outta him. My baby is six years old and has a whole life ahead of him. The hoe cake ass nigga better hope my child pull through this, whoever he is! I will find out! You know ninjas run their mouths like little bitches. Somebody gonna leak something, watch." Poochie was clearly and seriously distressed.

"You gotta know that Pooh." Ceria responded wiping the tears from Poochie's eyes as well as her own. "My lil cuz gon' be good and when he gets outta here, I'm gonna take him to Six Flags." Ceria had a big smile on her face.

"Yeah that would be fun." Poochie showed a small smile.

"I'm going to the restroom. I'll be back. Do you want something from the cafeteria while I'm down there?" Ceria asked leaving out of the waiting room.

"Naw I'm good. I just want my son to be okay," she genuinely confirmed.

"He will cuz, he will," said Ceria before disappearing down the hallway.

While sitting there waiting on the doctors, Poochie's phone rang to the sounds of The O'Jays' "Family Reunion". She knew it was her grandparents wanting an update. "Hello," she answered.

"Is there any new information on my grandboy?" her granny inquired, concerned.

"No, nothing since y'all left."

"You need to go back to that damn nurse's station and demand some damn answers!"

"Okay granny I will but could you hold on?" She looked at the name that appeared on her cell phone. "Wow!"

"Granny, I'm going to call you back okay?"

"Alright baby. I love you."

"I love you too granny." She clicked to the other line. "Hello."

"Hey, is this Mahoganee?" the sexy voice asked.

"Yes, it is and who is this?" she asked knowing goodness well it was Tyron.

"This is Tyron and I wanted to know if I could take you out tonight"

"Just straight and to the point but unfortunately tonight will not be a good night. My son was shot and I'm at the hospital on pins and needles hoping my child is going to be okay." The tears began to roll down her face as she broke down once again.

"I'm sorry to hear that Mahoganee. What hospital are you at? I would like to come and be with you, if you don't mind," Tyron sincerely stated.

"That won't be necessary."

"Yes it will be necessary," Tyron interjected. "Now do I have to find you or are you going to tell me what hospital you're at?" he demanded, clearly serious.

"I'm at Children's Hospital," she finally replied.

"On Kingshighway right?"

"Yes," Poochie responded getting herself together.

"Okay, I'm on my way," he told her, disconnecting the call.

Just as Poochie disconnected the call from Tyron, Dr. Jackson walked into the waiting room. Poochie had a worried look on her face. She had a gut feeling that the news she was about to receive wouldn't be good. "Man Doc, I was going crazy out here waiting to know about my baby." The palms of her hands were sweating something terrible. *"Lord you never failed me. I'm depending on You and only You Lord. Is this life?"* She talked to God as the words escaped Dr. Jackson's mouth. "Paso didn't make it. I'm extremely sorry. I did everything in my power to save his life." Dr. Jackson once again has to explain to a parent, why his or her child didn't survive it in this cruel world of violence. Poochie's entire body froze. The huge tears slowly trickled down her red cheeks.

Ceria walked in as Poochie hit the wall screaming, "NOOOO!" She knew her cousin needed her. Ceria ran over and hugged Poochie extra tight as well as restraining her. She was trying to conceal the hurt Poochie felt, only a mother could understand. She just didn't want Poochie to hurt herself. Dr. Jackson now directed his attention toward Ceria while she held Poochie in her arms.

"I'm sorry," Dr. Jackson expressed, extending his hand for a hand shake. "And you are?" he asked.

"I'm Ceria, Poochie's cousin, I mean Mahoganee's cousin."

"This is one of the defaults of my job and I don't care for it, not one bit," he declared firmly. "The bullet to the chest damaged many organs and his little body couldn't take the trauma. Even if young Paso survived, he would have been helpless, a vegetable as some people call it," he clarified before he was cut off.

"I don't give a shit! My baby boy would have been here!" Poochie shouted. "Is this life? Hell naw!" Poochie beat on her breasts with the palm of her hand. "Not for me! I don't have a reason to be alive anymore!" She continued to cry loudly.

"I understand Mahoganee and I wish that I could have saved him but it wasn't my battle. I did all that I could do," Dr. Jackson told her, feeling her pain fully.

"Doc, she's upset right now. Thanks for everything." Ceria showed her appreciation and shook Dr. Jackson's hands again. As Dr. Jackson exited the waiting room, Tyron stood at the door.

"How's it going?" Tyron asked.

"Not so good young fellow, not so good," Dr. Jackson replied sadly, walking away shaking his head with a dark expression plastered across his face.

Poochie's head was buried in Ceria's chest, crying her soul out when Tyron made an appearance. *"Damn who is this fine ass brotha?"* Ceria thought to herself as Tyron walked over to her and Poochie. "Damn, cuz didn't give me the 411 on him. Thumbs up!" she thought silently.

"Hey how's it going?" Tyron asked Ceria, looking at Poochie. "I'm Tyron, Mahoganee's friend," he confidently confirmed.

"I'm good and I'm Ceria, Poochie's cousin, nice to meet you." They shook hands.

Tyron looked at Ceria as if to say, "*May I?*" and grabbed Poochie from behind and hugged her tightly. Poochie fell right into his arms, fitting like the perfect glove. Ceria watched with jealously but was happy for her cousin at the same time.

"I'm so sorry, Mahoganee. How did this happen?" Tyron continued to hold her. She explained the story again to him crying non-stop. "Its okay baby, take your time. I'm not going anywhere." He laid her head back on his chest gently, walking over to the sofa by the window. Poochie took in the aroma of his I Am King cologne by P. Diddy. He smelled amazing and she savored the scent, letting it abuse her nostrils.

"If you both will excuse me, I'm gonna go call the family and bring them current." Ceria proceeded to walk away.

"No," Poochie broke loose of Tyron's embrace. "I think that they should hear it from me Ce Ce." She wiped her eyes pulling herself together. "Thanks cuz but let me handle this." She released her cell phone from the case Paso bought her for her birthday. It had dollar signs covering it with *PASO* written on it in bold letters front and back. She broke back down but she held her composure well, covering her mouth to muffle the sounds of her crying. Tyron rubbed her back to comfort her and it helped somewhat. She proceeded to dial her grandparents' number to deliver the bad news, thinking to herself, "Is this life? If so, it sucks right now. Seriously."

Chapter 6

GETTING THROUGH THE STORM!!

Poochie finally laid her six year old son to rest. One of the toughest things a mother could ever imagine. The turn out for Paso's visitation and homecoming was enormous. Faith Miracle Temple was filled to capacity and that's a hefty sized church. She doesn't know how she ever would have made it through such a wearisome time without the Lord on her side and the help of her family not to overlook Tyron. He walked with her every step of the way. In just a few weeks' time, they were inseparable. Her granddad thought things were moving high-speed while her grandma thought just the opposite. She wanted Poochie to stay busy. Mrs. Patrick was glad Poochie had found someone to keep her mind occupied after the senseless death of her son.

The following week:

Tyron called and informed Poochie that they would be double dating with Tyron's cousin Chance and his girlfriend Shakira. They went to the Moolah Theater and Lounge on Lindell Boulevard to see the movie *The Blind Side*. Poochie found that she straight liked Tyron and he liked her even more. Ceria informed Poochie the other day that it was something memorable about Tyron but she didn't know *what*. However, she did explain to Poochie that when she finds out she would enlighten her.

The date was going well and Poochie loved the attention. Tyron took the loneliness away but he didn't discontinue her thoughts of her sweet boy. To swoop Poochie up, Tyron selected his red Monte Carlo that his mother bought him years ago. Poochie got in the car rocking a pair of dark demin *SSO* straight legs with a colorfully flared blouse with balloon sleeves, cleavage sitting right and tight. Although she'd had a child, her body was stacked. Poochie got in the car smelling sweet, promoting Kim Kardashian's perfume, Dash. She also swagged out a pair of black Polo boots she'd purchased weeks ago while at the mall with Paso. She stepped with pride wearing those boots knowing that her six year old son had done everything within his power to persuade her to buy them and she did. She also purchased him a pair of black and a brown pair.

She could remember it as if it was yesterday. They were in West County Mall at the Kid's Foot Locker store. They were also scheduled to take photos at Sears Portrait Studio. For some strange reason, young Paso was addicted to Polo, maybe because that's all Poochie really dressed him in. "Ma, why don't you buy you a pair of Polo boots. They would look fly on your feet." He threw his charm at her, something he was rather good at. He continued, "If you let me, I can buy them for you. I got money in my bank." He became excited.

"I *have* money in my bank," Poochie corrected her son's grammar. "Thanks lil daddy. You keep your money for something else. I'm glad to know that you would buy them for me."

"Ma when I get big, I'm going to buy you whatever you want, buy you the biggest house I can find, the best car in the world," he stretched his arms as wide as they could go to express the love he held for his mother. That warmed her heart and Tyron gave her the same feeling but in a different approach and manner and that's how she ended up with her Polo boots.

"You look nice as usual." Tyron leaned over and kissed her on the cheek.

"You look and smell nice, as usual," she threw back at him, leaning over kissing him back on his cheek.

"I hope you don't mind hanging with my peeps."

"I don't mind. It should be fun." She smiled at him. Tyron wanted nothing more than to put a smile on Poochie's face. After witnessing the hurt she felt after the passing of her son, he wanted nothing but happiness for her and he wanted to be the person to bring pleasure to her and so far it seemed to be working. Nothing would be more pleasing to Poochie's soul than to find the person or persons responsible for her son's death. She made a promise to herself and she would accomplish it by any means necessary, even if it meant her life, then so be it, she was getting it in. And Tyron was on her level. Don't hurt the kids.

Shakira and Poochie hit it off well. Shakira did take in Poochie's fashion game when she and Tyron walked into the theater lobby. Her gear game was tight and on point. Tyron made a swift introduction. After that he and Chance headed straight for the game room and left the ladies. "Girl I like that bag, where did you get that from if you don't mind me asking?" Shakira inquired flossing the same exact bag but in a different color.

"I got this from Macy's a few weeks ago on clearance. I think it ran close to two hundred dollars but there was a fifty percent off sticker on it with another fifteen percent off, if I'm not mistaken, if you used your Macy's card." She clarified. "I'm a bargain shopper, always have been."

"Girl it's hot!" she said revealing her bag as they both laughed. "Mahoganee," Shakira became serious. "Baby Ty told me what happened to you. I'm beyond sorry." She displayed her sorrow and pain. "I can't imagine what it must feel like to lose someone you love more than life itself."

"You have no idea. But through the grace of God, He's helping me through this trying time and of course Tyron," she finished with an extensive smile spread across her face.

"That's what's up. He's a good guy, they both were raised well," she stated with pride knowing that she had a good guy, too. "Mahoganee, if you ever want to talk, holla at a sista." They both smiled.

"Of course, you know good people when you see them. He and I have been dating a short period but it seems as if I've known him awhile. He's cool people and you is too, Shakira. Thanks huh." They smiled as they walked to the game room to get the fellows.

After the movies, Tyron, Poochie, Chance and Shakira stopped by Tyron's mother's house. She lived in the suburbs of Chesterfield, MO. Once they reached the house, Poochie was in awe. She approved of the lifestyle in which his mom lived. This was her dream, to one day to take her son out of the hood and show him a different way of life. That's why she worked as hard as she did and continued her education in Journalism. She knew it was better than where she was living. Don't get it twisted; they lived better than most in the hood but they were still *in* the hood, where drugs, rape, murder and prostitution was obvious and unkind to their community. She would never forget where she came from. She wanted to show her child something more diverse from what she knew.

Tyron's mother and sister were sitting in the family room when they entered from the side door. Tyron kissed his mom and sister on the cheek and Chance and Shakira did the same. "Hey nosy rosy," he greeted his sister Kaneesha.

"That's not my name lil big head boy." She hit him and ran. She loved when her big brother came over. He always played with her and showed her much love.

"Ma, this is Mahoganee, the young lady I've been telling you about," he happily said.

"Hi, Mahoganee," Libra replied.

Poochie yelled, shocked and at a lost of words. "Tyron you didn't tell me that your ma was Libra. A.K.A Scale's the singer!" She hit him in his arm playfully.

She was past excited. "I love your CD's!" She stopped to breathe, covering her mouth. "Oh wow and the clothes!" She stopped and went at it again. "She's your sister!" Her eyes grew big, "Essence right?" She shook her head and carried on. "Which is your aunt?" Poochie said, pointing to Ty. "She's the brain behind the clothing line!"

"You have it all mapped out," Tyron told her, kissing her on the cheek, happy to see Poochie beaming. He'd achieved his goal. "That's what's up."

Libra fixed dinner for Poochie and Tyron. Chance and Shakira declined dinner because they had early morning appointments the following day and they wanted Tyron to spend the remainder of the night with his lady. They didn't want to cock-block, meaning stopping things from going down.

Libra served grilled T-bone steaks, baked potatoes with sour cream, broccoli and cheese and a salad. For dessert they shared a piece of lemon cake. After dinner Tyron and Poochie went into the family room and watched movies. She felt a sense of comfort with him. She was safe and satisfied but most importantly she was undisturbed. Tyron made Poochie want to share her deepest thoughts. He made her feel things she never considered were possible. She had never been in a real relationship, not even with Paso's dad. Poochie was silent and Tyron wanted to know why. "Baby what's wrong?" He slid closer to her on the couch wrapping his arms strongly around her.

"Nothing's wrong. I was thinking that my baby boy would have loved you too." She looked him in his coal black eyes.

"Why do you say that?" he retorted.

"What's not to love about you?" she answered with a question. "You're considerate, caring, compassionate and sweet. Now who wouldn't love that?"

"So, what are you saying, you love me?" he inquired in a solemn tone.

"What I'm saying is that I can see myself falling in love with you." She answered back truthfully not having control over the words that rolled off her tongue.

"Real talk," he faintly retorted.

"Real talk," Poochie uttered, kissing him on the mouth using her tongue, demanding that he kiss her back.

Libra walked in the room informing Tyron that she needed to leave to go pick up her husband, Keke. "I was wondering if you would stay here with your sister while I go and get my hubby from the airport or until Miracle arrivals."

"Sure ma."

"Mahoganee, it was nice meeting you. I hope to see a lot more of you. And also know that losing somebody you love takes time to get over. It will get easier. Know that some days will be harder than others but you have to keep it moving. It's called getting through the storm."

"Thank you so much." Poochie's eyes watered.

"You're more than welcome." Libra emerged from the doorway and hugged Poochie. "I'll see you kids later. Love you Baby Ty." She walked out of the room smiling. She knew that he hated when she called him Baby Ty but what was he going to do? She was the parent and he was the kid. She would always tell him that.

Chapter 7

FACING THE TRUTH!

Things were going good with Tyron and Poochie. She had been off work and school for a month now but things were going back to its normal routine the following Monday, work from 9-5 and school from 6-9. She knew her life had to go on and she was doing everything she could to make that happen but a part of her was missing. Facing the truth is never easy when death is involved. Poochie dreaded gathering Paso's belongings. For him to only have been six years old this kid had everything a kid his age wanted and most adults for that matter. But all in all he earned it.

Poochie kept all of Paso's first holiday's outfits, such as his first Christmas, Easter, New Year's and 4th of July ensembles. When I say Paso was the Polo kid, Ralph Lauren himself should have adopted him, literally. As she cleaned out his closets, tears fled her eyes. Her kid that she had major dreams and hopes for was gone and wasn't ever coming back again. There wasn't a come back from death and she would never wish that on anyone except the punk that killed her baby. She wanted to let him have it way beyond thought. She would keep some of Paso's things but she would give the remainders to the Frank L. Banks Foundation. Pulling the clothing out of the closet, she had a memory for each piece she purchased. Poochie thought her son looked exceptionally fine in his blue Polo sweater with the blue and black down vest and dark Polo jeans. He thought he was looking good as well. His barber Jay hooked him up with a

Mohawk haircut. Jay was one of the toughest barbers in the Lou. He kept fresh designs in Paso's head. He visited Jay once a week faithfully. If Poochie couldn't get him there, her papa took him. Once again this kid was fresh to death everyday, even lounging around the house in his Polo pajamas and slippers accommodated by a robe. By the time Poochie finished packing his things, there were fifteen trash bags.

Monday Morning

The big colorful Welcome Back banner was the first thing Poochie saw upon entering the office. The flowers also looked nice on her station. Everybody welcomed her back with open arms. Her co-workers were very supportive in her time of sorrow. They sent flowers, cards and money. Things quickly went back to usual at work but for some reason they were different but better in a sense. It had to be the new man in her life. A special feeling sustained her being.

Poochie was about to go to lunch when Tyron walked in.

"What's up with it Mahoganee?" His tone sent shock waves through her body.

"Hey, Ty." She blushed uncontrollably.

"What are you doing for lunch?"

"Nothing much, why?" she asked curiously.

"Come go with me. I'll have you back in an hour," he told her.

"Let me get my purse." She walked in the back office and Ty watched as she disappeared behind the secured doors. He enjoyed the way the pink *SSO* dress enfolded her full figure. The four inch heels went perfectly and defined her big sexy legs.

Tyron drove his black Suburban down 40 West to Clayton. The underground parking lot was exclusive and Poochie had never seen anything like this. This was how she wanted to live but she had to complete school first. Little did she know, if she inquired about the lofts, she'd discover that she could afford one on her income. They took the underground elevators to the fourth floor. She was surprised to know that Tyron occupied the entire floor. Once inside, she immediately fell in love. Ty took his shoes off at the door and she followed suit. "Baby you don't have to take off your shoes," he told her. 'This is something I do all the time. It's just a bad habit." Just as he ceased his sentence, Maxwell's single "Bad Habits" played on satellite radio. They both broke into laughter.

"Do you want something to eat Mahoganee?" he asked, taking off his shirt going to the kitchen.

"Do you have some fruit or something healthy?" she answered back. Tyron went into the refrigerator and removed some strawberries. He then took a bowl from the cabinet and placed some in there.

"Do you want some whipped cream on them?" he asked being flirtatious spreading it across the strawberries.

"That's not healthy for me, now is it?" she replied being more flirtatious. "It really doesn't matter at this point due to the fact that you took it upon yourself and covered them. So I guess I *do* want whipped cream." She smiled.

"It can be." He moved in closer kissing her passionately. She went with the flow. "Do I have to take you back to work?" he whispered. "Why don't you call and tell them that you need to take the rest of the day off." He stared into her eyes.

"Now why would I do that? I just went back today," she uttered.

"Because I asked you to before you would be late." He placed miniature wet kisses on her neck. It felt so good to her. She didn't want him to stop.

"I will not do this again Tyron. Some of us do have to work for a living." She told him grabbing a hold of his face with both hands, looking into his eyes. He respected and admired her drive.

"That's what's up. You betta handle your business my baby." He smiled moving as she confiscated her cell phone from her purse.

After Poochie made her call, they went into the living room. Ty went into the back and came out with a huge envelope. Poochie wondered what he had going on. He took a seat next to her and positioned her leg across his lap. "I want to ask you something but I know how you are about missing work. But with everything that has went on with you in the last month, I think it's much needed. Before you turn me down, please give it some thought." Ty passed her the envelope. She looked over the contents carefully. It was a pair of first class airline tickets to New York. Underneath the airline tickets were a set of tickets to a Jay-Z concert for the following weekend. Poochie didn't say anything. She was at a loss for words. She felt guilt for enjoying the company of this man while her child was six feet under. Little did she know it was more than okay to enjoy herself. She did what she could do as a mother to protect her son. It was just his time.

Tyron didn't want to pressure her but he felt this was a good chance for her to relax her mind. They could get to know each other better. He was straight digging her and he could see himself with a woman such as Poochie. She wasn't a knucklehead. She had goals and dreams. "So what's good with it?" Tyron broke the stillness.

"I don't know. I just met you and..." She stopped.

"And what Moo." He gave her a pet name.

"I guess I feel guilty," she confessed, becoming teary eyed. The name caught her off guard as well.

"Guilty about what, that I like you and you like me? You have nothing to feel guilty about. We're two people that digs the hell out of each another. It's just unfortunate circumstances. Baby it's time to face the truth." He chose his words cautiously but remained firm. "Your son is gone and he isn't coming back. I don't mean to sound unconcerned or harsh but your life must go on. I'm sure your son is smiling down on you." He lifted her chin confidently with the tips of his three forefingers. "And plus I'ma likable kind of brother." They both smiled and he wiped the single tear that fell from her eye. "He will approve." He beamed displaying his dimples.

"How can you be so sure?" she whispered sounding innocent.

"You're here with me now, right?" He shook his head.

"Yes, but what does that mean?" she asked, confused.

"You answered your own question then shawty."

"You right." She rolled her eyes at him. "But on the real, facing the truth can hurt most times."

"Yep!" Tyron said rubbing her leg in his Trey Songz style.

Chapter 8

THE PAST!!!!

Mrs. Patrick missed her grandboy tremendously. With Poochie not being at home, she had nothing to do. Yes, she had to take care of Mr. Patrick but she loved doing for her grandbabies. She never wanted Poochie to move out. She knew how badly Poochie wanted to break away from the hood and she wanted Poochie to stand up and be her own woman, don't get it twisted. Mrs. Patrick knew one day she would leave this earth and prayed to God it was before her granddaughter. She wanted to make sure Poochie was totally prepared for whatever in this world. In her heart, she knew Poochie could handle herself in any situation, as she'd proven so many times in the past. It's just that motherly love. Poochie had proven that she was a responsible young parent. She finished high school and continued her education. She's held down a decent job and her attendance is excellent. And Mrs. Patrick knew she was going to move out one day, but she wanted to hold on for as long as she could.

Mrs. Patrick was stunned that Poochie was home on a weekday so early in the evening. "What's wrong sweetie? You and your boy toy mad at one another?" she joked.

"No ma'am," Poochie clarified. "I wanted to talk to you about something ma. I know I've been preoccupied lately and I haven't spent any time with you. You seem lonely."

"Baby, I am. I miss Paso so much. I miss him begging me to play the racing car game with him. *MeMa please come play the game with me.*" She gave a slight smirk. "It's just not the same around here. Your paw-pa misses him too. He still goes looking in his room in the middle of night. That's how I know you're never here. And tell me this?" Mrs. Patrick froze with her hands on her hip. Mrs. Patrick was very out-spoken.

"What's that MeMa?" Poochie referred to her granny imitating Paso also trying to smooth the blow she was about to give.

"Why didn't you ask me to help you gather his things?" She was stern and to the point.

"That was something I wanted to do alone." She hugged her granny. "I'm sorry, that was my closure on the situation." They held each other for awhile.

Mrs. Patrick released Poochie and went into the living room. "It freaked me out the other day when I went in there and his things were gone. But I knew it was coming." She sat down on the couch patting the spot next to her for Poochie who did as she was told, sitting Indian style. "How's everything going with you and that boy, what's his name?"

"Tyron." Poochie paused, making sure her granny heard his name. "Things are good. I'm taking it one day at a time," she explained.

"That's exactly what you do. But baby its okay to go on with your life. As much as I hate to admit it, Paso is not coming back and you need to live your life. I feel in my spirit that you have a good man, you better hold on to him. I'm not telling you what I heard; I'm telling you what I know. A good man is hard to find. Why you think I'm still with your paw-pa?"

"Cause you love him I hope." Poochie looked confused.

"No, because he made me smile, *then* I fell in love with him. Yes there's going to be times when things seem tough but work through it. Let the past be the past and move forward. You're young baby, live your life and enjoy it to the fullest," her granny finished.

"So I should go out of town with Tyron?" Poochie asked, showing a warm smile.

"Yes, you should go and have fun," Granny told her.

"As long as you approve, I'm going. Ma, I really like him. I've met his mom *and* sister. His cousin and his cousin's girlfriend are cool, too." Her eyes beamed as she spoke of Tyron.

"I can see that you really like this fellow. Just be careful. Where does he want to take you?" Granny wanted to know.

"To a Jay-Z concert in New York." Poochie was extra excited.

"You talking about the fellow that sings that song, 'In New York' with that Alicia Keys girl your paw-pa drools over?"

"Yes, him Ma." Poochie busted out laughing looking up to heaven, knowing her son was the reason for that. Her grandparents would let him look at videos one hour a day with them supervising.

"Have fun." Mrs. Patrick couldn't do anything but laugh with Poochie. They both shared a special memory.

"Thanks, MeMa." She kissed her on the cheek and strolled to her room.

Tyron was working at the BP gas station he and Chance bought together on the North Side. One of his employees called off with an emergency so he decided to go in. His day was laid back and he needed to do inventory anyway. He knew that Poochie would be at home talking with her grandparents about her going out of town with him so he wasn't going to bother her until she called him. He was stocking the cooler when he got a small crowd. He stopped what he was doing and went behind the bulletproof glass. He made a mental note to call the contractors to set up an appointment to expand the place.

He did, however, get the customers in and out in record time. Finally, he got to his last customer. Before he could ask, "How may I help you," she stated what she wanted.

"Can I have a box of Chocolate Ty?" Quitta seductively requested as she licked her lips seductively.

"Hey, what's good Quitta?" He was caught off guard.

"I know you don't have a woman. Not working in this station. You got too much time on your hands. I came up here on the humbug and I'm glad I did."

"Oh yeah," Ty replied.

"Boy, come from back there and give me a hug." She waved her hand and he obliged her request. Quitta didn't give him time enough to get from behind the door before she wrapped her arms around his neck. He didn't stop her. Quitta was once his girlfriend, his first love at that. He didn't know what happened to Quitta, as he'd once remembered she wasn't giving it up; now she was all over him like a furious bull.

"Wait a minute Quitta, hold all that down. On the real ma." He stopped her.

"What's that all about? You got a lil chick now?" She continued as if he hadn't said anything to her. He firmly removed her arms from around his neck and placed them at her side.

"Now you can talk to me without all of that," he announced defensively. His phone indicated that he had a voicemail message. He released Quitta's arm and looked at his phone realizing that he's missed a call from Poochie. He tried to call her back but it went to her voicemail. He wanted to get Quitta out of the store. "Quitta what do you want?" he asked as he looked at the text message Poochie sent: *Baby, I'm on my way around there.* Tyron looked at the time of the text and asked Quitta again what she wanted. He knew it wouldn't take Poochie long to get there. She lived on Red Bud Ave and the gas station was on the corner of Red Bud Ave and North Florissant. She could walk out of her door and be there in two minutes.

After Ty looked at his phone, his entire demeanor changed. Quitta was going to have to play her cards right. She wanted Ty back but he wasn't fucking with her at all. He went back to stocking the cooler.

"Let the games begin," she silently thought. "Do you have any cold Red Bulls?"

She deliberately asked for something she didn't see.

"Let me go check in the back cooler. I'm sure we do." He proceeded to the back, checking the stock, making sure not to lock himself out of the booth.

"Stall tactic," she thought out loud as she quickly looked for Tyron's keys to lock the store doors. Ty was in the back a few minutes searching for the cold Red Bull. "Here we go," he whispered, retrieving a six-pack to take up front. He then replaced the six-pack in the back cooler, something that was supposed to be stocked after every shift. He caught a quick glace at the camera and was stopped dead in his tracks. "What the fuck?" Ty shouted out loud. Quitta was behind the bulletproof glass naked, standing there dancing to "I Invented Sex" by Trey Songz. He walked to the front at a fast pace. "What in the hell are you doing girl?! This is my place of business, and my lady is on her way around here! What the fuck?" It all played in slow motion and he tried to retain his composure.

Ty looked up and Poochie was at the door looking at everything. "Ahh shit! This is what I was trying to prevent!" he told Quitta as he got his keys from under the counter. "Get your shit on and get the fuck out!" He then left the booth and unlocked the door for Poochie. She entered looking from him to Quitta. "What's *this* all about?" She moved her finger to Ty, then Quitta. She displayed a sense of coolness.

"This ain't about shit Moo. Quitta was getting her shit and she's gonna keep it moving." He looked at Quitta, kissing Poochie on the lips.

"You know if she wasn't here, you would have been all up in between my thick thighs," Quitta interjected pulling her *SSO* jeans up.

"I guess we'll never know then?" His face displayed composure. Quitta walked past Ty tucking her shirt into her jeans rolling her eyes. Poochie stood in the door as Quitta exited.

"Bitch move outta the way." She tried to bump Poochie.

"Sweetie don't get cute with me. Your beef is clearly with Ty so please direct your anger toward him and keep me out of this. Thank you," Poochie told her nicely with a smirk on her face as she made a check mark with her index finger. Quitta was about to say something but Ty gave her a gaze that stopped her at once. She sashayed past Poochie furiously.

"Now, what was all that about?" she asked with a pleading expression.

"Moo it was nothing. I promise," he tried to explain.

"Who was the back burner bitch?" she laughed snobbishly.

"It was all a fabrication. She's my past and nothing else. I don't even talk to her." He walked over to Poochie.

"You better not be lying to me either or next time I'm gonna whip both of y'all asses." She chuckled. She felt in her soul that it was nothing up with that situation. Ty was too calm and didn't a nervous bone show in his body.

Poochie sat in the booth with Ty as he finished up inventory. The night worker was coming in early to cover the remainder of the shift. "Hey Moo, I'm glad you believed me. You had that look like, trip if you wanna and I'ma beat yo ass. You should have seen the expression you had on your face." Tyron chuckled. "Man." He wiped his forehead.

"Tyron I wasn't tripping off of that girl. If that's your past then that's what it is. I'm on something different." Poochie became excited. Tyron knew he had a winner. This is the rider he needed on his team. "What, why are you looking at me like that?" She ceased her conversation.

"Nothing Moo. And what has you so hyped?"

"I'm going to New York with you!" She provocatively danced around him snapping her fingers.

"That's what's up, Moo." He approved of her decision. "I promise you will have so much fun."

"I better," she walked up to him kissing him ever so gently but meaningfully.

Chapter 9

YOU WITH ME OR NOT!!

The streets were hush, hush about Paso's killer. Poochie's family knew people in high places and her uncle Lester knew the OG's and gangsters from way back. He's good friends with the owner of London and Son's, a family owned restaurant that sat on the corner of Prairie and Martin Luther King Dr. that served the best chicken in St. Louis back in the day. Poochie knew before long somebody was going to run their dick or pussy suckers. St. Louis is small, you gotta know that.

Poochie hadn't talked to LaTona in a minute and wanted to holler at her cousin. See, the difference between LaTona and Ceria is LaTona was a go-getter. She made shit happen. She didn't wait on a ninja to do anything for her. She was an only child and ran the streets with her daddy. So if Poochie wanted something done about her son's murder, she had to do it herself and she has a gutter bitch on her team. LaTona got down like she lived. Her daddy taught her that.

Poochie had two days left before she departed with Ty. She was overly enthusiastic about this trip. She made up her mind that they would take their relationship to the next level. Ty was getting some of her juice box. But before she left, she wanted to put something in motion such as finding her son's murderer. She met LaTona at West County Mall to hang out and talk to her. LaTona was about her money and played no games about it. You know what they say; money is the root to all evil and some. You gotta know that.

Poochie spent freely at the mall, not worrying about her budget she always set for herself. After her baby's death, her bank account grew fifty K strong. She knew Tyron's financial status was enormous but she was a woman that stood on her own two feet. She didn't want him to think that she was a gold digger or a knucklehead. She wanted bigger things out of life. She was determined to make it happen. Just to let Ty know that she wasn't a selfish person and thought of others, she'd purchased him a Polo jacket, something she would have gotten for Paso.

LaTona met Poochie for lunch in the food court. LaTona was waiting for Poochie when she arrived with her hands filled. "Hey what's up with it cuz?" LaTona hugged Poochie. "You look fabulous."

"No, bitch, you look fabulous. What's with the new haircut? You getting dick put to you on a regular, zoom, zoom!" Poochie started doing the dance to Lil' Boosie's "Bad Ass" song before she busted out laughing with LaTona not finding that so funny. Her private life was nobody's business.

"No, bitch, I hear you the one getting dick on the regular. You're never home when I call the house. Granny be like, *child she's with that boy. I don't see her until she comes and change for work.*" LaTona imitated Mrs. Patrick. They both laughed again.

"Yeah I be booed up and Ty is good people." She smiled harder thinking of him. "I've met his mama *and* sister." She spat eagerly. "Bitchhh," she dragged out. "Guess who's his mama?"

"Girl, who?" LaTona impatiently asked.

"Libra," she paused, letting Tona digest the news. "The singer with the sister Essence, the fashion designer, *SSO*, Sista' Sista' Original." She stood and turned around pointing to the butt of her jeans.

"Word." LaTona approved.

"Word Tona, but enough about that." Poochie's tone changed to a serious nature. "That ninja Fatman knows who killed my baby." She got right to the point. Her exterior turned sober.

"I was thinking the same thing." Tona gave Poochie her undivided attention.

"Do you still talk to his friend Trap?" Poochie asked in an anxious tone. She wanted Paso's murderer or murderers in prison, if not dead.

"Yeah, we kick it from time to time. And he kicks down real proper like. His pockets runs deep. That's my baby but we only get along when we're fucking," she concluded.

"That's a start." Poochie pushed her chair closer to the table. "Dig, you need to get as much info about Fatman'em. Find out about his boys and get back with me. I gotta find these clowns. I can't let that go down cuzo." Her eyes watered.

"It's already done cuz. I want them as bad as you do, if not badder." Tona reached over and wiped the tear about to fall from her cousin's eye. "I got this. No more of these." She wiped the tear on the napkin. "It's time to make some noise." LaTona loved this type of conversation. "Cuz, we don't have to go any further with this conversation. I got you. I'll have some news for you when you get back from out of town," Tona assured her.

"How you know I'm going out of town?" Then they both said in unison, "Grandma," laughing once again.

"Thanks cuz." She took a deep breath. "The way I feel right about now, you either with me or you're not. I have this good feeling that Tyron is down with me no matter what and if I have to, I'll ask him to help me find the killer." Her face showed coldness as well as hurt.

"Shit, I know their family gets down. All that shit I read in the Evening Whirl newspapers about them a few years back." She went on to elaborate. "Tyron's mama's current husband Keke faked his death. Tyron's dad was abusive and almost made her lose her child by beating her half to death. His auntie Reesie's boyfriend Caelin killed her while she was pregnant with twins, Miracle and Chance, that was supposed to be his. The craziest thing about this story is that Miracle is Caelin's child but Chance is Lorenzo's child, Libra's sister Essence's husband."

Poochie was absolutely astonished. LaTona carried on. "Libra just found out that Essence is her dad's daughter some years ago. And the fucked up twist is that Miracle's daddy is Libra's best friend Mya's brother, which makes Mya Miracle's auntie. Crazy I know." LaTona rapped it up.

"Yeah, pretty much so," Poochie finally replied.

"Girl that was the talk of the Lou. Where were *you?*" LaTona wanted to go on but had already given her an earful.

"I'll get all of that information when we go on our trip, but in the meantime please try to make something happen. Just know when I get back I'm going to get my gun license and it's on."

"Girl, just because you have your license doesn't mean you can go around shooting people," LaTona joked.

"Shit why not?" Poochie showed no remorse and was serious. "They shot and killed my baby." LaTona understood her cousin's attitude completely. They talked awhile longer and hugged each other before LaTona told Poochie to be safe on her trip. They then promised to stay in touch before parting ways.

Chapter 10

U Gotta Know That!!

Ty and Poochie stayed in Libra's high-rise condo in Manhattan, compliments of Big Tyron. She was awarded a million dollars plus of Big Tyron's money and property in their divorce settlement. The place was cozy and romantic. Even though the condo looked huge, it only had one gigantic bedroom. "Where should I put my bags?" Poochie asked Ty, wanting to hear his response.

"You can put them in the bedroom," he yelled to her from the kitchen looking for something to eat in the black Subzero refrigerator.

"Where are you going to sleep?" she chuckled to herself knowing where he's sleeping, right next to her.

"I can sleep in the living room. The couch lets out into a bed, very comfortable. Moo don't carry me like I'm some lame. That was my plan from the beginning. Nothing is gonna happen that you," he stopped looking through the refrigerator and pointed his finger at her. "Don't want to happen, straight up Moo" and continued on his expedition.

Poochie went into the bedroom and went through her bag. While situating her things, Ty's voice echoed through her head. "Moo don't carry me like some lame." She didn't know how to take that statement but she did understand that he was serious as hell. Damn, she was digging this cat! She strolled into the living room, retrieved Ty's bags and placed his clothes in the drawers and closet with her things.

"Moo, are you hungry?"

"Yeah, what you got up in this piece?" she imitated Paso, smiling at Ty. They both laughed.

"You have a variety of things to choose from. I can grill some streaks and we can eat out on the deck or we can go out. I know you want to see the city of New York, concrete jungle where dreams are made of." He sang Jay-Z's song which made them both laugh again.

"We can stay in. I want to get to know Tyron a little better. Is that okay with you?" She grabbed him in his collar delicately and kissed his lips tenderly.

"You gotta know that Moo. It's cool. Let me call Chance to see what's poppin'."

"Is Shakira with him?" Poochie inquired washing the steaks off, seasoning them, letting Ty know she can burn as well.

"Yep! And his twin, Miracle." He seemed pleased. "You can finally meet her." He held the phone up to his ear.

Poochie cooked dinner and they were joined by Chance, Shakira, Miracle and Denise. They also resided in the condo below Tyron and Poochie. Ty invited everyone over to break bread with them their first night in town. Ty had the music grooving to Jay-Z's "Blueprint III". Poochie was happy with Ty but felt somewhat uncomfortable in Miracle's presence. Miracle displayed a snobbish demeanor toward her. Poochie was to some extent accustomed to this type of behavior from females. She tried not to let it affect her.

"Now that everyone is here, let's eat!" Ty shouted leading them to the table.

"Miracle I'm so glad you decided to fuck with your people." Ty joked with her. "I thought you threw a nigga to the curb."

"You know it ain't never like that cousin." She replied meaning every word. "Just trying to maintain, that's all," she finished looking in Poochie's direction.

"Shit, I feel you on that sista. I used to think that working for the family business would be easy. Shiiit," he drugged it out. "Tete make you earn every dime she drops down, she paid lovely, I'm not saying that, but I'm just saying." Tyron explained with a slight smirk.

"Yeah, I get so tired of people talking about 'I wish I had your job'." Chance interjected. "They don't know half of the shit we go through" He finished taking a bite of his tender steak.

"Banana you can get off my moms." Ty told him making fun of the nickname Miracle gave him. They all laughed at Ty's silliness. "Tete E makes a nigga get theirs extra hard. I think she has mom's beat." Ty continued. "If the shoot is scheduled for 6:00am, she wants you there at 4:45am. What type of shit is *that*?" They clowned around.

"Tete is the same way," Miracle butted in. "Baby Ty what you thought?" She rolled her eyes playfully causing them all to bust out laughing again. Miracle didn't like Essence, her father's wife and Libra's sister not one bit at the beginning of their relationship. Now that she's older, she loved Essence to pieces. She filled the emptiness of her mother's love, since Reesie was taken from her at birth by the hands of her abusive father Caelin.

Dinner was going well and everybody seemed to be enjoying themselves. Miracle really didn't have anything against Poochie but she did want to know her motives toward her little cousin. Yes, they all were twenty plus years old but Miracle knew how females were. If she could help it, neither her brother nor her cousin would ever get played by these hungry heffas. Shakira genuinely loved and had love for her brother and he felt the same exact way about her. "So Poochie, what do you do for a living?" Miracle started with the twenty questions.

"I'm a bank teller." She answered Miracle's question without hesitation.

"How long have you been doing that?"

"I started my senior year of high school and when I received my diploma, I was hired on permanently." She gave Miracle a smile and continued proudly. "I'm also up for a promotion to become head teller." She bragged letting Miracle know she had her own money. It may not equal up to their money but she had her own. And she worked even harder to get hers.

Miracle gave Poochie a look as to say *"bitch so what."* Shakira, Chance and Ty of course were happy for her. "How long have you known about the promotion Moo?" Ty asked excitedly.

"I knew the day you kidnapped me from work." She smiled extremely hard. Miracle didn't want to like Poochie but she'd witnessed how Ty lit up when he talked to her. She realized at that moment that she didn't have a reason to dislike her, so she decided be happy for them both and stop being so shallow minded.

"Congrats Poochie, that's what's up." She displayed a pleasant smile.

"Thanks Miracle." Poochie returned the smile. "I like her attitude," Poochie thought to herself as she made a mental note to holla at LaTona about this chick.

After dinner, Chance and Ty sat on the deck blowing a Dutch sipping on some Goose. "Cuz, old girl seems to be coming around from her son's murder," Chance noticed.

"Naw cuz, she's still very much fucked up about it," he sincerely stated, passing Chance the blunt.

"Naw, cuz, I'm not saying it like that. I'm just saying she's smiling more." Chance smirked, keeping his eyes on his cousin. "You must be putting it down fam."

"Cuz, I'm not gone even lie. I ain't even smashed it yet. Man, I dig the shit out of her company and she has a strong drive. Cuz you know how these ratchet ass hoes is." He sipped his drink making a funny face as he swallowed it. "They all about them pockets; wanna know who's pockets got the mumps," he continued. "But you see, I like a woman that's on her grind. Shakira gets it in too," he complimented.

"Tru that, but I'm hitting that for breakfast, lunch and dinner. It also comes with a snack too." He loudly laughed, causing Ty to do the same. But he liked Poochie to take the lead.

"Man you stupid as a muthafucka'," Ty told him. "Shit you gotta know that cuz."

The ladies were in the house discussing what they were rocking to the concert the following day. "I went shopping before I left the Lou." Poochie told them, going to get her outfit out of the closet. They didn't wait for her to bring it back to the living room; they all followed her to the bedroom. Miracle observed her fashion statement when she walked through the door. She was pleased. The *SSO* jeans and shirt with a black scarf wrapped around her neck and 5-inch Jessica Simpson heels perfectly accommodated her full figure body amazingly. Now Miracle, she was in a class all by herself. She had the body of a goddess. Reesie blessed her with a too tiny waist, wide and enormous hips, followed by a nice size peach ass, carried by a beautiful face. Caelin on the other hand blessed her with gorgeous hair, creamy chocolate skin and a bad ass attitude. Don't get it twisted not one bit Miracle was the truth and could have any man she wanted. You gotta know that.

Denise loved the black short bubbled *SSO* dress with a pair of black tights and red 5-inch Jimmy Choo heels. "I watched Aunt E design this dress. I fell in love with it on paper, real talk. I bought the same dress in red and I have black shoes." Denise didn't seem thrilled about having the same dress as Poochie.

"What's the problem D?" Miracle asked, knowing the problem just as well as the other ladies.

"Poochie, I don't mean any harm but I don't like dressing like other bitches," Denise spat.

"Say what?" Poochie tone increased.

"No, disrespect in your direction. I just like to be different and I have my own style," she confirmed.

"It's cool, I guess," Poochie said, demonstrating a displeased look on her face. Miracle knew that Denise could be a bit much at times so she tried defusing the conversation. Pointing to them all, she said, "Why don't us ladies get up in the morning, hit some of these stores, find us something to wear and go hard tomorrow night. No matter what we rock, we gone swag it out and be fly." Miracle danced around the room.

"You gotta know that Mimi." Shakira co-signed and danced around the room with her. Before long, Denise and Poochie were swagging it out.

Chapter 11

Gettin' It In!

The night ended at three in the morning. Miracle and Chance were on teams and Denise and Shakira matched up getting their asses whipped by Ty and Poochie in a game of spades. Tyron talked much shit while he smacked the king of spades, ace of spades and the big joker on the table. "Let me have those," he shouted. Chance dropped his cards and removed himself from the table. "Where you going man? Take that, take that," Tyron joked.

"Man fuck you. I'm going to the bathroom," Chance cursed waving his hand at Ty.

"You the man daddy," Poochie told Ty reaching over kissing him on the lips.

"Of course I am Moo," he bragged.

"Boy whatever," Miracle shouted walking over poking him in his head playfully.

"I don't give a damn what y'all say, Banana you and your sista betta take y'all shots, losers." He laughed pouring Ciroc into both shot glasses. Shakira laughed knowing that Chance would let her take his shot since he didn't care for Ciroc that well. They sat around and talked about the concert a while longer. Before long, Ty's people all left the condo, tipsy as hell. Once everybody was gone, Ty and

Poochie sat in the living room talking and joking around. "Did you enjoy my people tonight Moo?" Ty wanted to know.

"I really did enjoy myself tonight. I have not laughed this much in a while, since... you know." Poochie cut her conversation off looking down.

"No go ahead and say it. It may make you feel better and not guilty about enjoying your life. You can always express yourself around me. You just don't get over something as tragic as losing your kid so easily." He looked her in the eyes.

"Tell me something Moo?" Ty reached for both of her hands and held them in his. "What do you think Paso would'a thought of me if he was here?" He exhibited his famous smile with the likeable dimples.

"That right there," she smiled kissing his dimple, "Your warm smile." He moved in closer to face her. He then leaned in to kiss her and she assisted him by moving closer as well. Next thing you know, a kissing match developed. Ty kissed Poochie's entire body. He didn't miss a spot. Poochie broke loose of his embrace and grabbed his hand and lead the way to the bedroom.

Ty was shocked by Poochie's actions. He had no intention of smashing her on this trip but he wasn't turning her down either! He never dated a full figure chick but he heard they give good love. "Stay in here until I tell you otherwise," she demanded. Ty did as he was told. Poochie went into the master bathroom and let the Jacuzzi fill with warm water. She then went into the kitchen and retrieved the strawberries and whipped cream from the refrigerator before removing the scented candle from the cabinet. Poochie walked back into the room with her hands filled. "You need any help Moo." Ty laid on the bed with his hands behind his head half looking at the basketball game.

"Nope, I got this lil daddy. You just sit on back and chill out until I give you further instructions. How does that sound?" She winked her eye walking back into the bathroom.

"That's what's up." He fired up again, relaxing his mind.

Ty heard Chrisette Michele serenade in surround sound with her poignant voice. He then saw the reflection from the candle as she turned the light down. She went back into the bedroom and Ty was taking a drag from his blunt.

"Moo, you wanna hit this?" He held the blunt out to her. She had an embarrassed look on her face. "My bad Moo, you don't get down do you?"

"No."

"It's cool, I didn't know." He took another puff. She walked over to him and took the blunt out of his hand.

"Let me see what this do do's about," she joked taking a pull.

"Girl, that's that good good. You betta be careful, you don't know what you're doing for real ma." Poochie had already puffed the blunt and was coughing uncontrollable. Her eyes watered while Ty laughed and patted her on the back. "I told you Moo." She handed the blunt back to him. "You wanna hit it again?" he joked.

"Yeah, as soon as I get myself together." She said in between coughs. "Ain't no punk in me, don't get it misconstrued." She had to laugh at herself.

Poochie finally got things under control and lead Ty to the bathroom. Once inside she unclothed him and did away with her clothing as well. Ty didn't want to appear discombobulated but Poochie had him flabbergasted. Her body was perfect, no stretch marks or anything, just right. His dick grew twice its normal size. Poochie took notice of the width as soon as his Polo briefs hit the floor. "Damn not only good looks but a nice body and pretty teeth. He's caked up and he's hung nicely," she thought. Ty must have sensed what she was thinking. He chimed right on in and told her.

"You can be the judge on how I put it down, Moo. Do know that I gets it in baby," he assured her.

"Where did that come from?" she replied with an odd expression on her face.

"Don't worry about it. Just come over here." He tried to be in charge of the situation.

"You gotta know that Baby Ty." She removed a strawberry from the bowl of whipped cream and Ty opened his mouth on cue. He bit the strawberry and Poochie licked the whipped cream from his lips, once again igniting a tongue war. Ty braced himself in the Jacuzzi while Poochie positioned her legs around his waist. She felt his dick touching her juice box in the water. She wanted so badly to jump down on it but she wanted to remain a lady.

She felt Ty massage his hard device against her juice box. "You feel so good. I've never been touched this way." She uttered in complete bliss.

"First time for everything Moo. Just ride with a nigga and you're gonna experience things you never knew existed."

"That's a ride I'm willing to take," she whispered. "Let's go lil daddy." She straddled him, reaching for the condom. Ty put the condom on and entered Poochie. "Ahhhh." Poochie released.

"Ah what?" Ty whispered feeling what Poochie was feeling. "Damn Moo you tight as a muthafucka'," he sighed loudly.

"I was saving it for you baby. Here baby take it like you own it!" she commanded.

"You gotta know that." He went as deep as he could with both of their performances displaying pleasure. Poochie held on for dear life. Ty took her on an advantageous journey that she didn't mind traveling ever and he felt the same exact way.

Chapter 12

Hating Bitches!

The next morning was even more beautiful than the night before. Poochie woke up to nine inches of hard, strong and long dick assaulting her insides but she refused to press charges of any kind. She was having more fun than she projected. Poochie had never had dick put to her in this fashion. She received it without fault. "Moo, this pussy is the truth girl, damn," Ty indicated with great enjoyment.

"This all for you baby. Take it and do what you wanna do to it," she announced rotating her hips to the beat of their love. The melody was soft and sweet. Poochie reached up and took hold of Ty's face and stared him straight in the eyes. "Ty please don't hurt me. I don't think, no fuck that. I *can't* accept another heartbreak in this lifetime," she sweetly murmured.

"Moo, I never intended to do anything that would hurt you. You gotta know that baby." He stopped his rhythm. "But life is about chances and heartbreaks with shortcomings. You can't stop, you gotta keep pushing. Don't let me hear you talking that way again. I do understand why you would feel this way, but you gotta stay pushing." He kissed her gently on her lips.

Poochie felt the tears welling in the corner of her eyes but she refused to let them fall. She had cried enough. Here she was, in New York, with a successful young black man with his own money, houses and cars, including two Harley Davidson motorcycles. He also treated her with much respect and he's legal. What more could a girl ask for? Except for losing her son, she was happy beyond her wildest dream. She thought the world would end without Paso but Ty exposed her to nothing but happiness on this trip. "Baby thanks for believing in me." She kissed his bottom lip provocatively. "I know why I'm in love with you," she revealed.

"Inform me," he replied. Every time she was about to say something, he would kiss her.

"Stop Ty, you play too much, with your crazy self." She punched him in the back teasingly.

"Crazy about you." He stole another kiss.

The Next Morning

Poochie was getting ready to go shopping with the girls when Ty walked in the room with a plate of breakfast. He sat the tray on the night stand. Poochie stopped what she was doing to eat with Ty. She removed the cover from the plate and the delicious aroma of steak, eggs, rice and biscuits invaded her nostrils. Sitting to the left of the tray laid a red card in the shape of a shoe. The inside of the card carried a Visa credit card.

"Baby you didn't have to do this." Poochie was speechless.

"Moo, I never do anything I don't wanna do, you gotta know that." He paused. "Go 'head and buy what you want." He downed the steak.

"I have money, Ty," she threw at him.

"It's no good with me. I asked you on this trip, so therefore, I'm responsible for everything." Poochie didn't argue his point.

"Yes, sir," was her answer.

"Moo, don't trip off of Miracle. She tends to give new girlfriends a hard time. She means well though ma." He tried to justify her actions.

"Miracle is cool people. I can totally understand where she's coming from. I can even more so respect that. It shows the close bond you all share but Denise is a different story," she unashamedly stated.

"Did something happen that I don't know about?" He grew concerned.

"Naw, nothing I can't handle, just a small misunderstanding about a dress that we have alike." She played it off. "It's nothing; I have a few fits to switch into."

"That's what's up," Ty answered back as they finished breakfast and then they got dressed.

At the Mall

"These shoes are hot to death! I *got* to have these bitches!" Poochie said, holding up a black leather Michael Kors claw shoe, admiring the 5-inch wooden heel. "Damn they're in red too!" She became more excited.

"Damn can somebody else buy a pair *too?*" Denise shouted at Poochie in a nasty manner.

"You can buy what the fuck you wanna buy. That has nothing to do with me." Poochie continued to admire the shoes.

"Denise, what's wrong with you?" Miracle asked pulling her to the side.

"Shit, I just wanna know can somebody else buy something? That bitch is parading around this store like she's the only one that has cake!" Miracle looked in Poochie's direction and knew that she heard Denise.

"Cuz, it ain't even like that, chill out." Miracle tried to reason. Shakira wanted the situation defused as quickly as possible. She didn't know what Denise's problem was but she needed to get it together quick, fast and in a hurry.

"Look Poochie, don't pay Denise any attention. She's always on some stupid shit," Shakira explained.

"I don't give a damn what she be on but she betta get it together. Know this, I don't give a damn what anybody thinks of me. I'm dating Ty, not his family, so whoever don't like me, so muthafuckin' what!" she said loud enough to be heard. Denise heard Poochie and began to walk in her direction, with Miracle on her heels thinking to herself, *"Man I hope I don't have to whip Poochie's ass about my lil cousin."*

Shakira stood in between the two as did Miracle. "Come on cuz this is *not* the place!" Miracle was becoming irritated with Denise's actions.

"Bitch let me tell you something!" Denise jumped in Poochie's face. "You're walking around here like you all that and innocent and shit, but did you tell my cousin that you were a hoe and got pregnant by your high school gym teacher? You fake ass wanna be!" Denise blew her out the bag.

"Let's get something straight lil girl. First off, who my son's father is is none of your business. Secondly, why are you worried about it? Thirdly, you don't know what your cousin and I discuss, so once again stay the fuck outta my business." Poochie was ready for war. She also knew she stood alone and if she fought Denise, she knew she would have to fight Miracle too and Shakira for that matter.

"Come on you guys!" Shakira shouted. "We're gonna get put out of here."

"So what! This lil chick doesn't know anything about me so she can stop poppin' off at the mouth at me!" Denise balled her fist and swung on Poochie but not before Poochie caught her with a right to the jaw. Miracle then pushed Poochie back. "Miracle, don't put your fuckin hands on me!" Poochie pushed her back harder. Now this was something that Shakira didn't want to see go down. She didn't know whether to call Ty, Chance or the mall security.

Shakira knew how nasty Miracle's attitude was. She'd hoped that she wouldn't fall into her old ways. "Look Poochie I'm not trying to make the matter worse. I'm trying to calm the situation down. Now if you want to throw'em, then let's get it." She stood toe to toe with Poochie.

"Don't put your hands on me then. I know y'all relatives and all, and y'all fall together so its whatever." Poochie stood her ground.

"It doesn't even have to go down like this." Shakira grabbed Poochie's arm. "Let's walk so you can calm down." Poochie snatched her arm away from Shakira.

"I'm not going any damn where. I came here to shop and that's what I'm going to do. I'm about to go to the cash register and cash out. Once I'm done with that, I will be going to find me a bag to go with my shoes. I'm a big girl I can shop alone. I understand that that's your peeps and you have to fall with them," Poochie bitched at Shakira.

"It's not even like that Poochie," Shakira barked at her. Poochie felt a sense of genuineness from Shakira.

"It's cool, Shakira. I tell you what." She stopped walking. "Go holla at your peoples and when y'all really to go, go 'head. I'll get a cab back to the condo," she clarified.

"Naw that's not cool. We came together so we gonna leave together and plus Ty is gonna have our heads if we come back to the condo and you're not with us. I'm not against you Poochie. If anything I'm with you."

"That's what's up. I'll be in the purse department. Hit me on my cell." Poochie walked away to pay for her shoes.

Miracle finally got Denise under control and she was ready to go. The tantrum Denise displayed toward Poochie was taking a lot out of Miracle who was trying to change her attitude but how *could* she when being surrounded by negativity? "Look Denise, this is supposed to be a nice trip. Lil cuz wanted us to meet his chick and it's evident that he digs the shit outta her and there's nothing you can say or do to change that. So just chill. We will get back on the subject of the baby's daddy later but for now fall back. We gon' kick it tonight, you acting like a hating bitch right about now cuz. I'm telling you what God loves." They both laughed.

"Yeah aight cuz, but I'm watching that bitch." She tightened her eyes shaking her head deviously.

"I know you are." Miracle commented and they continued shopping with Shakira in tow. Glad that Denise was calm now, Shakira thought to herself, *"Denise is a hating bitch."*

Chapter 13

EITHER YOU WANT ME OR NOT!

Back in St. Louis

    LaTona was back home gettin' it in. The fellows from around the way kept her up on everything. They knew that she was a real chick and got down for what she believed in. LaTona was also linked to that nigga Trap. Trap was feared by many and respected by all. He was a good dude and was loved tremendously. He'd liked LaTona ever since they were kids and promised himself that she would be his girl one day. Trap lived by any means necessary. He was a hustler by nature and his family wanted for nothing. He hit the streets at an early age. He lived and gained great knowledge on how to come up in this cruel cold world.

    As children they couldn't stand each other. They always bumped heads. Their relationship resembled the movie *Love and Basketball*. The only difference was, they weren't in college and they lived the street life to the fullest. They had an open affiliation and could do what either one of them wanted to do as long as they were there when the other needed them. They both were true to their word, they dated once a week and they slept together at least three nights a week if not all seven of them.

    LaTona wanted to take care of her cousin's request immediately. She jumped right on it. She was chilling at her crib, sitting on the couch looking at "The Monique Show" when Trap came strolling through the door. She hadn't seen him since he'd left the day before. LaTona respected the relationship they shared but her feelings were forming into something more and Trap was only following *her* rules. LaTona didn't want to make a commitment but she didn't want him to get away in the same token. Trap had done everything he could to wife LaTona but she was on something else, so he played his position. Trap perceived the change in LaTona's attitude but she made the decision and he was going to let her make the call.

Trap walked over to her and kissed her on the lips. "What's good wit' it ma?" he asked flopping down next to her reaching for the remote changing the channel to ESPN.

"Shit, chilling," she dryly responded reaching for the remote to change it back to "The Real Housewives of Atlanta". "Don't come in here changing the channels and shit," she fussed.

"What's wit' the 'tude ma?" he asked wanting to know where this was coming from.

"I don't have no tude!" she nastily replied.

"Shit, I can't tell!" he threw back at her.

"Whatever Trap." She waved her hand.

"Whatever ma." He got up to go in the kitchen. "What you cooking?" He looked through the refrigerator.

"Nothing, you should'a came home last night," she bitched again, rolling her eyes.

"Okay, *that's* what this is about." He shook his head understanding the attitude. "Damn Tona I gave you what you wanted man so don't be looking me upside my head when I don't do what you want me to do!" he released. LaTona didn't say anything. She continued looking at her show.

After watching Trap pull pots and pans out of the cabinet, trying to make him some breakfast, she walked into the kitchen and took over. "You knew I was going to take over, that's why you acted like you were about to cook. You play too much. You don't even know how to boil water for a damn hot dog so what the hell you know about scrambling eggs and frying bacon? Get outta here stunner." She pushed him out of the small kitchen.

Trap sat down on the couch and pulled his shirt over his head. Tona's temperature increased a bit. Her mid-section became extra wet. Her intentions were to feed Trap, sex Trap and then get all the information she wanted from Trap. He shared a lot of things with her. He knew he had a bitch that would go to bat for him. He didn't have to worry about her selling or bailing out on him, she was gutter. Tona put the bacon in the oven, whipped the eggs up in a bowl, buttered the pan for the biscuits and put them in the oven and had the water boiling for the rice. She then went and sat next to him on the couch. She lifted his head and positioned it on her lap and fondled his ear, something he loved for her to do. She then leaned down and kissed him on his forehead. "What's up with the forehead kiss ma?" He asked not understanding her change of attitude.

"It's nothing Trap. I don't get to spend as much time with you as I would like, so I've decided to take this time and enjoy you, instead a being of bitch." She continued to stroke his ear and head.

"Lift up a minute Trap." She gently moved his head to check the food.

Tona made Trap's plate and then her plate. "Trap, come sit at the table and break bread with me." She set their plates on the breakfast bar. He did as he was told. "Boy you better put that fork down and thank God for this food. What you thought?" she asked frowning at him. "Lord thank you for the food we're about to receive. Bless us that we may continue to chow down this way and bless the cook. Amen."

"God is good, God is great, thank you for letting me clear my plate. Amen." Trap followed joking. "Why didn't you ask God to watch out for me? Thugs need love too. What you thought?" he said, using her words against her.

"My bad, thug," she laughed, covering her mouth so the food wouldn't escape. "Trap." Tona called his name with much sincerity.

"What's good ma?" Trap noticed and put his fork down.

"Have you heard anything about who shot and killed my lil cousin? That nigga must pay. I can't let that ride." Tona's voice was very adamant.

"I heard something but I wanted to check it out first. I can get back with you." He put a fork full of eggs in his mouth. "Tona don't go searching for shit, let me get back with you. I've been on it since it happened. I got you girl, what you thought?" He chewed his biscuit.

"I'm going to fall back for a minute but that's it, a minute," she explained to him.

"I'll have something for you in a minute." He looked at her knowing that she was serious. "How's Poochie doing?"

"She's cool; she's out of town right now trying to get her head together." She wanted to close the subject.

Trap sat in the kitchen with LaTona while she cleaned it. After she was done they went into the living room. Being there only a few minutes, Tona informed Trap that she was going to lie down. Trap couldn't resist the blue Victoria's Secret boy shorts. Tona's ass bounced up and down as she made her way to her room. "I'm coming too," Trap told her turning the television off, heading in her direction. Tona was in the bed lying on her back when Trap took off his pants and hopped in the bed on top of her. Immediately Tona felt his dick harden against her midsection. "Tona this thing with your lil cousin got you straight zoned out." He informed her. "I can see that no matter what I say, you're going to do whatever it is that you want, with or without my help." She said nothing but looked him in his eyes. "But do know," he continued. "I got your back ma. Just let me know your moves. You can't be out here doing no crazy shit. These lil niggas is crazy," he finished.

"Do you fucking think I'm worried about some pussy ass niggas? They're cowards any muthafuckin' way to shoot a kid. I don't carry a pretty pink pearl .38 for nothing. I got something that will stop them in their tracks right where they stand." She became irate with tears in her eyes.

Trap took Tona and embraced her with a tight hug. She embedded her head in his chest and seductively licked his nipples. "Don't start Tona," he whispered rubbing his hands through her head.

"And if I don't, what's going to happen?" She continued licking.

"This is what's going to happen." He slid down her body removing her underwear before repositioning himself to slowly slide up to her midsection letting his tongue investigate her body. Erotic chills appeared over Tona's entire body. She reached for his head and he moved her hand. "Let me do this ma, just lay back and enjoy," he demanded giving her the best damn feeling she'd ever had. With his tongue flicking back and forth on her clit, she moaned in great pleasure. "Do you want to keep playing these bullshit ass games with me?" He released her clit. "Or do you want to make this thing official with us? I can't keep giving you my good magic stick," he explained to her.

"Damn Trap do we have to talk about this now? I love how you make my body feel." She looked at him crazy.

"Wow, wouldn't you believe that." Trap's attitude was visible at this point and LaTona noticed it.

"Come on Trap, not now." She rubbed his face. Trap removed her hand from his face and got out of bed. He then gathered his things to leave the room.

"Baby, don't do this!" she yelled behind him. *"Just when I was about to get mines,"* she said to herself. *"All into his feelings and shit."* She then got out of bed to follow him.

Trap was sitting on the couch putting on his shirt. He never looked at Tona when she entered the room naked. "So is this how we're gonna end our lovemaking session?" She sat next to him rubbing his back. He moved her hand.

"You damn right. You think it's a joke. I'm not out here in these streets for nothing; I'm trying to make shit happen. I thought you were down with me!" he yelled, clearly upset. "If you just wanna fuck then that's what it is, when *I* want to." He finished strapping his Polo boots.

"Boy get outta your feelings and come put it down as only you know how baby," Tona joked around, reaching for his arm. Trap looked at her and couldn't believe Tona's arrogance. He jerked away from her grip roughly. "Damn ma, you really don't get it do you?" He shook his head walking to the door.

"What!" She threw her hands in the air, taking a deep breath.

"I'm out here in these grimy ass streets, trying to make sure that you continue the lifestyle your dad provided for you and it's about some dick to you. I thought you carried me deeper than that lil mama. Either you want me or not." He opened the door and exited. Tona wanted to follow behind him to deeply express how she felt about him. She wanted to tell Trap she wanted him, just as he wanted her, maybe even more. But her pride wouldn't allow her to and she may have lost out on a good dude. She walked over to lock the door behind him. "I'll give him so time to cool off," she stated loudly.

Chapter 14

SOME THINGS SHOULD NEVER BE TOLD!

New York

Poochie arrived at the condo in a cab. Ty and Chance were posted at the 52" flat screen television betting on the Lakers and Celtics basketball game. Poochie rang the bell and Ty helped with her bags. "Damn Moo, did you buy out the mall?" he asked with Chance co-signing.

"No," she frowned kissing him on the lips. "What's up Chance?" she spoke walking to the kitchen.

"What's good Poochie? Where's the crew?" he inquired.

"I guess they're still at the mall," she answered, turning in his direction to face him.

"What you mean you guess? Y'all left here together right?" Ty chimed in.

"Yes, but we didn't leave together." She turned to open the refrigerator. Both Ty and Chance looked at each other.

Poochie waited for the questions to begin. "Five, four, three, two, one." She counted down in her head.

"What happened?" Ty inquired.

"Denise got to tripping with me about some shoes," she answered back, taking a sip of water.

"And," Ty egged her on while Chance co-signed.

"And she swung on me and I was about to beat her ass." She paused. "Let me make a long story short. Miracle pushed me and I pushed her ass back." She looked from Ty to Chance. "Once I cooled down, I realized that she was only trying to smooth out the situation."

"So where was Shakira when all of this was going on?" Chance finally asked a question.

"She was there trying to resolve the matter. I did inform her that I was taking a cab and she didn't agree but I left anyways." She ended.

Chance had heard enough and pulled out his cell phone, heading for the door. "I'll get at you in a minute cuz." Chance left. Poochie sat on the couch and Ty came and sat next to her. "Moo what popped off?"

"I really don't know. She just doesn't like me and I just don't care." She stared him in the eyes. "She first tripped over a dress and then some shoes. Talking about I think I'm all of that. I'm not the only one that has money." She smirked. "Shit I have to grind hard for mines. I work for the white man, she work for the family. What she thought?" She frowned, displaying wrinkles in her forehead.

"Are you kidding me?" Ty looked shocked as if to say, *"This some petty shit, but what's really good."*

"I am so not kidding you. Baby, I'm never fucked up about some shit as simple as clothes. I'm never caught up on materialistic shit. I can get that shit back in a heartbeat. Shit, give me my baby back. We can beef about *that*; this other shit, no time for it in my life." She then moved away from the subject. "What are you wearing tonight?" she asked Ty leaning over kissing him on the lips. That wasn't enough for him so he stuck his tongue down her throat.

Poochie grabbed his face and climbed on top of him on the couch. "Don't start anything you can't finish," he uttered.

"I got you lil daddy." She shoved her tongue further down his throat removing his wife beater, exposing his perfect torso.

Back at Denise and Miracle's Condo

Denise was blasting the sound of Monica's new single, "Everything to Me". Miracle had a blunt blazing grooving to the tune as well. "Hey Denise, what's good with you and Poochie?" she asked passing her the blunt watching her closely.

"What you mean cuz? It ain't shit. The bitch just thinks she better than everybody." Denise became irate and Miracle wondered why Poochie got under Denise's skin so badly.

"So what does that have to do with *you*?" she asked again.

"Look Mimi stop with all the questions, will you? I don't like the bitch and that's that. She better be glad that bullet missed her. But the pain she's feeling is all the same." Denise's words made her smirk conniving.

"You say what?" Miracle couldn't accept as true the words that were coming out of Denise's mouth. "Tell me you didn't have anything to do with that baby's murder." Miracle stood to her feet and went to turn the stereo down. "Now, let me hear you say that again." Miracle repeated looking at her oddly. "Let me make sure I heard you correctly. Now what?" She shook her head waving for hand for Denise to continue.

In Chance and Shakira's Condo

Shakira was getting her gear ready for the concert. She loved Chance's fashion tips and she allowed him to dress her on many occasions. Shakira had three outfits on the bed to pick from, a colorfully long flowing dress with a pair of 4-inch triangle heels, a black pinstripe pantsuit with matching shoes or a pair of hip hugging, skinny jeans with a tank top and half jacket with 6-inch heels. Yes, they all were brand as *SSO*. Chance took one look at the clothing and knew what she was going to wear.

He wanted to know what took place at the mall. "Slim Goody, what happened at the mall that Poochie had to take a cab back to the crib?" he asked sharply.

"I wish *I* knew what happened! You know how it is when Ty brings a new woman around. Denise has a tendency of getting too overprotective of her big cousins. She's gonna let your next bitch have it," she laughed loudly.

"What was with the pushing and shit?" His concern was without a doubt, large.

"A few words were passed about Poochie thinking she's all that and some other shit. Next thing I knew, Denise swung on the girl and she pushed her. Then of course, Miracle pushed Poochie and Poochie pushed her back. But all in all baby, I think Miracle was trying to stop the situation before it got out of hand. You know any other time she gets it in," Shakira explained. Chance knew she'd spoken the truth. He made a mental note to holler at Denise and Miracle later.

Shakira disrobed and tried the jeans, tank top and jacket on. She absolutely loved the way it grasped and enfolded her small frame. She pranced in the mirror doing her model pose. Shakira tried another pair of shoes she'd purchased with her outfit. She retrieved the box from the bag and observed that she had Miracle's shoes. As she removed the jeans and jacket, Chance reappeared. "Slim Goody, you think a nigga can get a bump before we head out?" He kissed the back of her neck. He appreciated the way Shakira's body harmonized with his.

"You can have whatever you like boy." She kissed him sloppy.

"Just let me take your sister her shoes. I don't want any disruption while you're beating this thang up." She licked his lips while reaching for his hand putting it in the front of her panties to fondle her.

"Hurry up and get on back girl. Look at what you did to me!" They both followed his eyes. Shakira kissed Chance once more and threw a pair of shorts on and headed across the hall.

Chapter 15

MESSED UP POSITION!

Across the hall

Shakira heard voices as she neared her neighbor's door. The door was cracked open but she decided to listen in before she knocked. "Mimi it's like this. One day I was riding with my homeboy from around the way. He and his boys was talking about this chick that thinks she's all that and of course it was Poochie. Well, his homeboy wanted somebody to whip her ass," Denise explained.

"Why?" Miracle questioned.

"Homeboy was out on the block handling his business, getting his grind on." She paused making sure Miracle was following her.

"Right, right." Miracle's tolerance level was zero.

"You know this bitch had the nerve to tell dude that he needs to go somewhere to make his paper." She looked at Miracle in disbelief. "She told him that she wanted her son to come outside and play and not be exposed to the hood life."

"What's so wrong with that?" Miracle asked becoming more upset by the second.

"Who the fuck does she think she is? She don't own the block, just a house on the block."

"No, correction, that's where you're wrong. That girl's grandparents have lived there before *we* were born. Now for future reference, sweetie, they do own most of the block. Her granddad is a wise man and he invested his money well," Miracle interrupted truthfully. "Now carry on."

Shakira was in the hallway gasping for air. Her lungs were losing oxygen. She needed air badly. She had grown real fond of Poochie and Shakira knew if Poochie knew Denise knew who killed her baby that that would be the end of Poochie and Ty's relationship. She didn't know what to do. She was in a messed up position or should I say fucked up position.

Denise was getting fed up with Miracle's disruptions. "Do you want me to finish or what?" Irritation was splashed around Denise's face.

"No, not really, but go ahead." Miracle knew what she was doing.

"Well the argument escalated and the bitch threatened to involve the cops and you know how that sits with the hustlers. That's like playing with their livelihood!"

"Was that a reason to take her son's life?" Miracle shrugged her shoulders. "Just because she wanted better for her kid? I don't understand lil cuz. It's something so absolutely wrong with this picture and if you don't see it, something's wrong with you too Denise!" Miracle shouted hoping that her cousin wasn't involved in this madness.

"No, that's not it Miracle. She put herself in a man's position and couldn't stand or deliver on it." Denise defended her homeboy.

"But what does that have to do with you, is what I'm not understanding Denise."

At this point Shakira had tears rolling down her face. She didn't know that Denise was this cold hearted. Maybe it was the fact that she lacked the love she needed from her mother, with Mya being on drugs and partying all night when she should have been home taking care of her daughter and husband.

Just when Shakira thought she'd heard enough. "I shot the gun that day cuz," Denise confessed.

"Say what!" Miracle yelled.

"What!" Shakira mouthed, quickly covering her mouth with her forearm. She didn't want them to hear her.

"What the fuck were you thinking? Do you know how serious this shit *is* girl?" Miracle got in Denise's face pointing her finger. "*Do you?!?*"

"I'm not worried about a muthafucka' doing anything to me." She freely stated with no remorse.

"You think that shit is fly, trying to get the approval of a nigga? You gone fuck around and damage your life if you haven't already. You done took a baby's life, not only that, Lil Cuz straight like the chick! Damn, all this drama over a nigga?!? Little girl please get your mind right!" Miracle headed to her bedroom but before leaving she turned and said to Denise. "You have me in a messed up position cuz, know that" and went to her room. Denise didn't say a word. Her conscience was bothering her. She was speechless and dumbfounded.

Shakira tried to compose herself before she knocked on the door. She had already been gone longer than she'd anticipated; knowing Chance would walk over and get her if she took too long. He was demanding when it came to her pussy. She finally knocked lightly. "Who is it?" Denise asked walking to the door.

"It's me, Shakira," she answered back holding the bag in her hand.

"What's up, Kira?" Denise opened the door before walking away.

"Shit, bringing this bag over. These have to be either yours or Miracle's shoes." She dropped the bag at the door.

"That's cool." Denise said never turning around to face Shakira. Shakira left feeling angrier in her heart, knowing that she too was in a messed up position. *"Damn you Denise,"* she thought, wondering how she would face Poochie, knowing who killed her son. This would be a compromising position for all parties involved.

TO BE CONTINUED!!!!

PART 3

GHETTO 4 LIFE!

Lea Mishell novels include:
Livin' Just Enough
Illusions: Things Are Not Always What They Seem...

Mary L. Wilson novels include:
Ghetto Luv
Still Ghetto

Teresa Seals novels include:
Taylor Made
Simply Taylor Made
Washed Up

Look out for more to come by **Myron A. Winston**

CPSIA information can be obtained
at www.ICGtesting.com
Printed in the USA
FSHW010753170919
62081FS